Betrayal of the
Mountain Man

Betrayal of the Mountain Man

William W. Johnstone
with J. A. Johnstone

PINNACLE BOOKS
Kensington Publishing Corp.
www.kensingtonbooks.com

PINNACLE BOOKS are published by

Kensington Publishing Corp.
850 Third Avenue
New York, NY 10022

PUBLISHER'S NOTE
Following the death of William W. Johnstone, the Johnstone family is working with a carefully selected writer to organize and complete Mr. Johnstone's outlines and many unfinished manuscripts to create additional novels in all of his series like The Last Gunfighter, Mountain Man, and Eagles, among others. This novel was inspired by Mr. Johnstone's superb storytelling.

All Kensington titles, imprints, and distributed lines are available at special quantity discounts for bulk purchases for sales promotions, premiums, fund-raising, educational, or institutional use. Special book excerpts or customized printings can also be created to fit specific needs. For details, write or phone the office of the Kensington special sales manager: Kensington Publishing Corp., 850 Third Avenue, New York, NY 10022, attn: Special Sales Department; phone 1-800-221-2647.

PINNACLE BOOKS and the Pinnacle logo are Reg. U.S. Pat. & TM Off.

ISBN 0-7860-1691-4

First printing: December 2006

10 9 8 7 6 5 4

Printed in the United States of America

Chapter One

Smoke Jensen saw the calf struggling through a snowdrift. The little creature had separated from its mother and the rest of the herd, and was bawling now in fear and confusion. He also saw the wolves, two of them, about twenty-five yards behind the calf. They were inching up slowly, quietly, hunkered down on their bellies to reduce their presence.

Smoke snaked his Winchester from the saddle sheath, then jacked a round into the chamber. He hooked his leg across the saddle horn, rested his elbow on his knee, then raised the rifle to his shoulder and sighted on the lead wolf. He was about 150 yards away from the two wolves, and he was looking down on them so it would be a difficult shot. But he figured that even if he didn't kill them, he might at least be able to drive them away from the calf.

Smoke squeezed the trigger. The rifle kicked back against his shoulder as smoke bellowed from the end of the barrel. When the smoke rolled away, he saw the lead wolf lying on its side, a spreading pool of red staining the snow.

The other wolf turned and ran quickly toward the trees, kicking up little puffs of snow as it did so. Smoke jacked another round into the chamber and aimed at the second wolf. His finger tightened on the trigger; then he eased the pressure, and lowered his rifle.

"Don't reckon I should shoot you for doing what your instinct tells you to do," Smoke said quietly. "I just don't want you doin' it to my cows. Specially not this year."

Smoke rode down to the wolf he had killed, then dismounted. His bullet had hit the animal just behind his left foreleg, penetrated the heart, and killed it instantly. The wolf's eyes were still open, his tongue still hanging out of his mouth. Strangely, Smoke felt a sense of sadness.

"I'm sorry I had to do this, fella, but you didn't leave me any choice," Smoke said. "At least it was quick for you."

Smoke remounted, then rode on toward the calf. He looped his rope around the calf, then half-led and half-dragged it back to the herd. There, he removed the rope and watched as the calf hurried to join his mother.

What had once been a large herd was now pitifully small, having come through what they were calling the "Great Winter Kill." Hundreds of thousands of cattle had died out throughout the West this winter, and Smoke's Sugarloaf Ranch was no exception. He had started the winter with fifteen thousand head; he was now down to less than two thousand.

Smoke's only hope to save what remained of his herd was to push them into a box canyon and hope that it would shield them from any further winter blasts. He, Cal, and Pearlie were doing that very thing when he came across the wolves.

Looking up, Smoke saw Cal approaching him from the north end of the canyon opening, while at the same time Pearlie was approaching from the south. Even if he had not been able to see them, he would know they were coming toward him, because each of them was leaving a long, black trail in the snow.

Cal reached him first.

"What was the shootin'?"

"Wolves," Smoke answered.

"Yeah," Cal said. "Well, you can't much blame 'em, I guess. They're probably havin' as hard a winter as we are. Same with all the other creatures, which is why they're goin' after cattle, rather than deer."

"Wolves?" Pearlie asked, arriving then.

"Yes, they were after a calf," Smoke said.

"Too bad you didn't see them a little earlier."

"What do you mean?"

Pearlie twisted in his saddle and pointed back down the black smear that marked his path through the snow. "Three calves back there, or what's left of 'em. Killed by wolves."

"Maybe we ought to put out some poisoned meat," Cal suggested.

Smoke shook his head. "I don't care to do that. Besides, there are enough animals around, frozen to death, that they probably wouldn't take the bait."

"You'd think they'd go after the dead ones, and leave the live ones alone," Pearlie said.

"The dead ones are frozen hard as a rock. They want something alive because it's warmer, and easier to eat," Smoke said.

"Speaking of something warm and easy to eat, you think maybe Miss Sally fixed us up any bear claws?" Pearlie asked.

"Does the sun come up in the east?" Cal asked.

Smoke chuckled. "I expect she did," he said. He stood in his stirrups and looked down toward the small herd. "We've got them in the canyon now; that's about all we can do for them. Let's head for the house."

The three started back toward the house, which was some five miles distant. A ride that, in good weather, would take no more than thirty minutes stretched into an hour because of the heavy fall of snow. The horses labored to cut through the drifts, which were sometimes chest high, and their heavy breathing formed clouds of vapor that drifted away into the fading light.

The three riders said nothing, lost in their own thoughts as they rode back toward the main house.

The oldest of the three, and the ranch owner, was Kirby "Smoke" Jensen. Smoke stood just over six feet tall, and had shoulders as wide as an ax handle and biceps as thick as most men's thighs. He had never really known his mother, and when he was barely in his teens, he went with his father into the mountains to follow the fur trade. The father and son teamed up with a legendary mountain man called Preacher. For some reason, unknown even to Preacher, the mountain man took to the boy and began to teach him the ways of the mountains: how to live when others would die, how to be a man of your word, and how to fear no other living creature. On the first day they met, Preacher, whose real name was Art, gave Kirby a new name. That name, Smoke, would one day become a legend in the West, and after a while, even Kirby thought of himself as Smoke Jensen.

Smoke was in his thirties, a happily married landowner whose ranch, Sugarloaf, had the potential to be one of the finest ranches in the state. For the last three or four years, Sugarloaf had lived up to its potential, so much so that Smoke had borrowed money to expand the ranch. He bought more land, built a new barn and bunkhouse, added onto the big house, and bought more cattle.

Then the winter hit. Blizzard followed blizzard as the temperature plummeted to record lows. All across the West cattle died in record numbers. Tens of thousands of cattle froze to death, thousands more died of starvation because they couldn't get to the food, while nearly as many died of thirst because the streams and creeks were frozen solid under several feet of snow.

Ironically, the smaller ranchers were better able to ride it out than the bigger ranchers, who had more land, more cattle, and much more to lose. In one terrible winter, Smoke Jensen had gone from being one of the wealthiest ranchers in Colorado to a man who was struggling to hang onto his ranch.

"Smoke, if you want, I'll take the lead . . . let my horse break trail for a while," Pearlie called up to him. The three men were riding in single file, the two behind the leader taking advantage of the lead horse breaking a trail through the snow.

"Sure, come on up," Smoke invited, moving to one side of the trail to let Pearlie pass.

A few years earlier, Pearlie had been a gunman, hired by a man who wanted to run Smoke off the land so he could ride roughshod over those who were left. But Pearlie didn't take to killing and looting from innocent people, so he quit his job. He had stopped by to tell Smoke that he was leaving when Smoke offered to hire him.

Since that time Pearlie had worked for Smoke and Sally. He stood just a shade less than six feet tall, was lean as a willow branch, had a face tanned the color of an old saddle, and a head of wild, unruly black hair. His eyes were mischievous and he was quick to smile and joke, but underneath his friendly demeanor was a man that was as hard as iron and as loyal to his friends as they come.

"I'll ride second," Cal said, passing with Pearlie. "That way I can take the lead in a few minutes."

Not too long after Pearlie had joined the ranch, a starving and destitute Cal, who was barely in his teens at the time, made the mistake of trying to rob Sally. Instead of turning him over to the sheriff, Sally brought him home and made him one of the family, along with Pearlie. Now Calvin Woods was Pearlie's young friend and protégé in the cowboy life.

The three men rode on in silence for the next fifteen minutes, frequently changing the lead so that one horse wouldn't be tired out. Finally they crested a hill, then started down a long slope. There, half a mile in front of them, the ranch compound spread out over three acres, consisting of the main house, bunkhouse, barn, corral, and toolshed.

In the setting sun the snow took on a golden glow, and the scene could have been a Currier and Ives painting come to life.

The main house, or "big" house as the cowboys called it, was a rather large, two-story Victorian edifice, white, with red shutters and a gray-painted porch that ran across the front and wrapped around to one side. The bunkhouse, which was also white with red shutters, sat halfway between the big house and the barn. The barn was red.

A wisp of smoke curled up from the kitchen chimney, and as the three approached, they could smell the aroma of baking.

"Yep! She made some," Pearlie said happily. "I tell you the truth, if Miss Sally don't make the best bear claws in Colorado, then I'll eat my hat."

"Hell, that ain't no big promise, Pearlie," Cal said. "The kind of appetite you got, you eat anything that gets in your way. I wouldn't be that surprised if you hadn't already et your hat a time or two."

Smoke laughed.

"That ain't no ways funny," Pearlie complained. "I ain't never et none of my hats."

"But there ain't no danger of you eatin' your hat anyhow 'cause you're right," Cal said. "Miss Sally does make the best bear claws in Colorado."

Sally was a schoolteacher when Smoke met her, but she was far from the demure schoolmarm one most often thought of when picturing a schoolteacher.

Sally could ride, rope, and shoot better than just about any man, and yet none of that detracted from her feminine charms. She was exceptionally pretty and her kitchen skills matched any woman and surpassed most.

The bear claws that Pearlie was referring to were sweet, sugar-coated doughnuts. They were famous throughout the county, and some men had been known to ride ten miles out of their way to drop by the Sugarloaf just on the off chance she'd have a platter of them made up and cooling on the windowsill.

The three men rode straight to the barn, where they unsaddled their horses, then turned them into warm stalls with hay and water. They took off their coats, hats, and boots on the enclosed back porch, dumping the snow and cleaning their boots before they went inside.

The house was warm and cozy, and it smelled of coffee, roast beef, fresh-baked bread, bear claws, and wood burning in the fireplace. Sally greeted Smoke with a kiss and the other two with affectionate hugs.

Around the dinner table the four talked, joked, and laughed over the meal. And yet, as Sally studied her husband's face, she knew that, just beneath his laughing demeanor, he was a worried man. It wasn't so much what he said, as what was left unsaid. Smoke had always been a man filled with optimism and plans for the future. It had been a long time since she had heard him mention any of his plans for improving and expanding the ranch.

* * *

Sally had no idea what time it was when she rolled over in bed, still in that warm and comfortable state of half-sleep. She reached out to touch Smoke, but when she didn't feel him in bed with her, the remaining vestige of sleep abandoned her and she woke up, wondering where he was.

Outside, the snow glistened under the bright full moon so that, even though it was the middle of the night, the bedroom was well lit in varying degrees of silver and black. A nearby aspen tree waved in a gentle night breeze and as it did so, it projected its restless shadow onto the softly glowing wall. Smoke's shadow was there as well, for he was standing at that very window, looking out into the yard.

"Smoke?" Sally called out in a soft, concerned voice.

"I'm sorry, darlin'," Smoke replied. "Did I wake you?"

Sally sat up, then brushed a fall of blond hair back from her face. "Are you all right?" she asked.

"I'm fine."

"You're worried, aren't you?"

Smoke paused for a long moment before he answered. Then, with a sigh, he nodded.

"I won't lie to you, Sally," he said. "We may lose everything."

Sally got out of bed and padded across the room. Then, wrapping her arms around him, she leaned into him.

"No," she said. "As long as we have each other, we won't lose everything."

Chapter Two

The banker leaned back in his chair and put his hands together, making a steeple of his fingers. He listened intently as Smoke made his case.

"I'm sure I'm not the only one coming to you with problems," Smoke said. "I reckon this winter has affected just about everyone."

Joel Matthews nodded. "It has indeed," he said. "Right now our bank has over one hundred fifty thousand dollars in bad debt. I'll tell you the truth, Smoke. We are in danger of going under ourselves."

Smoke sighed. "Then it could be that I'm just wasting my time talking to you."

Matthews drummed his fingers on the desk for a moment, then looked down at Smoke's account.

"You have a two-thousand-dollar note due in thirty days," he said.

"Yes."

"What, exactly, are you asking?"

"I'm asking for a sixty-day extension of that note."

The banker turned at his desk and looked at the calendar on the wall behind him. The picture was an idealized night scene in the mountains. Below a full moon a train was crossing a trestle, its headlight beam stretching forward and every car window glowing unrealistically.

"Your note is due on April 30th," he said. "A sixty-day extension would take you to June 30th. Do you really think you can come up with the two thousand dollars by then?"

"I know that I cannot by April 30th, and I'll be honest with you, Joel. I don't know if I will have the money by June 30th either. But if any of my cattle survive the rest of this winter, I will at least have a chance."

"Smoke, can you make a two-hundred-dollar payment on your note? That would be ten percent."

Smoke shook his head. "Maybe a hundred," he said.

"A hundred?"

"That's about the best I can do right now."

Matthews sighed. "I'll never be able to convince the board to go along with it, unless you can at least pay ten percent on the loan."

Smoke nodded. "I understand," he said. He started to stand, but Matthews held out his hand.

"Wait a minute," he said.

Smoke hesitated.

"I know how you can come up with a hundred fifty dollars, if you are willing to do a job for me."

"A job for you?"

"Well, for the bank, actually," Matthews said. "It will take you about three days."

"Three days work for a hundred fifty dollars? I'll do it," Smoke said.

"Don't you even want to know what it is?"

"Is it honest work?"

"Oh, yes, it's honest all right. It might also be dangerous."

"I'll do it," Smoke said.

"Yes, I didn't think you would be a person who would be deterred by the possibility of danger. But just so that you know what you are letting yourself in for, we have a rather substantial money shipment coming by stagecoach from Sulphur Springs. If you would ride as a special guard during the time of the shipment, I will pay you one hundred fifty dollars."

Smoke gasped. "One hundred fifty dollars just to ride shotgun? It's not that I'm looking a gift horse in the mouth, Joel, but shotgun guards make about twenty dollars a month, don't they?"

"Yes."

"So why would you be willing to pay me so much?"

"We are bringing in over twenty thousand dollars," Matthews said. He sighed, then opened the drawer of his desk and pulled out a newspaper. "And the damn fool editor over at Sulphur Springs has seen fit to run a front page story about it."

Matthews turned the paper around so Smoke could see the headlines of the lead story.

HUGE MONEY SHIPMENT!

$20,000 In Greenbacks

TO BE TRANSPORTED
by Sulphur Springs Express Company
to BIG ROCK.

"Why in the world would he publish something like this?" Smoke asked.

"Well, if you asked the editor, I'm sure he would tell us that he is merely exercising his freedom of the press," Matthews said. "But I would call it idiocy. Anyway, the cat is out of the bag, and no doubt every outlaw in three states knows about the shipment now. Do you know Frank Simmons?"

"No, I don't think I do."

"Frank Simmons is the normal shotgun guard on this run. He's sixty-six years old and blind as a bat. Ordinarily it's not a problem. About the only thing the stage ever carries is a mailbag with letters from grandparents, a few seed catalogues, and the like. But this? Well, Frank just isn't up for the job."

"I see what you mean," Smoke said. "When do I go?"

"You can take the stage over Monday morning," Matthews said. "The money will arrive by train Tuesday night. Marshal Goodwin and a couple of his deputies will meet the train with the banker just to make sure it gets in the bank all right. Then, Wednesday, you'll take personal charge of it until you get it back here."

"Sounds easy enough," Smoke said.

Matthews laughed out loud. "For someone like you, I imagine it is," he said. "But I'll be honest with you, Smoke. If I had to guard that shipment, knowing that every saddle bum and ne'er-do-well from Missouri to California is after it, why, I'd be peeing in my pants."

Smoke laughed as well. "I'll have the money here Wednesday evening," he said. "And I'll be wearing dry pants."

* * *

"You want me to go with you?" Pearlie asked over the supper table that night.

"No, why should you?"

"Well, if it's like Mr. Matthews says, you're liable to run into some trouble between here and Sulphur Springs."

"No. I thank you for the offer, Pearlie. But I want you and Cal to stay here and look after what few cattle we have left. You'll have to take hay out to them, since they won't be able to forage. And you'll have to watch out for the wolves, and any other creatures that might have a yen for beef. The only chance we have of saving Sugarloaf is to keep enough cows alive that I can sell to raise the two thousand."

"All right, if you say so," Pearlie said as he reached for the last of the bear claws.

"That's four," Cal said.

"What's four?"

"That's four of them things you'n has had."

"Cal," Sally said sharply.

"What? You think I'm lyin', Miss Sally? I been a'countin' them."

"I'm not concerned about that. I'm talking about your grammar."

"That's four of *those* things *you have* had," Pearlie said, correcting Cal's grammar. "Not them things you'n has had."

"Have you had four of them, Pearlie?" Sally asked.

"Well, yes, ma'am, but I believe these are somewhat smaller than the ones you usually make," Pearlie replied.

Sally laughed, then got up from the table and, walking over to the pie saver, opened the door and pulled out an apple pie.

"Then you won't be wanting any of this, will you?" she asked, bringing the pie to the table.

"*I* sure do!" Cal said, licking his lips in anticipation as Sally cut a large slice for him.

"Maybe just a little piece," Pearlie said, eyeing the pie she was cutting. "With, maybe, a slice of cheese on top."

That night, Sally cuddled against Smoke as they lay in bed.

"You take care of yourself, Smoke," she said.

Smoke squeezed her. "I've spent a lifetime taking care of myself," he said. "I'm not likely to fall down on the job now."

"It was nice of Mr. Matthews to offer you the job," Sally said. "He did say we would get the extension?"

"Yes." Smoke sighed. "For all the good it will do."

"What do you mean?"

"We've got thirty days until the loan is due, with the extension ninety days. Then what? We are still going to have to come up with the money."

"You don't think we'll have enough cattle to sell?"

"What if we do?" Smoke said. "Then what? At best, we'll just be buying time. A cattle ranch without cattle isn't much of a ranch."

They lay in the quiet darkness for a long moment before Sally spoke again.

"I know a way we might be able to come up with it," she said.

"Oh, no," Smoke said.

"Oh, no, what?"

"I'm not going to let you go on the line for me. I mean, I appreciate the offer, but I just wouldn't feel right, you becoming a soiled dove."

"What?" Sally shouted, sitting up in bed quickly and staring down at him.

Smoke laughed out loud. "I mean, I have given that very idea some thought too, but I wasn't sure you would do it. Then I figured, well, maybe you would, but I just wouldn't feel right about it."

"Kirby Jensen!" Sally said, laughing at him as she realized he was teasing. She grabbed the pillow, then began hitting him with it.

"I give up, I give up!" Smoke said, folding his arms across his face as she continued to pound him with the pillow. Finally, winded, she put the pillow down.

"Truce?" Smoke asked.

"Truce," Sally replied. Then, she smiled wickedly at him. "How much do you think I would make?"

"Sally!" Smoke gasped.

This time it was Sally's turn to laugh. "Well, you are the one who brought it up," she said between giggles.

Sally lay back down beside him and, again, they were quiet for a moment.

"How?" Smoke asked.

"How what?"

"You said you may have a way to raise the money. How would we do it?"

"Light the lamp," Sally said as she got out of bed, "and I'll show you."

Sally walked over to the dresser and opened the top drawer. Removing a newspaper, she returned to the bed just as a bubble of golden light filled the room.

"Read this advertisement," she said, pointing to a boxed item in the paper.

Smoke read aloud. "New York Company desires ranch land to lease. Will pay one dollar per acre for one-year lease."

"If we leased our entire ranch to them, we could make twelve thousand dollars," Sally said.

Smoke shook his head. "No," he said.

"Why not?"

"Sally, you know why not. If we lease this ranch to some outfit like this"—he flicked his fingers across the page—"they'll send their own man in to run things. We'll be tenants on our own land. Only the land won't even be ours, at least not for a year."

"Smoke, you said yourself we are in danger of losing everything," Sally said. "At least, this way, we could hang onto the ranch. All right, we won't make any money this year because everything we get will have to go toward the notes. But next year, we could start fresh."

"Start fresh with no money," Smoke said.

"And no debt," Sally added.

Smoke stared at the advertisement for a long moment. Then he lay back on the bed and folded his arm across his eyes.

"Smoke?"

Smoke didn't answer.

"Smoke, you know I'm right," Sally said.

After another long period of silence, Smoke let out a loud sigh.

"Yeah," he said. "I know you're right."

"Then you'll do it?"

"Is this what you want to do, Sally?"

"No, it isn't what I want to do," Sally admitted. "But I don't see any other way out of this. At least think about it."

"All right," Smoke agreed. "I'll think about it."

The man standing at the end of the bar had a long, pockmarked face and a drooping eyelid. He picked up his beer, and blew the foam off before taking a drink. His name was Ebenezer Dooley, and he had escaped prison six months ago. He was here to meet some people, and though he had never seen them, he knew who the three men were as soon as they came in. He could tell by the way they stood just inside the door, pausing for a moment to look around the main room of the Mad Dog Saloon, that they were here to meet someone.

The room was dimly lit by a makeshift chandelier that consisted of a wagon wheel and several flickering candles. It was also filled with smoke from dozens of cigars and pipes so that it took some effort for the three men to look everyone over. Dooley had told them that he would be wearing a high-crowned black hat, with a red feather sticking out of a silver hatband. He stepped away from the bar so they could see him; then one of them made eye contact and nodded. Once contact was made, Dooley walked toward an empty table at the back of the saloon. The three men picked their way through the crowd, then joined him.

One of the bar girls came over to smile prettily at the men as they sat down. She winced somewhat as she got a closer look at them, because they were some of the ugliest men she had ever seen.

Dooley had been in town for a few days, so she had already met him. He was tall and gangly, with a thin face and a hawklike nose. He was not handsome by any standard, but compared to the other three, he was Prince Charming.

"Girlie, bring us a bottle and four glasses," Dooley said.

The bar girl left to get the order, returned, picked up the money, then walked away. None of the men seemed particularly interested in having her stay around, and she was not at all interested in trying to change their minds.

"You would be Cletus, I take it?" Dooley said to the oldest of the three men. Cletus had white hair and a beard and, as far as Dooley could tell, only one tooth.

"I'm Cletus."

"A friend of mine named McNabb told me you would be a good man to work with," Dooley said. "And that you could get a couple more."

"These here are my nephews," Cletus said. "This is Morgan." Morgan had a terrible scar that started just above his left eye, then passed down through it. He had only half an eyelid, and the eye itself was opaque. Morgan stared hard at Dooley with his one good eye.

"And this here'n is Toomey," Cletus continued. "Neither

one of 'em's too quick in the mind, but they're good boys who'll do whatever I tell them to do. Ain't that right, boys?"

"Whatever you tell us, Uncle Cletus," Toomey said. "Mama said to do whatever you tell us to do."

"His mama is my sister," Cletus said. "She ain't none too bright neither, which is why I figure she birthed a couple of idiots."

Neither Morgan nor Toomey reacted to his unflattering comment about them.

"Can I count on them to do the job I got planned?" Dooley asked.

"I told you," Cletus said. "They'll do whatever I ask them to do."

"Good."

"You said this would be a big job?"

"Yes."

"How big?"

"Twenty thousand dollars big," Dooley said.

Cletus let out a low whistle. "That is big," he said.

"The split is fifty-fifty," Dooley said.

"Wait a minute, what do you mean, the split is fifty-fifty? They's four of us."

"I set up the deal, I'm in charge," Dooley replied. "I take half, you take half. How you divide your half with your nephews is up to you."

Cletus looked at his two nephews for a moment; then he nodded.

"All right," he said. "That sounds good enough to me. Where is this job, and when do we do it?"

"Huh-uh," Dooley replied.

Cletus looked surprised. "What do you men, huh-uh? How are we goin' to do the job iffen we don't know what it is we're a'supposed to be doin'?"

Dooley shook his head. "I'll tell you what you need to know when the time comes. I wouldn't like to think of you gettin' greedy on me."

"Whatever you say," Cletus replied.

Chapter Three

Even though Smoke had nothing to do with the money yet, he was in the Sulphur Springs Railroad Depot when the eleven o'clock train arrived.

The depot was crowded with people who were waiting for the train. Some were travelers who were holding tickets, and some were here to meet arriving passengers, but many were here for no other purpose than the excitement of watching the arrival of the train.

They heard the train before anyone saw it, the sound of the whistle. Then, as the train swept around a distant curve, the few people on the platform saw the headlamp, a gas flame that projected a long beam before it.

The train whistled again, and this time everyone could hear the puffing of the steam engine as it labored hard to pull the train though the night. Inside the depot, Smoke stepped over to one of the windows, but because it was very cold outside, and warm inside, the window was fogged over. He wiped away the condensation, then looked through the circle he had made to watch the train approach, listening to the puffs of steam as it escaped from the pistons. He could see bright sparks embedded in the heavy, black smoke that poured from the flared smokestack. Then, as the train swept into the station, he saw sparks falling from the firebox and leaving a carpet of orange-glowing embers lying between the rails and trailing out behind the train. They glimmered for a moment or two in the darkness before finally going dark themselves.

The train began squeaking and clanging as the engineer applied the brakes. It got slower, and slower still, until finally the engineer brought his train to a stop in exactly the right place.

Much of the crowd inside went outside then, to stand on the platform alongside the train as the arriving passengers disembarked and the departing passengers climbed aboard. But Smoke and three men remained inside the depot. Smoke had met with the others earlier in the day when he had presented them with the letter from Joel Matthews, authorizing him to take possession of the money.

"Well, Mr. Jensen," the banker said, noticing Smoke for the first time that night. "On the job already, I see."

"I just came down to see if I would actually have a job tomorrow."

"That's probably not a bad idea," the young deputy said. "Coming down here now to watch us can give you a few pointers."

"Ha," the marshal said, laughing. "I can see Smoke Jensen picking up some pointers from the likes of us."

"Everybody can learn something," Smoke said.

The station manager stuck his head inside the door then.

"Mr. Wallace, you want to come sign for this now? The railroad is anxious to get rid of it."

"I'll be right there," the banker said.

The marshal and his deputy both drew their pistols, then followed Wallace out to the mail car. Smoke went outside with them, and he turned up the collar of his sheepskin coat as he watched Wallace take the money pouch from the express messenger. Then he followed the banker and his two guards down to the bank, where the money was put into the safe.

"There you go, Mr. Jensen," Wallace said when the money was put away. "All safe and sound for you tomorrow."

"Yes, well, I'll feel a lot better when it is safe and sound in the bank back in Big Rock," Smoke said.

Smoke was just finishing his breakfast the next morning, sopping up the last of the yellow of his egg with his last biscuit, when someone walked over to his table.

"You're Mr. Jensen?"

"Yes."

"I'm from the bank, Mr. Jensen. Mr. Wallace said to tell you to come over and get that . . . uh . . . package now," he said cryptically.

"All right," Smoke said, washing down the last bite with the end of his coffee. He put on his coat, turned up his collar, and pulled his hat down, then followed the messenger back to the bank.

"I didn't think the bank would be opened yet," Smoke said, his words forming clouds of vapor in the cold morning air.

"It isn't open yet," the young man said. "Mr. Wallace thought it would be better to give it to you before we had any customers."

"Sounds sensible," Smoke said.

Smoke thought they would go in through the front, but the young man walked alongside the bank until they reached the back. Then, taking a key from his pocket, he opened the back door and motioned for Smoke to go inside.

Wallace was sitting at a desk in his office when the young man brought Smoke in. The pouch that the money had come in was open, and there were several bound stacks of bills alongside.

"You want to count this money?" Wallace asked.

"It might be a good idea," Smoke replied.

"Jeremiah, pull that chair over here for Mr. Jensen."

"Yes, sir," the young messenger said.

Thanking him, Smoke sat in the chair and began counting. When he finished, half an hour later, he looked up at Wallace. "I thought it was supposed to be twenty thousand dollars."

"How much did you come up with?" Wallace asked.

"Twenty thousand four hundred and twelve dollars," Smoke replied.

Wallace smiled, and slid a piece of paper across his desk. "That exact amount is recorded here," he said. "It's good to see that you are an accurate counter. Sign here, please."

With all money accounted for, Smoke took the pouch and walked down to the end of the street to the stage depot. The coach was already sitting out front and the hostlers were rigging up the team.

Although it had not snowed in nearly a week, there were still places where snow was on the ground in many places, some of which could not be avoided. As a result, Smoke had snow on his boots, but he stomped his feet on the porch, getting rid of as much as he could.

The stage depot was warm inside, and he saw five people standing around the potbellied stove, a man, two women, and a young boy. There were three more men over by the ticket counter and one of them, seeing Smoke, came toward him. He was an older man, with white hair and weathered skin. He stuck his hand out.

"Good morning, Mr. Jensen. I'm Frank Simmons."

"Call me Smoke," Smoke said. "You would be the shotgun guard?"

"Yes, sir, normally that would be me," Simmons said.

"Normally?"

"Well, the truth is, if you have that much money to look after, ever'one figures it'd be better if you'd just go ahead and ride shotgun yourself." Simmons held out his hands and both were shaking. "I got me this here palsy so bad, why, I couldn't no ways hold a gun to shoot. Only reason I go along now is to keep Puddin' company. We don't never carry nothin' worth stealin'. That is, until now."

"Puddin'?"

"That would be me," another man said, coming over to shake Smoke's hand. "Puddin' Taylor is the name.

I'm the driver. You'll be sittin' up on the high board with me, if you don't mind."

"No, I figure that's probably the best place for me," Smoke said. "Not looking forward to getting that cold," he said.

"Ah don't worry none 'bout gettin' too cold," Puddin' said. "We keep us a really warm buffalo robe up there. Why, you'll be as warm as the folks down in the box with their wool blankets."

"Puddin'," someone called from the front door. "Your team is hitched up, you're all ready to go."

"Thanks, Charlie," Puddin' replied. "All right, folks, let's get on the stage. I'm 'bout ready to pull out."

Smoke went outside with the others and watched as the passengers boarded the coach, then wrapped themselves in blankets to ward off the cold. Smoke climbed up onto the high seat alongside Puddin', who then released the brake and snapped the ribbons over the team. The coach jerked forward, then moved at a clip faster than a brisk walk through the town and onto the road.

Dooley stood on a rock and looked down the road.

"What we stayin' here for?" Cletus asked. "It's cold up here."

"We're here because by the time the coach reaches this point, the driver will have to stop his team to give 'em a breather. That's when we'll hit them," Dooley said.

Cletus, Morgan, and Toomey were sitting on a fallen log about forty yards away from the road. Morgan got up and walked over to a bush to relieve himself. He began to giggle.

"What are you laughin' at?" Toomey asked.

"Lookie here when I pee," Morgan said. "There's smoke comin' from it."

"That ain't smoke, you idiot," Dooley said. "It's vapor, same thing as your breath when it's cold."

"That don't make no sense," Morgan said. "There ain't no breath a'comin' offin' my pee."

"Wait," Tommey said. "I'm goin' to see if I can piss smoke too."

"Quiet!" Dooley said sharply. "I think I hear somethin'."

In the distance, Dooley could hear the whistle and shouts of the driver as he urged his team up the long grade.

"They're comin'. Ever'one get ready," Dooley said, climbing down from the rock.

"Git up thar, git on with ya'!" Puddin' shouted, urging the straining team up the grade. He leaned over to spit a chew, and a wad of the expectorated tobacco hit the right front wheel, then rotated down.

"Will you be stopping at the top of the grade?" Smoke asked.

"Yeah," Puddin' answered as he wiped his mouth with the back of his hand. "We got to, else the team'll give out before we reach the next way station."

Smoke pulled his pistol and checked the loads.

"What you doin' that for?" Puddin' asked.

"If I were planning to hold up this stage, this is where I would do it," Smoke said.

"Yeah," Puddin' said, nodding. "Yeah, you're prob'ly right."

It took another ten minutes before the team reached the crest of the grade.

"Whoa!" Puddin' called, pulling back on the reins.

The team stopped and they sat there for a moment, with the only sound being the heavy breathing of the horses. Vapor came, not only from their breath, but from their skin, as the horses had generated a lot of heat during the long pull up the hill.

Suddenly three armed men jumped out in front of the stage. One of the men fired and his bullet hit Puddin' in the arm.

Even before the echo of that shot had died out, Smoke was returning fire, shooting three times in such rapid succession that all three of the would-be robbers went down.

"Puddin', are you all right?" Smoke asked.

"Yeah," Puddin' replied, his voice strained with pain. "It just hit me in the arm, didn't do nothin' to any of my vitals."

"What's happening? What's going on up there?" someone from inside the coach called. The door to the coach opened.

"No!" Smoke shouted. "Stay inside!"

With his pistol at the ready, Smoke climbed down from the driver's seat, then moved slowly, cautiously toward the three men he had just shot. That was when he heard hoofbeats and looking toward the sound, he saw a rider bending low over the neck of his horse as he kept the horse at a gallop.

Smoke raised his pistol and started to shoot, but decided that whoever it was offered no immediate danger, so he eased the hammer back down and examined the three men.

All three were dead, their faces contorted in grimaces of pain and surprise.

"Did you kill the sons of bitches?" Puddin' called.

"Yeah," Smoke said.

"Good."

"Keep everyone on the stage until I have a look around," Smoke said.

Smoke followed the tracks of the three would-be robbers back into the edge of the woods. There, he saw a fallen log. There was also enough disturbed snow around the log that he knew this was where the men had been waiting. He also saw three horses tied to a branch. He walked over to the animals and patted one of them on the neck.

"Don't worry," he said. "I'm not going to leave you out here. You didn't try to hold up the stage."

Further examination showed that there had been a fourth horse, and Smoke was satisfied that that was the horse of the man he had seen running away. Nobody else was here, or had been here.

Smoke came back out of the tree line leading the three horses. He stopped at the bodies of the three outlaws.

"See anyone else back there?" Puddin' asked.

"No, it's all clear," Smoke said. He began putting the bodies on the horses, belly down. "Don't know which one of you belongs to which," he said to the horses. "But I don't reckon it matters much now."

Puddin' tied off the team, then climbed down. "You folks can come out now," he called to his passengers. "If you need to, uh, rest yourselves, well, there's a pretty good place for the ladies over there," he said.

"Let me take a look at your arm," Smoke said. He tore some of Puddin's shirt away, then looked at the wound.

"How's it look?"

"It went all the way through. If it doesn't get festered, you should be all right." Smoke tore off another piece of the driver's shirt. "Give me a chaw of tobacco," he said. "I'll use it as a poltice."

The driver chewed up a wad of tobacco, then spit it into the cloth.

"Here too. I'll need it on the entry and exit wound."

Puddin' complied, then Smoke wrapped the bandage around his arm, putting the tobacco over each wound.

"There was another'n, wasn't there?" the driver asked as Smoke worked.

"Yes. But I don't expect we'll have any trouble with him."

The passengers came back from their rest stop then, and the boy, who was about eleven, walked back to look at the bodies draped over the horses.

"Timmy, come back here," the boy's mother said.

"Wow," Timmy said to Puddin'. "There were three of them and just two of you, but you beat 'em."

Puddin' shook his head. "Not two of us, son," he said.

"Just one." He nodded toward Smoke, who had already climbed back up into the seat. "He did it all by himself."

"What kind of man could take down three armed outlaws all by himself?" one of the male passengers asked.

"Well, a man like Smoke Jensen, I reckon," Puddin' replied.

Dooley rode his horse at a gallop until he feared that the animal would drop dead on him. Then he got off and walked him until the horse's breathing returned to normal.

He had told Cletus and his nephews to stay out of sight until he gave the word to confront the stage. He'd had it all planned out, which included staying separated so as to deny the stage guard any opportunity to react.

But before he knew it, all three jumped up in front of the stage. At first, Dooley couldn't understand why they would do such a damn fool thing. But as he was riding away from the scene, he began thinking about it, and he was fairly certain that he had figured it out.

Dooley was convinced that Cletus and his two nephews had planned to rob the stage, then turn on him, keeping all the money for themselves. But it didn't work out that way for them because the shotgun guard killed all three.

What sort of man could take on three gunmen and kill all three? Dooley wondered.

From the moment he had learned of the money shipment, he had begun planning this robbery. He'd even taken a trip on the stage, just to make certain that he knew the route it would travel. That's how he'd learned about the long grade and the necessity of stopping to rest the horses.

But the shotgun guard on the trip he took was an old man with the shakes. He wouldn't have presented any trouble at all. In fact, Dooley even watched the coach depart two more times, and it had been the same guard for each trip. This guard today was new and, as it turned out, deadly.

Dooley resented the fact that he didn't get the money, but he was just as glad that Cletus and his nephews got themselves killed. As it turned out, they were nothing but a bunch of double-crossing bastards anyway.

Chapter Four

"Folks, can I have your attention please?" Sheriff Carson called.

At the sheriff's call, everyone in Longmont's Saloon grew quiet and turned to see what he had to say.

Sheriff Carson smiled, then nodded toward a table where Smoke was sitting with Sally, Pearlie, Cal, and Louie Longmont, owner of Longmont's Saloon.

"As you all know, our own Smoke Jensen here foiled a robbery last week, and that's why we're here celebratin' with him and Sally." Sheriff Carson turned toward Smoke, and held up his mug of beer. "Smoke, if those no-'counts had managed to steal the money you were guarding, the folks around here would be in a lot more trouble than we are. I thank you, and the town thanks you."

"Hear, hear," Longmont said, and the others in the saloon applauded.

"Mr. Longmont, another round of drinks if you please," Joel Matthews said. "The bank is buying."

"All right!" someone shouted, and there was a rush to the bar.

"I'll get ours," Pearlie said, getting up from the table.

"I'll have a beer," Cal said.

"He'll have a sarsaparilla," Sally declared.

"Miss Sally I . . ." Cal began, but Smoke cut him off with a steely gaze. Cal was about to say that he drank beer all the time when he was out with just Smoke and Pearlie, but he knew that if he told her that now, Smoke would curtail those privileges.

"May I join you?" Matthews asked, coming over to the table.

"Yes, please do," Sally said with an inviting smile.

Matthews sat down, then pulled an envelope from his inside jacket pocket.

"Smoke, the board voted to give you a reward of three hundred dollars, in addition to the one hundred fifty you earned," Matthews said, handing the envelope to Smoke.

"Smoke!" Sally said happily. "That will pay our interest, plus allow us to keep the money we were going to use."

Smoke nodded. "Thanks, Joel."

"I just wish it could be more," he said. "I wish it could be enough to pay off your entire note."

"Well, with the extension this will buy for me, maybe we'll come up with a way of handling that note," Smoke said.

At that moment, Emil Blanton came into the saloon, carrying a large pile of papers. Blanton was publisher of the local newspaper, the *Big Rock Vindicator.* Smiling, he brought one of the newspapers over to Smoke.

"Since you are the star of my story, I thought I might give you a free copy," Blanton said, holding it up for Smoke and the others to see.

SMOKE JENSEN
FOILS ROBBERY ATTEMPT.

On the 9th instant, the well-known local rancher Smoke Jensen volunteered his services as a shotgun guard for the Sulphur Springs Express Company. The reason for this was a special shipment of twenty thousand dollars, said money to be made available at the Bank of Big Rock in order to provide loans for those of the area who have been made desperate by the brutal winter conditions.

According to Mr. Puddin' Taylor, who was the driver of the coach, the would-be robbers accosted them just as they reached the top of McDill Pass. Before Taylor could question the intent of the three who had flagged down the coach, the highwaymen presented pistols, and opened fire with mixed effect. Mr. Taylor was wounded, but the other bullets missed. Smoke Jensen fired back, but not until after the robbers had fired first.

Smoke Jensen, as his reputation so nobly suggests, did not miss. Within scarcely more than the blink of an eye, all three outlaws were sent on their way to eternity, where they will be forced to plead their case before St. Peter and all the angels of heaven.

This newspaper joins other citizens of the fair city of Big Rock in congratulating Smoke Jensen for his quick thinking and courageous action.

* * *

Ebenezer Dooley was at the Cow Bell Saloon in the small town of Antinito, Colorado. A traveler had left a copy of the Big Rock newspaper in the saloon, and because Dooley had nothing else to do, he picked it up, took it over to an empty table, and began reading it.

The paper was over two weeks old, but that didn't matter because it had been several weeks since Dooley had read any news at all. He read about his botched robbery attempt.

"Smoke Jensen," Dooley said, scratching his beard as he read the weathered newspaper. "That's the name of the son of a bitch who stole my money."

Dooley folded the newspaper and put it in his pocket. "I'll be keepin' that in my memory."

"Beg your pardon?" the man at the next table over said.

"Nothin'," Dooley said. "I was just talkin' to myself, is all."

The man laughed. "I do that my ownself sometimes," he replied. "I guess when you're used to talkin' to your horse all the time, why, a man will sometimes just wind up talkin' to hisself."

"I guess so," Dooley said, not that interested in getting into a conversation with the man.

"You was readin' about Jensen, wasn't you? Smoke Jensen."

"Yeah," Dooley said. "Yeah, I was. How did you know?"

"You spoke his name."

"Oh, yeah, I guess I did."

"You know him?"

"No, I, uh, ran across him once," Dooley replied.

"So you wouldn't say he's a friend of yours?"

Dooley shook his head. "He ain't no friend. Do you know him?"

"Well, we ain't ever actual met, but I know who the son of a bitch is. He kilt my brother."

"He killed your brother? Why isn't he in prison for that?"

"Well, my brother was rustlin' some of Jensen's cattle at the time."

"Where were you when that happened?"

"I was in prison."

Suddenly Dooley smiled. "I'll be damned," he said. "I know who you are. You're Curt Logan, aren't you?"

Logan smiled, then picked up his glass and moved over to join Dooley. "I was wonderin' when you would recognize me. I mean, I recognized you right off. Course, we was in different cell blocks, so we didn't see each other all that many times. Then I done my time and got out." Logan looked puzzled. "What are you doin' out? I thought you was supposed to be doin' twenty years."

"Well, let's just say that the State of Colorado had its idea of when I should leave, and I had mine," Dooley said.

Logan chuckled. "I'll be damned. You escaped, didn't you?"

"Yes, I did. Fact is, you could get five hundred dollars just for turning me in to the law."

"Is that a fact?"

"It is," Dooley said. "But I'm not worried about you doin' that."

"Why not?"

"Because I know somethin' that would be worth a

lot more than five hundred dollars to you. That is, if you are interested."

Logan nodded. "I'm interested," he said.

"What have you been doin' since you got out?" Dooley asked.

"Tryin' to make a livin'," Logan said. "I've punched some cows, worked at a freight yard, mucked out a few stalls."

"Haven't found anything to your likin', though, have you?"

Logan chuckled. "What's there to like about any of that?"

"I might have an idea," Dooley said, "if I can get enough men together."

"How many do you need?"

"Besides the two of us, I'd say about four more."

"Six men? Damn, what you plannin' to do? Rob a bank?"

Dooley smiled again. "Well, that's where the money is, ain't it?"

Smoke sat in his saddle and watched as his hands dragged the dead cattle into large piles, then burned them. It was the only way to clear away the carnage left from the brutal winter just passed. He and all the cowboys were wearing kerchiefs tied around their noses to help keep out the stench.

When the pile was large enough, Pearlie and Cal rode around the carcasses, soaking them with coal oil. Their horses, put off by the smell of death, were skittish, and would occasionally break into a quick gallop away. Cal's horse did that, reacting so quickly that Cal dropped the can of kerosene.

"Whoa! Hold it, hold it!" Cal shouted, fighting his mount. Cal was an exceptionally skilled rider who sometimes broke horses for fun. Because of that, he generally rode the most spirited horses, and not many of the other riders would have been able to stay seated. Cal rode easily, gracefully, until he got the horse under control again.

When the gallop was over, Cal brought his reluctant horse back to the task at hand, bending over from the saddle to retrieve the can he had dropped.

Finally, when the pile of dead cows had been sufficiently dosed with kerosene, Pearlie lit a match and dropped it onto one of the animals. The match caught, and within a few minutes, large flames were leaping up from the pile.

Pearlie and Cal rode back to where Smoke was, then reined up alongside him and turned to watch the fire.

"It's like a barbeque," Cal said.

"If it is, it's the most expensive barbeque you'll ever see," Pearlie said.

"Yeah," Smoke said, answering in one, clipped word.

"Sally," Smoke said that night as they lay in bed. There was agony in the sound of his voice.

"Yes?"

"I had to let all the men go today."

"I figured as much. I saw them all riding off."

"I even let Pearlie and Cal go."

"Oh," Sally said.

"Don't worry. They aren't going anywhere. I explained that I cannot pay them, but they said they would stay anyway."

"Yes," Sally said. "I figured they would."

"We can't do it," Smoke said. He sighed. "We lost too many head. Even if we sold every cow we have left, we wouldn't make enough money to pay off the note on the ranch."

"Oh, Smoke," Sally said, putting her head on his shoulder.

"I've let you down," Smoke said. "I've failed you."

"No, you haven't let me down, and you haven't failed. You had no control over the weather."

"That's true, I had no control over the weather," Smoke said. "But if I hadn't borrowed so much money against the ranch, we could have ridden out this winter. Now, we're going to lose Sugarloaf. And I know how much you love this place."

"Oh, you silly darling," Sally said. "I do love this place, but don't you know that I love you much more? In fact, I love this place because of you. And no matter where we go, or what we have to do, it will be fine as long as we are together."

"Yeah," Smoke said. He tightened his arm around her. "That's good to know, but it doesn't make me any less a failure."

They lay in silence for a moment longer before Sally spoke again.

"We don't have to lose this place," she said.

"You have an idea as to how to save it?"

"Yes. Don't you remember? I told you about it last winter."

"You're talking about leasing the ranch, aren't you?"

"Yes."

Smoke sighed. "I don't want to do that. I don't want to give up control of my own place."

"But it would only be temporary. You would give up control for one year. Surely that would be better than losing the ranch, and giving up control forever?" Sally insisted.

Smoke didn't answer for a moment, and Sally thought about pressing her case, but she held back. She had lived with Smoke long enough to know that he was thinking it through.

"All right," he finally said. "Suppose I decide to do this, what would be the first step?"

"There is a land broker's office in Denver," Sally said. "I saved the address. We can go there and talk to him."

"No, you stay here with the ranch," Smoke said. "It's ours for thirty more days. I wouldn't want to give anyone the wrong idea that we were abandoning it, and someone might think that is exactly what is happening if we both leave."

"All right, I'll stay."

"Besides, if we do lease the ranch, I expect the tenants will want to live in this house. So you, Pearlie, and Cal need to find someplace for us to go. The line shack over on Big Sandy might work. It's the biggest of all of them."

"We'll get it in shape while you're gone," Sally said.

"I hate having to ask you to live in such a place."

"It will be fine, Smoke, you'll see," Sally said. "I'll

have it looking really nice by the time we move in. And it's only a year; then we'll be back in our own house."

"The Lord willing," Smoke said.

"Smoke, when you make the deal, don't forget that you must get the money in advance, in order to be able to pay the note."

"I know," Smoke said. "Don't worry, I will."

"It's going to be all right, Smoke," Sally said. "I know it will."

"Pearlie?"

Cal got no response.

"Pearlie?" he called again.

Although the bunkhouse had beds enough for twelve cowboys, Cal and Pearlie were the only two occupants at the present time.

Cal sat up in the darkness. He couldn't see Pearlie, but he could hear him snoring.

"Pearlie!" he said again.

"What?" Pearlie answered, sitting up quickly. "What's happening?"

"Are you asleep?" Cal asked.

Pearlie let out an audible sigh, then fell back in his bed.

"Well, I *was* asleep," Pearlie said.

"Oh. Well, then, I won't bother you."

Pearlie got out of his bunk, then walked over to Cal's bunk. He jerked all the covers off Cal.

"Hey, what did you do that for?" Cal shouted, reaching for the covers that Pearlie was holding away from him. "Give me my covers."

Pearlie handed him his covers, then sat back down on his bunk. "I'm listening now," he said. "So tell me what was so important that you had to wake me up." Pearlie ran his hand over the puff of purple flesh that was on his chest, the result of a bullet wound.

"We was goin' to bury you under the aspen trees," Cal said.

"What?"

"Last year, when we was down to the Santa Gertrudis Ranch, helpin' out Captain King, you got shot, remember?"

Pearlie laughed. "Well, Cal, that ain't somethin' that you just forget all that easy."

"Anyway, we didn't figure you'd live until we got you home, so we was already plannin' your funeral. We decided to, that is, Miss Sally decided to bury you under the aspen trees. That would'a been a real pretty spot too."

"Sorry it didn't work out for you," Pearlie said, teasing. "Cal, please tell me you didn't wake me up just to tell me where you had planned to bury me."

"Miss Sally planned."

"All right, Miss Sally planned. Is that why you woke me up?"

"No."

"Then why did you?"

"I'm worried," Cal said. "What if Smoke can't get the money? I mean, he's got to come up with all that money in less than a month. I can't see no way he's goin' to be able to do that."

"He's been in some tough spots before," Pearlie said. "I reckon it'll work out all right."

"What if he don't?"

"What do you mean?"

"What if he don't get the money? Then he'll lose the ranch. And if he does, then where will we go? What will become of us?"

"Cal, are you worried about Smoke? Or are you worried about us?" Pearlie asked.

Cal ran his hand through his hair. "I guess I'm worried about both," he said.

"Well, at least you are honest about it," Pearlie said. "Truth is, I don't know what will become of us."

"You know what I think? I think we ought to leave," Cal said.

"Leave? You mean run out on Smoke and Miss Sally?"

"No, not run out on them," Cal said. "Just leave, so they don't have us to have to feed and worry about."

"Yeah," Pearlie said. "Yeah, I see what you mean."

"I think we ought to go now," Cal said.

"You mean just leave, without so much as a fare-thee-well?"

"Yes," Cal said. "Think about it, Pearlie. If we stick around long enough to tell them good-bye, you know what they are going to do. They are going to try and talk us into stayin' on."

"Maybe they need us to stay on."

Cal shook his head. "No, right now, we're a burden to 'em. I know how it is, Pearlie. I was on my own when I was twelve 'cause I didn't have no family to speak of, and I didn't want to be a burden to nobody."

"All right, we'll go," Pearlie said. "But I ain't goin' without leavin' 'em a letter. There ain't no way I'm goin' to just run out on 'em. Not after all the things they have done for us.'"

"I agree," Cal said. "The least we can do is leave 'em a letter tellin' 'em what happened to us."

Chapter Five

"Smoke!"

Smoke was in the bedroom, packing for his trip, but the anguish in Sally's call to him caused him to drop the saddlebags on the bed and hurry to the kitchen. He saw her standing just inside the kitchen door, leaning against the counter. She was holding a letter in one hand, while her other hand was covering her mouth. Her eyes had welled with tears.

"What is it?" Smoke asked. "What has happened?"

"They are gone," Sally said in a strained voice.

"Who is gone? What are you talking about?"

"It's Pearlie and Cal," she said. "When I went out to the bunkhouse to call them in for breakfast, they weren't there, and all their stuff was gone. I found this lying on Pearlie's bunk." Sally handed Smoke a sheet of paper.

Smoke read the letter.

Dear Smoke and Miss Sally,
    By the time you get this letter, me and Cal will be gone. We figure, what with all the problems you're havin' with the ranch and all, that you

don't really need two more mouths to feed. And since you ain't got no cows to speak of, why, there ain't enough work to justify you keepin' us on just so's you can feed us.

We are both grateful for all the good things you two has done for us, and for all the good times we've had together. I know you ain't either one of you old enough to be our parents, but it's almost like that's just what you are, the way you have took care of us and looked out for us for all this time.

I hope you can save the ranch somehow. We'll be looking in now and again to see how it is that you are faring, and if we see that you got the ranch all put back together again, why, we'll come back and work for you again. Fact is, if we can find work now, why, me and Cal has both said that we'll be sending some money along to help you out.

> *Your good friends,*
> *Pearlie and Cal*

"I can't believe they would do something like that to us," Smoke said.

"Oh, Smoke, I don't think they believe they are doing it to us. I think they believe they are doing it for us."

"Well, that's just it. They didn't think," Smoke said. He sighed. "That means you are going to be here all alone while I'm gone. Will you be all right?"

"Why, Kirby Jensen," Sally said. "How dare you ask me such a question?"

Smoke chuckled. "You're right," he said. "That was

pretty stupid of me. I pity the poor fool who would try and break in here while I'm gone."

"Did you pack your white shirt and jacket? I think you should wear that when you talk to the broker."

"I packed it," Smoke said. He put his hands on her shoulders. "It's a long ride to Denver," he said. "I'll be gone for at least two weeks, maybe a little longer. I'll send you a telegram when I get there, just to let you know that I arrived all right. Then I'll send you another one when I get something worked out with the broker."

"I'll miss you terribly, but I'll be here when you get back," Sally said. "I'll spend the time while you are gone getting the line house ready for us. I intend to move some of my favorite pieces of furniture down there."

"How are you going to move them with Pearlie and Cal gone?"

"I'll go into town and ask Mr. Longmont to find someone to help me," Sally said. "Don't worry, I'll take care of it."

They kissed, and as the kiss deepened, Sally pulled away and looked up at him with a smile on her face.

"What would it hurt if you left an hour later?" she asked.

Smoke returned her smile. "Why, I don't think it would hurt at all," he said as he led her toward their bedroom.

It was just after dark when Pearlie and Cal rode into Floravista, New Mexico Territory. From the small adobe houses on the outskirts of town, dim lights flickered through shuttered windows. The kitchens of the houses emitted enticing smells of suppers being cooked, from the familiar aromas of fried chicken to the more exotic and spicy bouquets of Mexican fare.

A barking dog ended its yapping with a high-pitched yelp, as if it had been kicked, or hit by a thrown rock.

A baby cried, its loud keening cutting through the night.

A housewife raised her voice in one of the houses, launching into some private tirade about something, sharing her anger with all who were within earshot.

The main part of Floravista was a contrast of dark and light. Commercial buildings such as stores and offices were closed and dark, but the saloons and cantinas were brightly lit and they splashed pools of light out onto the wood-plank sidewalks and on into the street. As Pearlie and Cal rode down the street, they passed in and out of those pools of light so that to anyone watching, they would be seen, then unseen, then seen again. The footfalls of their horses made a hollow clumping sound, echoing back from the false-fronted buildings as they passed them by.

By the time they reached the center of town, the night was alive with a cacophony of sound: music from a tinny piano, a strumming guitar, and an out-of-tune vocalist, augmented by the high-pitched laughter of women and the deep guffaw of men. From somewhere in the Mexican part of town, a trumpet was playing.

Pearlie and Cal dismounted in front of the Oasis Saloon, tied their horses to the hitching rail, then went inside. Dozens of lanterns scattered throughout the saloon emitted enough light to read by, though drifting clouds of tobacco smoke diffused the golden light.

As they stood for a moment just inside the door, Cal happened to see a pickpocket relieve someone of his wallet. The thief's victim was a middle-aged man who was leaning over the bar, drinking a beer and enjoying his conversation. While he was thus engaged, the nimble-fingered pickpocket deftly slipped the victim's billfold from his back pocket. Instead of putting the billfold in his pocket, though, the thief walked down to the end of the bar and, casually, dropped it into a potted plant. Then the thief ordered a beer and stood there, drinking it casually.

"Pearlie, did you see that?" Cal asked.

"Yeah, I saw it," Pearlie answered.

"Maybe we should. . . ."

"Wait," Pearlie said. "Let's see what happens."

The victim ordered a second beer, then reached for his pocket to get the money to pay. That's when he realized that his billfold was gone.

Puzzled by the absence of his billfold, the man looked on the floor to see if he had dropped it. Then he picked up his hat, which was lying on the bar, to see if it was there.

"Hey," the man called. "Has anybody seen my billfold?"

"I know where it is," Cal said.

Cal and Pearlie were still standing in the middle of the floor, having just come in.

"You know where my wallet is?" the man replied in disbelief.

"Yes, sir, I know where it is."

"Well, where is it?"

Cal pointed to the potted plant that sat on the floor at the end of the bar.

"It's down there under that plant" Cal said.

The victim looked toward the plant; then he turned back toward Cal. "Now how in the hell would it wind up down there?" he asked. "I haven't moved from this spot since I got here."

The pickpocket, suddenly sensing danger, put his beer down and started walking toward the door. As he did, Pearlie stepped in front of him to stop him.

"Here, get out of my way," the pickpocket growled. "What are you doing."

Cal pointed to the pickpocket Pearlie had stopped. "Your billfold is in that pot, because this fella put it there. Only, he didn't put it there until after he took all the money from it and stuck it down into his own pocket."

"What?" the pickpocket said. "Mister, are you crazy? I just come in here to have a beer."

"And steal some money," Pearlie added.

By now the confrontation had stopped all conversation as everyone looked toward Pearlie, Cal, and the pickpocket.

"I ain't goin' to stand around here and be accused of stealin'," the pickpocket said. He pointed toward the bartender. "What kind of place are you running here anyway? Do you just let anyone accuse an innocent person of picking someone's pocket?"

The barkeep brought a double-barrel shotgun up from under the bar, and though he didn't point it at anyone, its very presence lent some authority to his next comment.

"Mr. Thornton, you want to step down there and look in the potted plant and see if your wallet is there?" the bartender asked.

The men who were standing at the bar between Thornton and the potted plant stepped back to let him by. He walked to it, then looked down inside.

"I'll be damned!" he said. "He's right! My wallet is here!" Thornton reached down into the pot, then came up with the wallet, holding it high for everyone in the saloon to see.

There was an immediate reaction from all the other patrons.

"Any son of a bitch who would steal another man's wallet ought to be strung up," someone said.

"Or at least tarred and feathered," another added.

"I don't know what you are talkin' about," the pickpocket said, his voice and expression showing his anxiousness. "I didn't put that there."

"Is your money gone, Mr. Thornton?" Pearlie asked.

Thornton opened his wallet and looked inside.

"Yes!" he said. "Every dollar of it is gone."

Pearlie stuck his hand down into the pickpocket's vest pocket and took out some folded bills. He handed the bills to the bartender.

"Hey! That's my money!" the pickpocket said. "You all seen it. He just stole my money!"

"How much money did you have in your billfold?" Pearlie asked.

"I had nineteen dollars," Thornton answered. "Three fives and four ones."

The bartender counted the folded bills, then held them up. "Three fives and four ones," he announced to all.

The pickpocket tried to run, but two men grabbed him, then hustled him out of the saloon bound for the sheriff's office.

"Well, now, I would like to thank you two boys," the victim said, extending his hand. "The name is Thornton. Michael Thornton."

"I'm Pearlie, this here is Cal," Pearlie said, shaking Thornton's hand.

"Pearlie and Cal, eh? Well, I reckon that's good enough for me. Could I buy you boys a drink?"

"Later, perhaps, after we've had our supper," Pearlie replied. "That is, if a fella can get anything to eat in here," he added to the bartender. "Do you serve food?"

"Steak and potatoes, ham and eggs, your choice," the bartender replied.

"Yes."

"Yes, which?"

"Yes, we'll have steak and potatoes, ham and eggs," Pearlie said.

Thornton laughed. "These young men are hungry," he said. "Bring them whatever they want. I'll pay for it."

"You don't need to buy our supper," Pearlie said. "We were just doin' what we figured was right."

"I know I don't need to. It's just my way of thanking you."

"If you really want to thank us, you can tell us where we might find a job in this town," Cal said.

"You two boys are looking for a job?"

"Yes, sir," Cal answered.

"You aren't afraid of hard work, are you?" Thornton asked.

"Not if it's honest."

"Good enough. I own the livery," Thornton said. "I can always use a couple of good men if you are interested."

"We're interested," Pearlie said.

"Then the job is yours."

Chapter Six

Ebenezer Dooley turned in his saddle and looked at the five men who were with him. Buford Yancey, Fargo Masters, and Ford DeLorian were men he had worked with before. He had never worked with Logan, but he vaguely remembered him from their time together in prison. Curt Logan had brought along his brother, Trace, as the fifth man. Curt and Trace Logan were wearing identical red and black plaid shirts.

Dooley spit out a wad of tobacco as he stared at the two brothers.

"Logan, would you tell me why in the hell you and your brother are wearing those shirts? Don't you know they stand out like a sore thumb? Ever'one in town is goin' to see 'em, and remember 'em."

"There's likely to be some shootin', ain't there?" Curt Logan asked.

"I told you there might be. Robbin' a bank ain't like stealin' nickels off a dead man's eyes."

"Well, I already lost me one brother when he got hisself kilt by Smoke Jensen, and I don't plan to lose me another'n. That's why Trace 'n me is wearin' these here plaid shirts."

Dooley shook his head in confusion. "What's wearing a shirt like that got to do with it?"

"Things gets real confusin' when there's a lot of shootin' goin' on, and I don't plan for me'n my brother to shoot each other by mistake. As long as we're wearin' these here shirts, that ain't likely to happen."

"If you lead the posse to us 'cause of them shirts, I'll be doin' the shootin' my ownself," Dooley growled.

"Dooley," Fargo said. "The sun's gettin' on up. I figure it's nine o'clock for sure. The bank'll be open by now."

"Right," Dooley said. "All right, men, anybody got to take a piss, now's the time to do it."

Three of the men dismounted to relieve themselves, then all remounted and looked at Dooley.

"Fargo, you, Ford, and Yancey will ride into town from the south end. Me'n the Logans will come in from the north. That way, we won't be drawin' no attention on account of so many ridin' together."

"All right," Fargo said. "Come on, boys," he said to the others. "We'll need to get around to the other side."

Jason Turnball, the city marshal for the town of Etna, was a big man, standing almost six feet six and weighing well over two hundred pounds. He was sitting in a chair on the porch in front of Dunnigan's General Store. Dunnigan had reinforced the chair just for the marshal, because he liked having the marshal parked on his front porch. That tended to keep away anyone who might get the idea to rob the store, almost as if he had hired his own personal guard.

Marshal Turnball had his feet propped up on the porch railing, and his chair tipped onto the back two legs. He was peeling an apple, and one long peel hung from the apple all the way to the porch.

Billy Frakes, an eighteen-year-old who worked as a store clerk for Dunnigan, was sweeping the front porch.

"I tell you true, Marshal Turnball," Frakes said. "I believe that's about the longest peel you've ever pared."

"Nah," Turnball said as he cut it off at the end, then held it up for examination. "I've done longer." He tossed the peeling to the bluetick hound that lived under the porch. The dog grabbed the peel, then backed up against the front wall to eat it.

"Look at them folks," Frakes said, pointing to the three riders who passed by in front of the store. "Two of 'em's got shirts just alike."

Turnball laughed. "Wouldn't think two of 'em would be dumb enough to wear a shirt that ugly, would you?"

Frakes laughed with him.

Fargo, Ford, and Yancey reached the bank just before Dooley and the Logan brothers. They stopped across the street from the bank and dismounted in front of a leather goods store. Yancey and Fargo examined a pair of boots in the window, while Ford dismounted and held the reins of the three horses. Dooley and the Logans arrived then, and Dooley nodded at Fargo, just before he and the Logans went into the bank.

* * *

"That's funny," Frakes said.

"What's funny?" Turnball replied.

"Them fellas over there in front of Sikes Leather Goods. How come you reckon that one is holdin' the horses, 'stead of tyin' 'em off at the hitchin' rail?"

"Maybe them other two just wanted to look at the boots and they was goin' to ride on," Turnball suggested.

"Well, if they're just wantin' 'em some boots, maybe one 'em would be interested in buyin' a pair of boots I just made," Frakes said. "I think I'll go down there an' see."

"If you go down there and sell your boots in front of Al Sikes's store, takin' business away from him, you never will get him to sell your boots for you," Turnball said.

"No, sir. I think it's just the opposite. If Mr. Sikes seen that folks would be willin' to buy boots that I've made, why, that might just make him want to sell 'em in his store," Frakes insisted as he stood the broom up against the wall. He stepped inside Dunnigan's for just a moment, then came back out carrying the boots he had made. He held them out for the marshal's inspection.

"What do you think of 'em?" he asked.

"They're good-lookin' boots all right," Turnball agreed. "Can't nobody say you don't do good work."

Smiling under Turnball's praise, Frakes started down the street toward Sikes Leather Goods.

Trace Logan stayed out front holding the horses, while his brother Curt and Dooley went into the bank.

There were only two people inside the bank, Rob Clark, the owner, and Tucker Patterson, the teller. Both were just behind the teller's cage, and Patterson looked up as the two men came inside.

"Yes, sir," Patterson said. "Can I help you gent . . ." he began. Then he paused and gasped as he saw that both men were wearing hoods over their faces. They were also holding guns.

"This here is a holdup," Dooley said in a gruff voice. He held up a cloth bag. "Fill this bag with money."

"Mr. Clark?" Patterson said. "What shall I do?"

Dooley pointed his pistol at Clark and pulled the hammer back. It made a deadly-sounding click.

"Yeah, tell him, Mr. Clark," Dooley said. "What should he do?"

"T-Tucker," Clark said in a frightened voice. "I think you had better do what the man says."

"Yes, sir," Patterson said.

"Now you're getting smart," Dooley said.

Patterson started taking money from the cash drawer and putting it into the sack.

"Take a look out in the street," Dooley said to Curt. "Anybody comin' in?"

"Don't see nobody," Curt answered.

"That's all the money we've got," Patterson said, handing the sack back.

Dooley looked down into the sack. "There's not more'n a couple hundred dollars here," he said. "I know you got more'n that. I want the money from the safe."

"I . . . I don't have the combination to the safe," Patterson said. "Only the bank president has the combination."

"Where is the bank president?"

Patterson glanced toward Clark, but he said nothing.

"I see," Dooley said. "All right, Mr. Bank President, I'll ask you to open the safe."

Clark didn't move.

Dooley pointed his gun at Patterson. "Open the safe or I'll kill him right now," Dooley growled.

"Mr. Clark, please!" Patterson begged.

Nodding reluctantly, Clark walked over to the safe. Within a few minutes he had the door open. Dooley could see several small, filled bank bags inside.

"Damn!" Curt Logan said with a low whistle. "Have you ever seen so much money?"

"Put them bank bags in the sack," Dooley ordered, handing the sack over to Clark.

"What's takin' 'em so long?" Yancey asked, looking back toward the bank.

"Maybe there's lots of money and it's takin' 'em a while to get it all," Fargo suggested. "You don't worry about them; you just do the job you're supposed to be doin'. Keep a lookout all around you."

"There ain't nobody payin' no attention to the bank," Yancey said.

"Fargo, Yancey, there's someone comin'," Ford called from his position holding the horses.

"Where? Who?" Fargo asked.

"Up there," Ford said, nodding. "He's comin' right for us."

"He's carryin' a pair of boots," Yancey said. "Maybe he bought some boots here and he's bringin' 'em back."

"This is a hell of a time for him to be doin' that," Fargo said.

At that moment, Dooley and Curt Logan ran from the bank, still wearing hoods over their faces. Clark appeared in the front door of the bank, right behind them. He was carrying a pistol, and he fired it at the three men as they were getting mounted.

"Holdup!" Clark shouted. "Bank robbery! These men just robbed the bank!"

Dooley and both of the Logan brothers shot back at the banker, and Clark dropped his gun, then fell back into the bank.

"Shoot up the town, boys!" Dooley shouted. "Keep ever'one's head down!"

Frakes, who was nearly to the leather goods store by then, was surprised to see that the three men he was coming to see were also part of the robbery. He dropped his boots and ran as they began shooting up and down the street, aiming as well at the buildings. Window glass was shattered as the bullets crashed through.

One of the bullets hit the supporting post of the awning in front of the meat market, just as Frakes stepped up onto the porch. Frakes turned, and dived into the watering trough right in front of the meat market. Sinking to the bottom, he could hear the continuing sound of shots being fired, though now it was muffled by the water. Frakes held his breath as long as he could, then lifted his head up, gasping for air. By that time he could see the six men just crossing over the Denver and

New Orleans railroad track. They galloped out of town, headed almost due west toward Thunder Butte, which rose some twenty miles away.

Frakes climbed out of the trough and stood in the street alongside, dripping water. The town was in a turmoil with men yelling at each other, dogs barking, and children crying. Several men were running toward the bank.

"Was anybody hit?" someone asked.

"Help me," Patterson was calling from the front of the bank. "Help me, somebody! Mr. Clark has been shot!"

By now there were several men gathered at the bank and as Frakes started toward it, he saw Dr. Urban going there as well. Urban was carrying his medical bag, and when he reached the bank he started shouting at the people to let him through.

"It's the doc," someone said. "Let him through."

Frakes went over as well, and because there were too many people crowded around for him to see, he climbed up on the railing. That gave him a good view, and he saw Dr. Urban kneeling beside Clark's prostrate form.

"How is he, Doc?" someone asked.

Dr. Urban put his fingers to Clark's neck, held them there for a moment, then shook his head.

"He's gone," Dr. Urban said.

"Somebody better go tell Mrs. Clark," Tucker Patterson said.

Dr. Urban looked up at Patterson. "Well, Mr. Patterson, I expect that should be you," he said. "You know her better than anyone else."

Gulping, Patterson nodded. "I expect that's so," he said.

"Did anyone get a good look at the ones who did this?" Turnball asked.

"Marshal, it was them same fellas we seen comin' into town," Frakes said. "The ones with them plaid shirts."

"Yeah, I seen them shirts too," one of the other townspeople said.

"That's right, Marshal," Patterson said. "Two of them were wearing red and black plaid shirts."

"Did you see their faces?" Turnball asked Patterson.

Patterson shook his head. "No, I didn't see their faces. They had their faces covered with hoods."

"The ones outside wasn't wearin' hoods," someone said.

"Yeah, well, wearin' hoods or not don't make no difference," one of the others said. "Near'bout all of us seen them shirts. You can't hide a shirt like that."

"You goin' after them, Marshal?"

"There are six of them," Turnball said.

"I don't care how many of 'em there is, they got our money. Hell, after this winter we just come through, that's near'bout all the money the town has left."

"I'll need a posse."

"I'll ride with you."

"Me too."

"You can count on me."

"I'll ride with you, Marshal," Frakes said.

"All right, men, get yourselves a gun, have your women put together two, maybe three days' food, get mounted, and meet me in front of my office."

"When?"

"I figure you should all be ready within an hour."

"An hour? Marshal, them outlaws can get a long ways in an hour," one of the men said. Like Turnball, he was wearing a badge, because this was Turnball's deputy.

"Pike, they've already got fifteen minutes on us," Turnball said. "If we go off half-cocked now, we ain't got a snowball's chance in hell of catchin' up to them. Best thing for us to do is be prepared. Now, are you plannin' on riding with the posse or not?"

"You know I'm goin'," Pike said. "I'm your deputy, ain't I?"

"Then get you some fcod, then get on back down to the office and wait until we are ready to go."

"All right, all right," Pike said. "I just don't want them sons of bitches to get away, that's all."

Turnball looked at the others, who seemed to be standing around awaiting further instructions. "What are you all a'waitin' on? Now!" he said gruffly, and with that, the posse scattered.

"Marshal, you want I should get some cuffs so we can cuff 'em when we find 'em?" Pike asked.

"Of course," Turnball said. "Unless you were plannin' on just askin' them not to try and get away."

"No, it's not that, it's just that I thought, well . . ." Pike hesitated.

"You thought what?"

"I wasn't all that sure we would be bringin' 'em back in, if you know what I mean."

"No, I don't know what you mean."

"I mean men like that, shootin' down Mr. Clark and stealin' all the town's money like they done. Well, some folks might think they don't have no right to be brought back in alive."

"Pike, I'm going to pretend I didn't hear that," Turnball said.

"It's not like I'm talkin' lynchin' or anything," Pike said. "I meant, uh, well, I meant, what if they put up a fight and we have to kill 'em? I mean, all legal like."

"Now, you get back down to the office and get ready, like I said."

"Sure, Marshal, sure," Pike said. "Like I said, I didn't really mean nothin' by it. I was just thinkin' on what might happen, is all."

"Do me a favor, will you, Pike? Don't think," Marshal Turnball said.

Smoke was riding north through a level forest. Just behind him a boulder-covered hillside rose almost ten thousand feet to the wooded and still-snow-covered peak of Thunder Butte. It was getting toward midday when Stormy started limping and Smoke had to stop. He had just lifted the left foreleg of his horse to look at the foot when he saw six men riding toward him.

Smoke didn't pay that much attention to them at first. He was on relatively level ground, which meant that anyone who was traveling through here would have to come in his general direction. Right now his biggest concern at the moment was the shoe. But the approaching horses made an obvious turn so that they began moving directly toward him.

Smoke had no idea what they wanted, so he kept an

eye on them as he examined Stormy's hoof. He saw that the horse had picked up a rock between the shoe and the hoof, so he started working to get it out.

The riders came right up to him, then reined to an abrupt halt. Smoke looked up at them again.

"Howdy," he said.

"Howdy," one of the riders—a man with a long, pock-marked face and a drooping eyelid—said, swinging down from his horse. The other five riders dismounted as well.

There was something peculiar about the riders, the way they all dismounted and the way they stared at him. It was also curious how they let one man do all the talking. Two of the riders were wearing identical red and black plaid shirts, and as he looked at them more closely, he saw that they looked enough alike that they must be brothers. He didn't have a good feeling about the whole situation, and he decided that the quicker they left, the better it would be.

"Are you havin' any trouble?" the man with the pock-marked face and drooping eyelid asked.

"Nothing I can't handle," Smoke answered. He squinted at the men. "You folks headed anywhere in particular?"

"Yeah, we're lookin' for work," the man with the drooping eyelid said.

Smoke shrugged. "Don't know as you'll have too much luck there. The winter was pretty bad on most of the ranches. What few spring roundups there were are probably over now. Far as I know, none of the ranches are hiring. Maybe if you go farther south, down into New

Mexico Territory where the winter wasn't so bad, you'll have some luck."

"What are you trying to do, mister? Put a shoe on a split hoof?" one of the men in a plaid shirt asked.

Smoke should have known better than to fall for an old trick like that, but out of concern for the horse, he looked at Stormy's foot. That was when one of the other riders stepped up and slammed the butt of his pistol down on Smoke's head. After that, everything went black.

Chapter Seven

Opening his eyes, Smoke discovered that he was lying facedown in the dirt. He had no idea where he was or why he was lying on the ground, though he sensed that there were several people standing around, looking down at him.

His head throbbed and his brain seemed unable to work. Who were these people and why were they here? For that matter, why was he here?

Smoke tried to get up, but everything started spinning so badly that he nearly passed out again. He was conscious of a terrible pain on the top of his head, and when he reached up and touched the spot gingerly, his fingers came away sticky with blood. Holding his fingers in front of his eyes, he stared at them in surprise. That was when he saw his shirt sleeve. He was not wearing the blue shirt he had started out with that morning. Instead, he was wearing a red and black plaid shirt . . . one of the shirts he had seen on the men who had accosted him.

"What happened?" Smoke asked. His tongue was thick, as though he had been drinking too much.

"I'll tell you what happened, mister. Looks to me like

there was a fallin'-out among thieves," a gruff voice said. "The other boys turned on you, didn't they? They knocked you out and took the money for themselves."

Smoke got up slowly, trying to make sense of things. He wasn't sure what the man was suggesting, so he just hesitated.

"That's right, ain't it?" the man asked. The man talking to him was a very big man, wearing a tan buckskin vest over a red shirt. Peeking out from just behind the vest was a lawman's star.

"I'm not sure I know what you are talking about, Sheriff," Smoke said.

"I'm not a sheriff, I'm marshal for the town of Etna. And lyin' ain't goin' to do you no good. Too many people seen you in that shirt you are wearing. And just because you wound up without any of the money, it don't make you no less guilty. You're going to hang, mister. I don't know which one of you killed Mr. Clark back there in Etna when you held up the bank, but it don't really matter none who pulled the trigger. Every one of you sons of bitches is just as guilty."

Smoke had been right in sensing that there were several people around him, because as he looked around now, he could see several more men glaring at him, all of whom were brandishing weapons, ranging from revolvers to rifles to shotguns.

Again, Smoke put his hand to the wound on his head. It was extremely painful to the touch, and he winced.

"Who are you?" Smoke asked.

"I'll be askin' the questions, mister," the big man replied. "But for your information, the name is Turnball." Turnball pointed to a thin-faced, hawk-nosed man who appeared to be in his mid-twenties. He was also wearing a star.

"This here is Pike, my deputy, and the rest of these men are temporarily deputized for posse duty. What is your name?"

"Jensen. Kirby Jensen, though most folks call me Smoke."

Turnball smiled broadly. "Smoke Jensen, eh?"

"You've heard of me?" Smoke said, relieved. Sometimes having a reputation could be an intrusive aggravation. But in a case like this, it would be helpful in preventing a case of mistaken identity.

"Oh, yes, I've heard of you all right," Turnball said. "Fact is, I've got paper on you tacked up on my wall."

"Paper?"

"You're a wanted man, Mr. Jensen."

"No," Smoke said. "If you've got wanted posters on me, they are old. Very old. All the dodgers on me have been withdrawn. I'm not wanted."

"Well, if you wasn't wanted before, you're sure wanted now, seein' as how you robbed our bank. I reckon you and your friends figured you could get away with it 'cause Etna is so small. But you got yourselves another think coming."

"I didn't rob any bank."

Turnball pointed to Smoke's shirt. "Anyone who would wear a plaid shirt while robbing a bank is just too damn dumb to be an outlaw," he said. "Hell, half the town of Etna described you."

"They may have described this shirt, Marshal, but they didn't describe me," Smoke said.

"Same thing."

"No, it isn't the same thing. This isn't my shirt."

Turnball laughed. "Oh, you mean you stole the shirt before you stole the money from the bank?"

"No. I mean whoever attacked me took my shirt and put this one on me."

Turnball and the others laughed.

"Now if that ain't about the dumbest damn thing I've ever heard. Why would anyone do that?"

"It's obvious, isn't it? They did it to throw the suspicion on me," Smoke explained. "I guess they figured the law around here would be dumb as dirt and buy into it. Looks like they were right."

Turnball laughed again. "You say I'm dumb, but you are the one who got caught. Quit lyin' and save your breath. I know what happened. You boys got into a little fight, and they lit out on you. I'm arresting you for the murder and bank robbin' you and the others done in my town," Turnball said.

Deputy Pike and one of the other riders grabbed Smoke roughly, and tried to twist his arms behind his back. Smoke broke loose.

"Oh, do it!" Pike said, cocking his pistol and pointing it at Smoke's head. "I'm just lookin' for an excuse to shoot you, you murderin' bastard!"

"Pike!" Turnball said gruffly. "I told you, we're takin' him back alive. You kill him here, we never will find the others."

Smoke glared at Pike. "If you want to shackle me,

just ask," he said. "No need for you to pull my arms out of their sockets."

"Put your hands behind your back," Pike ordered.

"Shackle his hands in front of him," Turnball said. "He's got to ride his horse back into town."

Smoke held his hands out in front, and Pike shackled them together.

"Help him on his horse," the marshal ordered. "And pick up them empty bank wrappers. Like as not, we'll be needing them as evidence."

"Marshal Turnball, my horse picked up a stone," Smoke said. "I was working on his foot when the bank robbers jumped me. He'll go lame if it isn't taken care of."

"Check it out, Frakes," Turnball said.

Frakes, who was the youngest of the bunch, had been staring unblinkingly at Smoke from the very beginning. He made no effort to move.

"Frakes?" the marshal said again.

Frakes blinked, as if just aware he was being spoken to. "What?"

"He said his horse picked up a stone. Check it out."

"Left foreleg," Smoke said.

Frakes lifted the horse's left foreleg. "Yeah, there's a stone here, all right," he said. He took a knife from his pocket and, after a moment, got the stone out.

"Thanks," Smoke said.

"You're welcome," Frakes said.

Pike held the reins as Smoke got mounted.

"You're making a big mistake," Smoke said. "I did not hold up any bank. I was on my way up to Denver to meet with a land broker. I own Sugarloaf Ranch down in Rio Grande County. I haven't even been in Etna before today."

"You want to explain these empty bank wrappers here?" Turnball asked, holding one of them out for Smoke to examine. Printed on the side of the wrapper was $1,000,00 BANK OF ETNA.

"They must've been left here by the men who jumped me. They're the ones you are looking for."

"Jumped you, you say?"

"Yes, I told you, I was seeing to my horse when they rode up. They started talking to me, and the next thing I knew, they knocked me out. That must have been when they took my shirt and left this one. That's also when they left these bank wrappers lying around. They set me up."

"You got any witnesses to that?"

"Well, no," Smoke answered. "The only witnesses are the ones who did it, and they certainly wouldn't testify against themselves."

"Too bad you got no witnesses, mister. 'Cause I do have witnesses. At least half a dozen of 'em. And they'll ever'one of 'em swear they seen you and the other robbers ridin' out of town."

"Your witnesses are wrong, Marshal. They are either mistaken, or they are lying."

"Mister, I am one of them witnesses," Turnball said. "And I don't cotton to being called a liar. So, don't you go tellin' me what I did and what I did not see." He pointed at Smoke's chest, adding, "I remember them plaid shirts you and one of the other robbers was wearin' like as if there was a picture of 'em drawn on my eyeballs."

"I told you, this isn't my shirt," Smoke said again. "You are making a huge mistake."

"No, friend," the lawman responded. "The only mistakes made around here was made by you. And you made three of 'em." Ticking them off on his fingers, he enumerated: "Your first mistake was in pickin' a bank in my town to rob. Your second was in havin' a fall-out with the other thieves, and your third was in getting yourself caught. Now, let's go."

The ride back to town took about two hours, and as Turnball and his posse rode into town, several of the town's citizens turned out along either side of the street to watch.

"They caught one of 'em!" someone yelled.

"Good job, Marshal!" another said.

"Hang 'im! Let's hang the son of a bitch now!" yet another shouted. "Ain't no need for a trial! Hell, the whole town seen him kill Mr. Clark!"

The last citizen had several others in the town who agreed with him, and the mood grew much uglier by the time Turnball got Smoke back to the jail.

"What you goin' to do with him now, Marshal?" someone asked as the riders all dismounted.

"I'm going to put him in jail and hold him there until Judge Craig can get down here and hold a trial," Turnball said.

"Hell, there ain't no need in wastin' the judge's time

or our time," one of the citizens said. "If you ask me, I say we hang the son of a bitch now, and get it over with."

"Fremont, I hope you are just mouthin' off to hear yourself talk," Turnball said. "I hope you aren't really talkin' about lynchin'."

"Come on, Jason, you seen what he did to poor old Mr. Clark. His wife has been grievin' something pitiful ever since it happened," Fremont said. "It ain't right that poor Mr. Clark is dead and the son of a bitch that killed him is still alive."

"Pike," Turnball said gruffly. "Get the prisoner in the cell."

"These folks are pretty worked up," Pike said. "Maybe Fremont's got a point. I mean, why should the town pay to feed the prisoner when he's just goin' to hang anyway?"

"Get the prisoner in the cell like I told you to," Turnball said. Turnball pulled a shotgun from the saddle boot of his horse. "The rest of you," he said to the crowd. "Get on about your business and let me get about mine."

"Marshal, you know damn well if we try him, the judge is goin' to find him guilty. Then we'll hang him anyway," Fremont said.

"Then you can afford to be a little paitent."

"To hell with patience. I say let's do it now and get it over with," Fremont insisted, still undeterred by Marshal Turnball's chastising.

Turnball pointed the shotgun at Fremont. "You aren't listenin' to me, are you?" Turnball asked menacingly.

"Whoa, hold on there!" Fremont said, his voice showing his fright. Fremont held his hands out in front of him and took a couple of steps back. "What are you doin', Turnball? You'd shoot an innocent man to save a murderer?"

"There's nothin' innocent about a lynchin', or about anyone who would suggest one," Turnball said. He pulled the hammer back on one of the barrels of the double-barrel shotgun he was holding. "Now if these here people don't leave in the next ten seconds, I'm goin' to blow your head off."

"Wait a minute! What do you mean you're going to blow my head off? I'm not the only one here," Fremont said, obviously frightened at having the gun pointed at him.

"No, you aren't. But you are the one doin' all the big talk, and you are the one I'm going to kill if the others don't leave."

"Why would you shoot me if *they* don't leave?" Fremont asked.

"'Cause I won't be able to kill all of them," Turnball said impatiently. "One, two, three . . ."

"Let's go!" Fremont said to the others. "Let's get out of here!"

Turnball watched as the townspeople left. Then he looked at the men who had ridden with him in the posse.

"You folks can go too," he said. "I thank you for ridin' with me."

The posse members left as well, some of them remounting and riding away, others leading their horses. Frakes remained behind.

"You may as well go on too, Frakes."

"You think the town would really lynch Jensen?" Frakes asked.

"It sounded for a few minutes there like they were giving the idea some thought," Turnball said. "But I don't intend to let it happen. I can't say as I blame them, though. Mr. Clark was a good man, and he carried a lot of people through the winter, givin' 'em time on their loans and all."

"What if we don't have the right man?" Frakes asked.

Turnball laughed. "What do you mean, what if we don't have the right man? Hell, you was right over there on Dunnigan's porch with me when they rode in. We commented on the shirts two of 'em was wearin', remember?"

"Oh, yes, sir, I remember all right," Frakes said.

"Then what makes you think we ain't got the right man?"

"I remember the shirt," Frakes said. "But I don't know as I remember the face. I know for a fact he wasn't the one standin' out front. And when the other two come out of the bank, why, they was both wearin' hoods."

"Well, don't worry about it. We got the right man, all right. And soon as he gets his day in court, why, we'll prove he is the right one. Then we'll build a gallows right here on Front Street, and all these people that's got a bloodlust out will have their hangin'. Only by then, it'll be legal."

"Yeah," Frakes said. "Yeah, I guess you're right." Frakes climbed onto his horse, then started riding it toward the livery.

Turnball watched him for a moment, then went inside.

He saw Pike standing over at the utility table by the wall. Pike was leafing through all the wanted posters.

"You got him into the cell with no problem, I take it?" Turnball asked.

"No problem," Pike said as he continued to page through the wanted posters. "I reckon his kind knows better than to mess with me."

"No doubt," Turnball replied sarcastically.

"Aha! You was right!" Pike said, suddenly holding up one of the posters. "We do have some paper on a fella named Smoke Jensen. Hey, Marshal, did you know there's a five-thousand-dollar reward on him!"

"No. I just remember having seen the name on a dodger, that's all."

Pike whistled. "Five thousand dollars," he said. "Damn that's a lot of money. Just think what we can do with that money."

"It don't do us any good to think about it," Turnball said.

"What do you mean it don't do us any good to think about it? We're the ones that caught him. I'd like to know who has a better claim on it."

"It ain't a point of havin' a better claim on it. We're the law," Turnball explained. "If you're the law, you can't collect on a reward. That's just the way of it."

"Well, that ain't right," Pike said, crestfallen. "That ain't no way right."

"Marshal," Smoke called from the cell at the back of the room. "Check the date on that poster."

Turnball looked at the poster, front and back. "There ain't no date," he said.

"Well, take a good look at the poster then," Smoke said. "Can't you see how the paper has already turned color? That alone should tell you how old it is."

Turnball shook his head. "It don't matter how old it is. I've never received anything cancelin' it."

"All right, it tells what county issued it, doesn't it?" Smoke asked. "Doesn't it say it came from Hinsdale County?"

"Hinsdale County, yes."

"Then it is easy enough for you to check," Smoke said.

"Check, how?"

"All you have to do is send a telegram to the sheriff of Hinsdale County and ask if the poster is still good."

Turnball stroked his chin for a moment. "I could do that, I suppose, but what difference would it make?"

"What do you mean, what difference would it make? It would prove that I'm not a wanted man."

"Oh, it might prove that you aren't wanted for this crime anymore," Turnball said, pointing to the poster. "Whatever the crime was. But that don't have anything to do with why you are in jail now. You are in jail now because you robbed a bank and killed a good man, and near half the town seen you do it. That's somethin' you can't get out of."

"I didn't do it," Smoke said.

"Yes, well, I guess we'll just have to let a judge and jury decide that, won't we?"

Dooley, the Logan brothers, Fargo, Ford, and Buford Yancey had watched from an elevated position near the place where they had encountered Smoke. They saw the posse arrive, confront Smoke, then ride away with him as their captive.

"Ha!" Yancey said. "That was smart leavin' them empty bank wrappers like that. They think he done it."

"Yeah, but this is what gets me. They got to know that there was more'n one person," Fargo said. "How come they're all goin' back with him? Why ain't they still searchin' for the rest of us?"

"Come on, Fargo, you know how posses is," Curt Logan explained. "When they first get started, why, they're all full of piss and vinegar, ready to chase a body to hell and back. But they run out of steam just real quick. Especially if they find just enough success to make 'em feel good about themselves. And what we done was give 'em somethin' to make 'em think they done good."

"Let's go," Dooley said, turning away.

Dooley led them up into the high country and through a pass that was still packed with snow.

"Damn, Dooley," Curt Logan said. "Couldn't you find a place that's easier to get through? The snow here is ass-deep to a tall Indian."

"Nobody who's looking for us will expect us to come this way," Dooley said. "And if they do come this way, it'll be just as hard for them as it is for us."

"Well, you seen 'em. They ain't even comin' after us at all," Curt Logan said. "I sure don't see no need to be workin' so hard just to get away from a posse that ain't even chasin' us."

"If you don't like followin' me, just go your own way," Dooley offered.

"Well, hell, we ain't got no choice now but to keep on a-goin' this way," Curt Logan said. "Now it'd be as hard to go back as it is to keep goin'."

"Besides which, we ain't divided up the money yet," Yancey said.

"We'll divide it up soon as we get through the pass," Dooley said. "Then we can all go our separate ways."

Chapter Eight

"Come on, Pearlie, why won't you go with me?" Cal asked.

"I just don't care that much about travelin' shows, that's all," Pearlie said.

"But they say that Eddie Foy is really funny."

"You go, Cal," Pearlie said. "Have a good time."

"You're sure you don't want to come? I mean, I won't go if you . . ."

"Go," Pearlie said. "We aren't joined at the hip. You can do something by yourself if you want to."

Cal smiled. "All right, if you're sure." He started down the street toward the music hall. A large banner that was spread across the front of the music hall read: EDDIE FOY—DANCER—HUMORIST.

"Cal?" Pearlie called.

Cal turned toward him.

"If you hear any good jokes, tell me tonight, will you?"

Cal nodded. "I will!" he said.

Pearlie watched his young friend walk away; then he headed for the saloon. It wasn't that he didn't want Cal's company, or even that he didn't enjoy his company. It was just that he intended to play a little poker tonight and he knew how Sally felt about such things. He didn't want to be blamed for getting Cal mixed up in a card game.

There was another reason Pearlie wanted to play cards tonight. On the few nights he had come in for a beer, which was all he could afford before his first payday working in the livery stable, he had noticed that the Oasis Saloon employed a woman as dealer for the card games.

The woman's name was Annie, and through the week, Pearlie and Annie had flirted with each other. She had invited him into the game several times, and Pearlie sometimes got the idea that the invitation might be for more than just a game of cards.

He had turned her down every time, not because he didn't want to, but because he couldn't afford to. Tonight, he felt like he could, so he nursed a beer at the bar, then went straight to the table the moment a seat opened up.

"My, my," Annie said, smiling up at him. "Look who has finally come around."

"I thought I might give it a try," Pearlie said, sitting in the open chair.

"New player, new deck," Annie said. She picked up a box, broke the seal, then dumped the cards onto the table. They were clean, stiff, and shining. She pulled out the joker, then began shuffling the deck. The stiff, new pasteboards clicked sharply. Her hands moved swiftly, folding the cards in and out until the law of random numbers became king. She shoved the deck across the table.

"Cut?" she invited Pearlie. She leaned over the table, showing a generous amount of cleavage.

Pearlie cut the deck, then pushed the cards back. He tried to focus on her hands, though it was difficult to do so because she kept finding ways to position herself to draw his eyes toward her more interesting parts.

"You aren't having trouble concentrating, are you?" Annie teased.

"Depends on what I'm concentrating on," Pearlie said.

Annie smiled. "You naughty boy," she said.

"Here, what's goin' on here?" one of the other players asked. "You two know each other?"

"Not yet," Annie answered. She licked her lips. "But I have a feeling we are going to. Five-card?" She paused before she said the next word. "Stud?"

"Fine," Pearlie said.

The cards started falling for Pearlie from the moment he sat down. He won fifteen dollars on the first hand, and a couple of hands later he was ahead by a little over thirty dollars. In less than an hour, he had already tripled the money he'd started with.

Eddie Foy, wearing a broad, outlandish black and white plaid suit, along with a bright red shirt and a huge bow tie, pranced and danced across the stage. He was a very athletic dancer who often twisted his body into extreme positions, but did so gracefully.

Sometimes he would stop right in the middle of his dance and look at one of his legs in a seemingly impossible position. When he did so, he would assume a look of shock, as if even he were surprised to see his leg there. Then, with that same shocked expression on his face, he would stare at the audience, as if asking them how this had happened.

The audience would react in explosive laughter; then the music would start again and his dance would resume.

Sometimes in the middle of his dance, the music would stop and Eddie would walk to the front of the stage, turn sideways, then stare out at the audience, almost as if surprised to see them there. He was carrying a cane, and he had a method of holding the cane behind him in such a way as to cause his hat to seem to tip on its own.

As he spoke, he affected a very pronounced lisp.

"Yethterday wath thuch a nith day that I went for a thmall thtroll," he began.

The audience grew quiet, and Cal leaned forward in anticipation of the upcoming joke.

"I took mythelf into the bank and gave the teller a twenty-dollar bill. My good man, I thaid, I would like to trade thith bill for two ten-dollar billth.

"The teller complied with my requeth.

"I then thaid, my good man, tho well did you perform that tathk, that now I would like to trade my forty-year-old wife for two ladieth of twenty."

Eddy Foy tipped his hat as the audience exploded with laughter.

Cal decided that would be one of the jokes he would have to remember to tell Pearlie.

* * *

Back in the Oasis Saloon, most of the other players were taking Pearlie's good luck in stride, but the one who had asked if Annie and Pearlie knew each other, a man named Creedlove, began complaining.

"Somethin' kind'a fishy is goin' on here," Creedlove said.

"Fishy, Mr. Creedlove?" Annie asked sweetly.

Creedlove looked at Annie, then nodded toward Pearlie. "I think you'n him's workin' together," he said.

"And just how would we be working together?" Annie asked. Almost instantly, the smile had left her face and her words were cold and measured.

"You think I believe that him winnin' all the time is just dumb luck?" Creedlove asked.

"It's not luck, it's skill," Pearlie said. "And the only dumb person in this card game is you. You need to calculate the odds so as to know when to bet and when to fold. That's somethin' you haven't figured out."

"You think you have me pegged, do you?" Creedlove asked. He stared across the table through narrowed eyes. "Suppose me'n you have a go at it? Just the two of us."

"Don't ask me," Pearlie said. "Ask the others if they'd be willing to sit it out."

"I come to play cards," one of the others said. "I don't plan to sit nothin' out."

"Twenty-five dollars to sit in," Creedlove said.

"That's too rich for my blood."

"Anyone else?"

"Play your game, Creedlove. I'll just drink my beer and watch," one of the others said.

"How about you?" Creedlove asked Pearlie.

"All right, I'll play. Name your game," Pearlie said.

"Five-card stud."

"I'm in," Pearlie said, sliding twenty-five dollars to the middle of the table.

Creedlove reached for the cards, but Pearlie stuck his hand out to stop him. "You don't think I'm going to let you deal, do you? We'll let the lady deal."

"Huh-uh," Creedlove said, shaking his head. He nodded toward one of the other players. "We'll let Pete deal."

"How do I know that you and Pete aren't in cahoots? Suppose we get someone who isn't at this table right now," Pearlie suggested.

"Who?"

Pearlie looked around the saloon and saw that there were at least four bar girls working the tables. "How about one of the ladies?" Pearlie asked. "You can choose."

"All right," Creedlove said. He looked over toward the nearest one. "You, honey, come here," he called.

The girl looked up in surprise at being summoned in such a way.

"It's all right, Sue," Annie said. "It'll just take a minute."

"We want you to deal a hand of cards," Creedlove said to Sue when she came over.

"She gets ten dollars from the pot," Annie said.

"What? Why should she get ten dollars?"

"If she gets ten dollars from the pot, it won't make any difference to her who wins," Annie said. "It will guarantee you that it's a fair game."

"That's fine by me," Pearlie said. "How about you?"

"All right," Creedlove agreed.

Sue dealt a down card to each, then an up card. Creedlove showed a king, Pearlie a five of hearts.

Creedlove laughed. "Not lookin' that good for you, is it? Bet five dollars."

Pearlie matched the bet.

The next card gave Creedlove a pair of kings showing. Pearlie drew a six.

"Bet ten dollars," Creedlove said.

Pearlie called the bet, and Creedlove's next card was a jack. Pearlie drew another six, giving him a pair of sixes.

Creedlove bet another ten dollars and Pearlie called.

Creedlove's final card was another jack. Pearlie drew another six.

"Well, now," Creedlove said. "I have two pair, kings and jacks, and you have three of a kind." Creedlove lifted his down card. "So the big question is, do I have a jack or a king as my hole card? Or do your three little sixes have my two pair beat?" He chuckled, and put twenty dollars in the pot. "It's going to cost you twenty to find out."

Pearlie called and raised him twenty.

The smile left Creedlove's face. "You're puttin' quite a store in them three sixes, aren't you? How do you know I don't have a full house?"

"I'm betting you have two pair, and I have you beat," Pearlie said.

Creedlove hesitated for a second, then, with a big smile, he pushed twenty dollars into the center of the table. "All right, I've got you right where I want you. I call." He smiled and flipped over his down card to disclose a king. "Well, lookie here, a full house, kings over jacks. It looks like you lost this one, friend. A full house beats three sixes."

Creedlove reached for the pot as Pearlie turned up his down card showing another six.

"Yes, but it won't beat four sixes," he said, reaching for the pot and pulling it toward him.

"What?" Creedlove gasped. He pointed at the table. "That's not possible!" he said.

"Of course it's possible," Pearlie said. "There are four of everything in a deck. Or hadn't you ever noticed that?" he added innocently.

By now, everyone in the saloon was aware of the high-stakes game and they had all gathered around to watch. They laughed at Pearlie's barb.

Creedlove slid the rest of his money to the center of the table. "I've got thirty-six dollars here," he said. "What do you say we cut for high card?"

Pearlie covered his bet; then Sue fanned the cards out.

"I'll draw first," Creedlove said.

Creedlove drew a queen.

"Ha!" he said triumphantly.

Pearlie drew a king.

"What the . . ." Creedlove shouted in anger. "You cheated me, you son of a bitch! Nobody is this lucky!"

"How did I cheat?" Pearlie asked. "You had the same chance I did."

"I don't know how you cheated," Creedlove said. "I just know that, somehow, you cheated."

Pearlie stood up then, and stepped back from the table. "Now, mister, you might want think about that for a moment," he said in a quiet but ominous voice. "You can always get more money, but you can't get another life."

"No," Creedlove said, shaking his head and holding his hand out in front of him as he backed away. "No. I ain't goin' to draw against you. But I ain't takin' back my words either. You are a card cheat."

"Both you gents just hold it right there," someone said loudly and, looking toward the sound of the voice, Pearlie saw the bartender pointing his shotgun toward them.

"Callin' someone a cheat is the kind of thing that can get a man killed if he can't back it up," the bartender said. "Annie, Sue, you been watchin' this. Was there any cheatin' goin' on?"

"Not a bit of it, Karl," Annie replied. "The game was aboveboard in every respect."

"All right, then that leaves you at fault, Creedlove. So I reckon you'd better get on out of here."

"You got no right to run me out of here," Creedlove said.

The bartender pulled back the hammers of the shotgun.

"This here scattergun gives me the right," the bartender said. "Now, you can either walk out, or your bloody carcass will be pulled out. Which is it going to be?"

Creedlove glared at the bartender for a moment. Then he glared at Pearlie.

"This ain't the end of it," Creedlove said to Pearlie. "Me'n you will run in to each other again sometime."

"I can hardly wait," Pearlie replied.

"Don't let the door hit you in the ass on your way out," Annie called to him.

A thunderous laughter from the saloon patrons chased Creedlove out of the saloon.

"Marshal?" Smoke called from the cell.

"What do you want, Jensen?"

"I appreciate you standing up to the mob like that."

"That wasn't a mob," Turnball said. "That was a group of concerned citizens. Maybe you don't realize this, Jensen, but folks around here had a hard winter."

"We all had a hard winter," Smoke said.

"Yes, well, a lot of the folks hereabout wouldn't have their homes or businesses if not for Mr. Clark. You picked the wrong man to kill."

"I didn't kill him."

"And you expect me to believe that?"

"Marshal, send a telegram to Sheriff Carson, back in Big Rock. He can tell you who I am."

"I might just do that," Marshal Turnball said. Turnball walked away from the cell and saw Deputy Pike standing at the front window.

"What are you lookin' at?" Turnball asked.

"Them fellas you run away is all standin' down there in front of the Bull's Head."

"I don't have any problem with them as long as they're standin' down there talkin' and not up here makin' trouble," Turnball said.

"That wasn't right, you runnin' 'em off like that,"

Pike said. "Ever' one of 'em is our friend. I can't believe you would'a shot Mr. Fremont over somethin' like this."

"I didn't shoot him, did I?"

"Would you have shot him?"

"I didn't shoot him, did I?" Turnball repeated.

Chapter Nine

"And then he said, 'I walked into thith church,'" Cal was saying.

"Thith?"

"This," Cal explained. "But that's how he talked. He would say words like Mithithippi instead of Mississippi. It was real funny the way he talked."

"All right, go on with the joke," Pearlie said. It was the morning after, and Cal and Pearlie were mucking out stalls in the stable.

"All right. So Eddie Foy says, 'Thith cowboy went into thith church and took a theat on a long bench, neckth to a pretty woman.' And then Eddie Foy asked everyone in the audience, 'What do you call that long bench that people thit on in a church?'

"And everyone in the audience yells back at him, 'Pew!'"

Cal laughed. "So then Eddie Foy says . . . he says, 'No, thath what the pretty woman thaid when the cowboy that down bethide her. Pew.'"

"So the pretty woman told him what the bench was called?" Pearlie asked.

"No!" Cal said in exasperation. "Don't you get the joke? She said 'Pew' 'cause the cowboy was stinkin' up the place."

"Oh," Pearlie said. He laughed. "Yes, that is funny."

"He was real funny," Cal said. "He told a lot of funny stories and I can remember most of 'em, but they aren't as funny when I tell them."

"Well, that's 'cause Eddie Foy does that for a livin', and he's good at it," Pearlie said. "You're a cowboy who . . ." Pearlie paused and looked at the rakes he and Cal were holding. "No, *we* are cowboys," he corrected, "who muck out horse manure for a living."

Cal laughed. "I reckon that's so."

"Cal, how would you like to go back?"

"Go back? Go back where?"

"To Sugarloaf."

"I thought we wasn't going to go back there as long as we were a burden on Smoke and Miss Sally," Cal said.

"Miss Sally would correct you and say weren't," Pearlie said.

"Well, but didn't you say we *weren't* going back to be a burden on Smoke and Miss Sally?"

"That's what I said all right," Pearlie said. "But if we go back now, we won't be a burden."

"How do you figure that?"

Pearlie stopped mucking and looked around the stable to make sure no one was close enough to overhear him.

"I played some cards last night," Pearlie said. "And I won some money."

"How much did you win?"

"Two hundred seventeen dollars," Pearlie replied with a broad smile.

"Two hundred dollars?" Cal asked in amazement.

"Two hundred seventeen," Pearlie corrected.

"That's a lot of money!"

"It sure is," Pearlie said. "It's enough to go back and help out."

"When do we leave?"

"Today," Pearlie said.

"Have you said anything to Mr. Thornton?"

"Yes, I told him we would be leaving today. In fact, we could leave right now if we wanted to, but I promised him we would finish with the stalls before we left."

"Yeah," Cal said. "That's only right."

The two men began raking with renewed vigor. Then, after a few minutes, Cal looked up.

"That's why you didn't want to go see Eddie Foy last night, isn't it?"

"Yeah," Pearlie said. "I just had a feelin' I was going to be lucky. And it turns out that the feelin' was true."

Creedlove sat nursing his drink in the back of the saloon in the little town of Solidad. He had left Flora-vista shortly after his run-in with Pearlie at the card game in the Oasis Saloon. He had lost so much money in the card game that he barely had enough money to get by, and wouldn't have any if he hadn't stolen twelve dollars from a stage way station.

That was three days and fifty miles ago, and he didn't figure he would ever see Pearlie again. But when he looked up as two men came in, there he was—Pearlie, and another cowboy who was even younger.

Because Creedlove was sitting alone, at a table in the back of the saloon, he was blocked from Pearlie's direct view by the cast-iron stove, which, though cold now, still smelled of its heavy winter use.

Creedlove watched as Pearlie said a few words to the bartender; then Pearlie and his friend took their beers to a nearby table.

Creedlove got up from the table, pulled his gun from his holster, then, holding it down by his side so it wouldn't be obvious that he had already drawn his weapon, stepped around the stove and started across the floor.

Pearlie was just pulling the chair out from the table when out of the corner of his eye, he saw Creedlove moving toward him. Pearlie wondered, briefly, what Creedlove was doing this far north of Floravista.

"Draw your gun, you son of a bitch! I aim to shoot you dead!" Creedlove shouted, raising his own pistol at the same time he was challenging Pearlie.

"Pearlie, he already has his gun out!" Cal shouted.

Pearlie didn't need Cal's warning because even as Creedlove was bringing his pistol to bear, Pearlie drew his own pistol and suddenly the room was shattered with the roar of two pistols exploding.

The other patrons in the saloon yelled and dived or scrambled for cover. White gun smoke billowed out from both guns, coalescing in a cloud that filled the center of the room. For a moment, the cloud obscured everything.

As the cloud began to roll away, Creedlove stared through the drifting white smoke, glaring at Pearlie.

Creedlove smiled and opened his mouth, but before he could say anything, there was incoherent gagging rattle way back in his throat. His eyes glazed over, and he pitched forward, his gun clattering to the floor.

That threat over, Pearlie looked around the saloon, checking to see if there was anyone else laying for him. Pearlie's pistol was cocked and he was ready to fire a second time, if a second shot was needed. He saw that Cal had drawn his own pistol and was also looking around the room for any potential danger.

Satisfied that there was no further danger, Pearlie holstered his pistol. Cal holstered his as well, and seeing them put their pistols back in the holsters, the other patrons began, slowly, to reappear from under tables, behind the bar and stove, and even from under the staircase.

A lawman came running in then, but seeing that it was all over, he put his gun away. He looked toward the body on the floor.

"Anybody know this man?" the lawman asked.

"His name is Creedlove," Pearlie said.

"Did you shoot him?"

"I did."

"It was a fair fight, Sheriff," the bartender said. "The fella on the floor drew first."

"That's right, Sheriff," one of the others said. "Fact is, this Creedlove fella not only drew first, he already had his gun out before he even challenged this man."

After that, several men at once began telling the story, each adding embellishments from his own perspective. When they were finished, the lawman came over to Pearlie and Cal.

"You got 'ny idea why he would come after you like that?"

"I won some money off him playing cards the other night," Pearlie said.

"Were you cheatin'?"

"No, sir, I wasn't."

"What's your name, mister?"

"Smith," Pearlie said. "John Smith."

Cal looked at Pearlie in surprise, but said nothing.

"Are you staying in town for the night, Mr. Smith?"

"I hadn't planned on it," Pearlie said. "My friend, Bill Jones, and I are heading toward California."

The sheriff realized then that Pearlie hadn't given his right name, and he sighed and shook his head.

"All right," he said. "No need for you to give me your right names, if what everyone here says is true. And there's no need for you to stay in town any longer. Fact is, it might be better all around if you just kept passing through."

"Soon as we finish our beer, we'll be on our way," Pearlie said.

The sheriff looked over at the bartender. "I'll get someone to come down here and get the body out of here," he said.

"Thanks, Sheriff," the bartender said. Looking around the saloon, he saw that several new customers had come in, drawn by the excitement. The bartender smiled.

"No big hurry, though," he said. "It seems to be good for business."

Carrying the wanted poster on Smoke Jensen, Marshal Turnball walked down toward the telegraph office.

"Good job catchin' that murderer and bank robber, Marshal," one of the townspeople said.

"Thank you," Turnball replied.

"Too bad he didn't have any of the money with him."

"Yes, it is. But at least we have him," Turnball said.

When Turnball stepped into the telegraph office, a bell on the door announced his entrance. Rodney Wheat, wearing a green visor and red suspenders, was sitting behind the counter reading a penny-dreadful novel. Wheat looked up as the marshal entered.

"I hear you caught one of the bank robbers," Wheat said.

"Yes," Turnball answered. He showed Wheat the poster. "It was this fella."

Wheat looked at the poster.

PROCLAMATION
$5,000.00
REWARD

For the Apprehension

DEAD OR ALIVE

Of the Murderer
KIRBY "SMOKE" JENSEN.

This Notice Takes the Place
Of All Previous
REWARD NOTICES.

Contact: *Sheriff,* Hinsdale County, Colorado
IMMEDIATELY.

"I want you to send a telegram to the sheriff out in Hinsdale County, telling him that we have this fella in custody," Turnball said.

Wheat shook his head. "I can't do that," he said.

"What do you mean you can't do that? Why can't you do it?"

"The telegraph line is down. It's been down for a couple of days now."

"Well, when do you think you'll get it back?"

Wheat shook his head. There's no way of telling. Last time it took two weeks."

"Two weeks?"

Wheat nodded. "Two weeks," he said. "And it might even take longer this time. If the line is out up in the higher elevations, there will still be so much snow that the line crew might not be able to get to it."

Turnball stroked his jaw as he contemplated the situation.

Then he nodded. "All right. I'll send a letter. What's the county seat of Hinsdale County?"

"Lake City," Wheat answered. "But I don't know if you are going to have any more luck with the letter than you are with sending a telegram. That's on the other side of the mountains, and I'm sure none of the high passes are open yet."

"Maybe not," Turnball replied. "But I'm going to try."

Smoke was lying on the bunk in his cell with his hands laced behind his head, staring at the ceiling. He had to admit that the cell was solidly built. The bars didn't go all the way to the ceiling, but came up only about six feet. Between the top of the bars and the ceiling itself was a two-foot wall of solid brick. At the back of the wall there were three small windows, enough to let in light and air, but not one of the three large enough for a man to pass through, even if there were no bars.

When he heard the marshal come back into the office, he sat up.

"Marshal?" he called.

"What do you want, Jensen?" Turnball answered.

"Did you send a telegram to Sheriff Carson, back in Big Rock?"

"No."

"What about the Sheriff of Hinsdale County? Did you contact him about whether or not the poster was current?"

"I told you, it doesn't matter whether or not the poster is current," Turnball said. "I'm only interested in the man you killed here, and the bank that you robbed here."

"I didn't do it," Smoke said. "I told you, contact Sheriff Carson. He'll vouch for me."

"I'll send him a letter," Turnball said.

"A letter?"

"The telegraph wire is down," Turnball explained. "Fact is, if Judge Craig wasn't scheduled to come into town tomorrow, we wouldn't even be able to send for him. At least, we can have us a fair trial."

"Hold on there, Marshal," Smoke said. "You aren't planning on holding a trial before you can check up on my story, are you?"

"We're holding your trial tomorrow," Turnball said. "We don't get that many visits from a judge, and I don't intend to waste this one."

"What about a lawyer?" Smoke asked. "Do I get a lawyer?"

"We got two lawyers in town," Turnball said. "If it's the way they normally do it, they'll flip a coin to see who prosecutes and who defends. It seems to work out all right."

Chapter Ten

There was no courthouse in the town of Etna, so the trial was held in the school. At the top of the blackboard in the front of the room, the alphabet was displayed in both cursive and block letters, in capital and lowercase. On the side panel of the blackboard were the work assignments for each of the six grades that attended the single-room schoolhouse. A stove sat in a sandbox in the corner of the room, and artwork of the children was pinned on the wall.

Two tables had been placed in the front of the classroom. One table had two chairs, and that was for Smoke and his lawyer. The other table was the prosecutor's table, and it had only one chair. The jury occupied the two first rows of desks in the classroom, while the citizens of the town squeezed into the remaining desks. Others were standing along the two side walls and the back wall. The judge's bench was the schoolteacher's desk, while Miss Garvey, the schoolteacher, was pressed into service as the court reporter.

Smoke felt a sense of melancholy as he looked around the schoolroom. His Sally had been teaching at a school exactly like this one when he met her. It was a cruel irony that his fate was about to be decided in a place like this.

"All rise!" Marshal Turnball shouted. In his capacity as city marshal, Turnball was also acting as the bailiff.

At Turnball's call, everyone seated in the classroom cum courtroom stood to await the arrival of the judge.

Judge Arlie Craig was a short, fat man who filled out his black robes. He was bald, except for a tuft of white over each ear. He took his seat at the bench, then looked out over the courtroom.

"The court may be seated," he said.

As the people sat, Judge Craig removed his glasses and cleaned them thoroughly. Then he put them back on, hooking them very carefully over one ear at a time. During this process the courtroom was very quiet, almost as if mesmerized by it. The only sound came from outside the courtroom, and that from a barking dog.

"Bailiff, would you call the case, please?" Judge Craig said.

"Your Honor, there comes before this honorable court one Kirby Jensen," Turnball said. "Mr. Jensen is charged with the murder of Robert J. Clark, said murder committed during the act of robbery of the Bank of Etna."

"Was this charge issued by a grand jury?"

"It was, Your Honor. The grand jury met this morning."

"Thank you," Judge Craig said. "And is the accused now represented by counsel?"

"He is, Your Honor," the lawyer sitting beside Smoke said. "I am Asa Jackson, duly accredited by the bar of the State of Colorado to practice law."

The judge looked over at Smoke.

"Is the defendant satisfied with counsel?"

"I am not, Your Honor," Smoke said.

His response surprised the judge and startled many who were in the court. Several reacted audibly, and one man shouted, "At least you have a lawyer! That's more than you gave Rob Clark!"

Others shouted out as well, and Judge Craig had to bang his gavel several times to restore order.

"Mr. Jensen, what complaint do you have against Mr. Jackson?"

"Your Honor, I have no complaint against Mr. Jackson personally. But I would prefer to select my own lawyer."

"There are only two lawyers in town," Judge Craig replied. "Would you rather have the prosecutor act as your defense counsel?"

"No, Your Honor. I ask for a delay so that I may get a lawyer from my own hometown of Big Rock."

"Mr. Hagen, you are the prosecutor," Judge Craig said. "How say you to this request?"

"Your Honor, the crime is still fresh upon the minds of all the witnesses. I fear that any delay may cloud their memories, perhaps even to the detriment of the defendant. All that is required by the law is that he be provided with counsel, and we have done so. I move that his request for a delay be denied."

Judge Craig nodded, then looked back at Smoke. "Due to my own busy schedule, it would be several weeks before I could return to Etna. And, as Mr. Hagen has pointed out, the closer the trial is held to the event, the sharper the memories of the witnesses who are called. Therefore, your request for a delay in the trial is denied. Has there been voir dire of the jury?"

"There has, Your Honor, and both defense and prosecution have accepted the jury as it is now constituted," Hagen said.

"Very good," Judge Craig replied. "Now, Mr. Jensen, how do you plead to the charge against you?"

"Not guilty," Smoke said.

"Very well," Judge Craig said. He cleared his throat. "The defendant represented and the jury accepted, I declare this case in session. Mr. Hagen, make your case."

Lester Hagen was a tall, gangly-looking man with a wild shock of hair and prominent ears. Standing, he turned to face the jury, which was seated just behind him.

"It won't take me long to do this," he said, speaking so quietly that those in the back had to strain to hear. "Practically everyone in this town was a witness to the robbery of the Bank of Etna on the sixth day of this very month. I could call any of them, and all would give compelling and damning testimony. Ten thousand dollars was taken, money that belonged to the fair people of this town."

Turning back to the table, he picked up the red and black plaid shirt Smoke had been wearing when he was arrested.

"Look at this shirt," he said. "It is not a shirt one can easily forget. And if you see this shirt on a man who is in the act of killing another, then the shirt becomes even more vividly burned into your memory. This shirt alone is enough to convict the defendant. No matter what he or his lawyer may say to obfuscate the issue, the facts are indisputable. A man wearing this very shirt killed Rob Clark. This man," he said, with a dramatic pointing of his finger toward Smoke, "was captured wearing this very shirt. I think that when this trial is finished, you will have no difficulty in finding Mr. Kirby Jensen guilty as charged."

As Hagen took his seat, there was a spontaneous outbreak of applause from the gallery.

"Hear, hear, there will be no such demonstration in this courtroom!" Judge Craig said with an angry bang of his gavel.

The court grew quiet; then all turned their attention to Asa Jackson. Like Hagen before him, Jackson stood to address the jury. Considerably shorter than Hagen, and with eyes made almost buglike by his thick glasses, Jackson made less of an impression by his appearance.

"The law states that before you can find someone guilty, you must be convinced beyond the shadow of a doubt that he is guilty. You will hear the witnesses say that there were three men shooting into the bank. Since three men were shooting, it impossible to say that Kirby Jensen was the one who actually murdered Mr. Clark."

Jackson sat back down and Smoke leaned over toward him.

"The way you presented that, it made it sound as if I was there," Smoke complained.

"It's going to be hard to say you weren't there, with the evidence that the prosecutor has," Jackson said. "Our best hope is to sew doubt as to who actually did the shooting."

"Prosecution, you may call your first witness," Judge Craig said.

"Prosecution calls Mr. Tucker Patterson," Hagen said.

Tucker Patterson walked to the front of the room and put his hand on the Bible.

"Do you swear to tell the truth, the whole truth, and nothing but the truth, so help you God?" Turnball asked.

"I do."

"The witness may be seated," Judge Craig said.

Hagen approached the witness chair. "For the record, Mr. Patterson, what is your employment?"

"I am the head teller of the Bank of Etna," Patterson replied.

"Hell, Tucker, you're the only teller," someone shouted from the gallery, and everyone laughed.

Judge Craig slammed his gavel down, then, with an angry scowl, addressed the gallery. "If there is one more outbreak, I will hold the person responsible in contempt of court. You will be fined, and you will spend time in jail."

Patterson looked at Hagen. "Mr. Barnes is right," he said, identifying the person who spoke up. "There is only one teller, but Mr. Clark had assured me that, if we were ever to hire a second teller, I would be the chief teller. Therefore my position, technically, was that of head teller."

"Mr. Patterson, were you in the bank on the sixth instant?"

"I was."

"Tell the court what happened that day."

"Mr. Clark and I were both behind the teller's cage,

counting the money to make certain that the books were balanced, when two men came in."

"Can you describe the two men?"

"One of the men was wearing a shirt like that one," Patterson said, pointing to the shirt that was still lying on the prosecutor's table.

"Let the record show that the witness identified the prosecution exhibit as the shirt worn by one of the robbers."

"Object, Your Honor," Jackson said. "The witness said it was a shirt like that one. He didn't say he was wearing that one."

"I stand corrected, Your Honor," Hagen said. "Mr. Patterson, you said there were two men?"

"Yes. The other man was wearing a white shirt."

"I object!" Smoke called out. "He is describing the clothes, not the men."

"Mr. Smoke, if your attorney cares to make that objection, he may do so," Judge Craig said. "But as the defendant, you are not allowed to object."

Smoke turned to Jackson. "Are you going to object?" he asked.

Jackson nodded. "I object," he said. "Mr. Jensen is correct. The witness is describing clothing, and not the men themselves."

"Sustained," the judge said.

"Mr. Patterson, could you see the men's faces?" Hagen asked.

"No, they were covered by hoods," Patterson replied.

"So, by looking at the defendant, you cannot say, as a

matter of actual fact, that he was not one of the robbers, can you?"

"I object," Jackson said. "He just said that the men's faces were covered."

"Listen to the question, Counselor," Judge Craig said. "He asked if he could positively say that Jensen was *not* one of the robbers."

"Oh," Jackson said.

"Objection is overruled."

"So, since you cannot positively say that he was not one of the robbers, it is possible that he was one of them?"

"Yes."

Hagen continued with Patterson, eliciting from him the details as to how Clark got a gun, then ran to the front door to challenge the bank robbers as they were leaving.

"I told him not to go, that there were too many of them," Patterson said. "But Mr. Clark was a brave man, and he wouldn't hear of it. He ran to the front door and started to shoot, but got shot instead."

"Thank you, Mr. Patterson. Your witness," Hagen said as he sat down.

Jackson stood, but didn't approach the witness. "Did you see who actually did the shooting?"

"No, I was inside the bank. I saw Mr. Clark get shot, but from where I was, I couldn't see who shot him."

"So even though you saw Mr. Jensen wearing this shirt in your bank, once the robbers got outside, you have no idea who did the actual shooting?"

"I object!" Smoke said loudly.

"You are objecting your own lawyer?" Judge Craig asked.

"Your Honor, I ask the court's permission to act as my own lawyer."

"Are you saying you wish to dismiss counsel?"

"Yes, Your Honor, that is exactly what I am saying."

"Court is going to stand in recess for half an hour," Judge Craig said. "Marshal Turnball, clear the court-room of everyone except you and the defendant."

"Yes, sir," Turnball said. "All right, people, you heard the judge. Everyone out."

"Your Honor, if there is going to be a sidebar, I request permission to remain," Hagen said.

"Permission denied," Craig said. "You will leave with everyone else."

"What about me?" Jackson asked. "Since the defendant is my client, shouldn't I be present?"

"You heard the defendant, Mr. Jackson," Craig said. "You have just been dismissed."

It took less than a minute for everyone to leave. Then Turnball, who had been standing at the door watching them leave, came back to the front of the room.

"They are all gone, Judge," he said.

Craig removed his glasses and cleaned them again. Watching him, Smoke realized that it was more of a nervous action than because the glasses actually needed cleaning.

"Mr. Jensen, there is a saying in the legal profession that a person who defends himself has a fool for a client." He put the glasses back on, again looping them very carefully over each ear, one at a time. "Do you know what I am saying to you?"

"Yes, sir, I believe I do," Smoke replied.

Judge Craig pointed at Smoke, and began shaking his finger. "Disabuse yourself of any idea that I will go easier on you because of your inexperience or lack of knowledge of the law. Regardless of your competence or incompetence, this case will be tried under the rules of law. Do you understand that?"

"Yes, sir, I do."

"Very well. Mr. Jackson is dismissed, and I hereby declare you sui juris."

"I beg your pardon?"

"Sui juris," the judge repeated. "It is a Latin term meaning that you have the capacity to act for yourself in legal proceedings. You are hereby acting as your own counsel."

"Thank you, Your Honor," Smoke said.

"Marshal Turnball, you may reassemble the court."

"All right, our take come to ten thousand dollars," Dooley said after he counted out the money. "That's a thousand dollars apiece for each of you."

"Wait a minute," Yancey said. "You think they can't none of us cipher? I make that over sixteen hundred dollars for each of us."

Dooley shook his head. "I set it up, I take half," he said.

"That ain't right," Yancey protested. "We all of us took our chances when we robbed that bank. We should all of us get the same amount of money."

"Tell him, Curt," Dooley said.

"Maybe you ain't never done nothin' like this before,"

Curt said to Yancey. "But the one that gets the job set up is always the one that gets the most money."

"There didn't nobody say nothin' like that when I got asked to join up," Yancey said. "And I don't intend to just stand by and get cheated like this."

"Look at it this way," Curt said. "You got a thousand dollars now, which you didn't have before. You know how long you'd have to cowboy to make a thousand dollars?"

Yancey shook his head. "I don't care, that ain't the point. I don't intend to be cheated like that."

While Yancey was talking, Dooley pulled his pistol. Yancey didn't notice it until he heard the click of the hammer being pulled back.

"Then I reckon you can't be reasoned with, can you?"

"What? What are you doin' with that gun?"

"Go, Yancey," Dooley said.

"Go? Go where?"

"Anywhere," Dooley said. "I don't want you around anymore."

"All right," Yancey said. "It ain't right, but give me my money and I'll be on my way."

Dooley shook his head. "No money for you."

"What do you mean no money for me?"

"One thousand dollars wasn't enough for you, so you get none. Now, get out of here."

Yancey glared at Dooley; then he started toward his horse.

Dooley pulled the trigger, the gun roared, and Yancey's horse dropped in its tracks.

"What the hell did you just do?" Yancey shouted. "You son of a bitch! You just killed my horse!"

"You're lucky I didn't kill you," Dooley said. "Curt, get his gun."

Curt walked up to Yancey and pulled his pistol from his holster.

"All right, Yancey, start walkin'," Dooley said, making a motion with his pistol.

"This ain't right," Yancey said.

"I thought we already had that settled," Dooley said. "I decide what's right."

Dooley shot again and the bullet hit the ground right next to Yancey's feet, then ricocheted through the valley, whining as it did so. Even before the echo died, Yancey was running back down the trail, chased by Dooley's evil laughter.

"Dooley," Fargo said. "Leavin' him out here without a horse or a gun . . . he could die."

"Yeah, he could," Dooley said. "Now, each one of you boys is two hundred dollars richer. That is, unless you don't want the money."

"Hell, I want the money," Ford said.

"Me too," Curt said.

"I'll take my share," Trace said.

"Fargo, that just leaves you," Dooley said. Dooley had not yet put his pistol back in its holster and a little wisp of smoke curled upward from the end of the barrel. The implication was obvious to Fargo.

"Yancey was a troublemaker," Fargo said. "You was right to do what you done."

"I thought you might see things my way," Dooley said as he counted out the money.

Chapter Eleven

As the trial continued, the prosecution called witness after witness to the stand to testify as to what they saw on the morning of the robbery. In every case the testimony was the same. They had seen two men leaving the bank; then they'd heard Clark shout out the warning that the bank had been robbed. They talked about seeing and hearing the exchange of gunshots, and seeing Mr. Clark go down.

"Did all of the robbers shoot at Mr. Clark?" Hagen asked a witness.

"No, sir, just the two who come out of the bank, and the one that was holdin' the horses in front of the bank. There was three more men across the street, waitin' in front of Sikes Leather Goods, but they didn't shoot at Mr. Clark."

"How do you know that those three men were involved with the robbery?" Hagen asked.

"'Cause they all left town together, and all of 'em was shootin' and hollerin' as they rode away."

"I see," Hagen said. "But as far as who actually shot Mr. Clark, it was the two men, who were wearing red and black plaid shirts, and the one man who was wearing a white shirt. Is that what you are saying?"

"Yes, sir."

"From your point of observation, could you tell which one of the three actually killed Mr. Clark?"

"No, sir, I could not."

"In fact," Hagen continued, "if I told you that there were four bullets in Mr. Clark's body, would you be able to believe that all three may have had a hand in killing him?"

"Yes, I would say so."

"Mr. Jensen," Judge Craig said quickly. "Counsel is leading the witness. Are you not going to object?"

"I'm not going to object, Your Honor, because I don't care which of the three, or if all three, killed him. I wasn't one of the three."

"Very well, I will disallow it myself. Jury will disregard counsel's last comment. You may continue, Mr. Hagen."

"I'm through with this witness, Your Honor."

"Did you see me in the street in front of the bank that day?" Smoke asked.

"Yeah, I seen you. I seen you in that shirt," the witness replied.

"I've no doubt but that you saw the shirt," Smoke said. "But I want you to look at my face closely. Is this the face of the man you saw in front of the bank?"

"No, you ain't the one that was standin' in front of the bank," the witness said. "But I done told you, and everyone has done told you. The faces of the two that come out of the bank was covered by masks."

"Thank you, that's all," Smoke said.

"But I seen that shirt you was wearin'," the witness added.

"Thank you, that is all," Smoke repeated.

Billy Frakes was Hagen's next witness.

Frakes was pointed out as having had a unique perspective on the robbery, because he had gone down to try and sell a pair of boots to three men who were waiting across the street from the bank, and who subsequently turned out to be in collusion with the robbers.

As the prosecutor had done with all the other witnesses, Hagen held up the red and black plaid shirt.

"Have you ever seen this shirt before, Billy?"

"Yes, sir."

"Where did you see it?"

Frakes pointed to Smoke. "He was a'wearin' it when we found him," he said.

"Let the record show that the witness has pointed out **that the defendant** was wearing this very shirt when he was captured," Hagen said.

"Had you ever seen the shirt before?"

"Yes, sir."

"When and where did you see it before?"

"I seen it on the sixth of this month," Frakes said. "I seen it when the two men who was wearin' them come ridin' into town. Then, I seen it again when the two bank robbers come runnin' out of the bank."

"Wait a minute," Hagen said in sudden interest. "Are you saying that you saw him when he rode into town?"

"Yes, sir."

"And this was before the robbery?"

"Yes, sir."

"So, you saw him without the mask?"

"Maybe," Frakes said.

"Maybe? What do you mean, maybe?"

"I seen their faces, but I didn't look at them that long. I couldn't tell you if this was one of the men or not."

"But you do remember the shirt, right?"

"Yes, sir."

"You saw this shirt on one of the men who came into town?"

"Yes, sir."

"And you saw it again when you were with the posse as they arrested him?"

"Yes, sir."

"No further questions. Your witness, Mr. Jensen."

"Did you get a good look at the man who was standing in front of the bank, the man wearing a shirt just like that one?" Smoke asked.

"Yes, sir, I got a good look at him."

"Am I that man?"

"No, sir, you ain't that man."

Smoke turned away as if to sit down. Then, getting an idea, he stopped and turned back toward the witness.

"You said you were going to try and sell a pair of boots to one of the robbers?"

"Yeah, I was. See, I make boots and I figured if I could sell a few pair, well, maybe Mr. Sikes would carry 'em in his store," Frakes said. "And I thought maybe one of them might buy my boots since I seen 'em lookin' at boots in Sikes's window."

"You make boots, do you?"

"Yes, sir."

"So, you must know quite a bit about boots."

Frakes smiled. "I know more'n most folks do, I reckon."

"Do you take notice of the kind of boots people wear?"

"Oh, yes, sir, I'm always lookin' at folks' boots."

"Can you tell me what kind of boots I'm wearing?" Smoke asked. He started to stick his boot out so Frakes could see it, but Frakes waved it off.

"You don't have to show me," he said. "I've done looked at 'em. Them boots you're wearin' is what's called black cherry brush-off boots. They're real nice boots, and kind of expensive."

"Were any of the bank robbers wearing boots like these?" Smoke asked.

"Ha!" Frakes said. "Are you kidding? None of 'em had boots like those."

"Not even the two men who were wearing the red and black plaid shirts?" Smoke asked.

Frakes shook his head. "No, sir." He chuckled. "They was wearing old, scruffed-up boots, the kind you can buy anywhere for no more'n two dollars."

Suddenly, the smile left Frakes's face, and he looked over at the judge. "That's right," he said. "They wasn't none of 'em wearin' boots like these here boots."

"Thank you. No more questions," Smoke said.

In redirect, Hagen tried to get Frakes to say that he couldn't be sure about the boots, that maybe one of them could have been wearing boots like the boots the defendant was wearing, but Frakes couldn't be budged.

"They was all six wearin' scruffed-up boots," he insisted.

When the prosecution finished its case, Judge Craig invited Smoke to call any witnesses he might have for his defense.

"Your Honor, in order to call any witnesses for defense, I would have to bring some people here from Big Rock."

"Could any of the people from Big Rock testify that you were somewhere else on the day of the robbery?" Judge Craig asked.

"No, sir. They would be more on the order of character witnesses," Smoke said.

"I see. Mr. Jensen, is there any witness, anywhere, who could testify that they were with you on the sixth of this month?"

Smoke shook his head. "No, Your Honor," he said. "I was on the trail for that entire day. I did not see a soul until I encountered the bank robbers."

Craig removed his glasses and polished them vigorously for a moment. Then he put them back on.

"If you cannot find a witness who can testify in direct contradiction to any of the witnesses the prosecution has brought to the stand, then I see no reason for granting a stay on this trial. I'll give you half an hour to compose your thoughts. Then I will expect you to make your closing arguments." Judge Craig slammed the gavel down on the desk. "This court stands in recess for one half hour."

As Smoke sat back down at his table, he saw the prosecutor summon Pike over to him. Hagen and the deputy spoke for a moment, then Pike left.

"Do you want me to help you with your closing argument?" Jackson asked.

Smoke shook his head. "No, thanks," he said. "I'm sure you mean the best, Mr. Jackson. But seeing as this is my life we're talking about here, I think I'd feel better if I did it myself."

"All right," Jackson said. He got up and started to leave. Then he turned and looked back at Smoke. "Mr. Jensen, don't try to make a speech. Just talk to the folks in the jury as if you were telling a friend what happened."

Smoke nodded. "Thanks," he said. "I appreciate the tip."

All too soon, it seemed, Marshal Turnball stepped up to the front of the room.

"All rise," he shouted.

Again, the gallery stood as Judge Craig came back into the court and took his seat.

"Mr. Jensen," Craig said after everyone was seated. "You may begin your closing argument."

"Thank you, Your Honor," Smoke said. He turned to face the jury.

"I must say that I am a little surprised that nobody in this town knows me," he began. "I guess this is a little far from Big Rock, so it's out of my home area. But I am well known back home. And, I'm proud to say, that I am known as a man of honesty and integrity. One of my closest friends in Big Rock is Sheriff Carson. I own a ranch there, a rather substantial ranch, and I am what you might regard as a pillar of the community.

"Now, normally, it isn't my style to blow my own horn, so to speak. But, since I don't have anyone over here to blow it for me, well, I reckon I don't have much choice." Smoke smiled broadly, and tried not to let it show when nobody returned the smile.

"I did not rob the bank here. I did not kill Mr. Clark. I did not know Mr. Clark, but from some of the testimony I've heard today, I'm sure he was a very good man. I can understand how having a good man killed so senselessly could get a town upset. But wouldn't it be better for you to find the person who actually did it?

"I wish I could tell you that I know who did it, but I don't. I was set upon by six men, two of whom were wearing shirts identical to the one prosecution is using as his evidence. While I was distracted, one of them knocked me out, and when I came to, I saw that my own shirt was gone, and I was wearing that shirt." He pointed toward the shirt.

"I was angry that someone had stolen my shirt, and puzzled as to why they would do it. But when Marshal Turnball and his posse came along a little later, I learned the reason. One of the bank robbers, perhaps even the killer, put this shirt on me to throw suspicion my way.

"Before you vote on your verdict, I want you to think about two things. Number one, nobody saw the face of the second man who was wearing the plaid shirt, and number two . . ." Smoke held out his foot. "We heard Mr. Frakes say that not one of the six was wearing boots like these."

Satisfied that he had done his best, Smoke sat down. Just as he did so, he saw Pike, smiling from ear to ear, come back into the school cum courthouse. He was carrying a bag, which he showed to Hagen. The two spoke about it for a moment, then looked over at Smoke.

Pike chuckled.

"Mr. Hagen?" the judge said.

"Please the court, I'd like one minute," Hagen said.

"Make it quick."

Hagen took the sack over to Frakes and showed it to him. Frakes looked into the bag, then nodded.

"Thank you," Hagen said. Hagen returned to the front of the room, facing the jury.

"Gentlemen of the jury," he began. "In Kirby Jensen's closing argument, you heard him say that he owned a large ranch near Big Rock. That is true, he does own a large ranch. However, according to papers found on him when he was arrested, that ranch is encumbered by a mortgage note of two thousand dollars, due in just over one month. If he fails to make that payment, he will lose his ranch.

"That, I submit, is incentive enough to make an otherwise honest rancher rob a bank.

"Where is that money, you may ask? Why was it not found on him? That is a good question, and the answer is as simple and as old as the sin of thievery itself. There is no honor among thieves, and he had none of the money when he was arrested because Jensen was beaten and robbed by his own fellow thieves.

"Did Kirby Jensen kill Mr. Clark? There were four bullets found in Mr. Clark's body, so it is likely that one of the bullets was his. But according to the law, it doesn't matter whether any of those bullets came from Jensen's gun or not. According to the law, everyone who was there is equally guilty of his murder.

"Now there comes only the question, was he there? You have heard witness after witness testify that they saw this shirt on the back of one of the killers. You also heard Billy Frakes testify that he saw the faces of the two men when they rode into town, and, having seen the faces, cannot rule out the possibility that Kirby Jensen was one of them. And not even Jensen can produce one witness who can testify that he wasn't there.

"So, what did Jensen do? He showed Billy Frakes a pair of fancy boots, and asked if any of the robbers were wearing such boots. Billy Frakes said no."

Hagen reached down into the sack and pulled out a pair of boots.

Smoke felt his heart sink. He had brought along those old and worn boots, intending to wear them to keep his better boots from getting scuffed. But they were uncomfortable as riding boots, so he kept them rolled up in his blankets.

"Mr. Pike took these very boots from Kirby Jensen's bedroll about half an hour ago," Hagen said, continuing with his closing argument. "You all saw me show these boots to Billy Frakes. Billy just told me that, if need be, he is prepared to testify that the two men in the red and black plaid shirt were wearing boots exactly like these.

"Gentlemen of the jury, your task is solemn, but it is simple. Your task is solemn, because you are charged, by your fellow citizens, with the responsibility of bringing justice to our fair town. But your task is simple, because there is overwhelming and irrefutable evidence to help you come to the right decision. And the right decision is to find Kirby Jensen guilty of murder in the first degree."

Hagen turned and started back toward his seat.

"Good job, Hagen, you got the son of a bitch!" a man shouted, and several others cheered and applauded.

It took Judge Craig several seconds of banging the gavel until he was able to restore order in the court. Finally, when the gallery was subdued, he charged the jury.

The jury filed out through the back door of the schoolhouse, then gathered under a shade tree to discuss the case. They returned in less than half an hour.

"Who is the foreman of the jury?" Judge Craig asked.

"I am, Your Honor. The name is Jeff Colfax."

"Mr. Colfax, has the jury reached a verdict?"

The jury foreman leaned over to spit a wad of tobacco into a spittoon before he answered. He wiped his mouth with the back of his hand.

"We've reached a verdict, Your Honor," he said.

"Would you publish the verdict, please?"

"We, the jury, find this here fella"—he pointed to Smoke—"guilty of murder and bank robbin'."

"So say you all?"

"So say we all."

"Thank you, Mr. Foreman," the judge said. "The jury is dismissed. "Mr. Turnball, you are hereby relieved of your duty as court bailiff, and may resume your duties as city marshal. Now, Marshal Turnball, bring your prisoner before the bench to hear his sentencing."

Marshal Turnball stepped over to the defense table and looked down at Smoke.

"Stand up and hold your hands out," he ordered.

Smoke did as he was directed, and Turnball clamped the manacles on his wrists before leading him up to stand before the judge.

"It is the sentence of this court that a gallows be constructed in the city street so that all may bear witness to the inevitable result that befalls a person bent on following the path of crime. Then, on Thursday next, at ten o'clock of the morning hour, you will be removed from your jail cell and taken to this public gallows where a noose will be placed around your neck, a lever will be thrown, a trapdoor will fall from under your feet, and you will be hurled into eternity.

"May God have mercy on your evil, vile, and worthless soul, sir, because I have none."

The judge ended his pronouncement with the banging of his gavel, and Marshal Turnball and one of his deputies led Smoke out of the court and down to the jail.

Chapter Twelve

"One hundred dollars!" the big man with the white, handlebar mustache shouted above the din in the saloon. "I'll bet one hundred dollars that no man can stay on Cannonball for one whole minut

Pearlie and Cal were on their way back to Big Rock, but had stopped in the town of Jasper. They were having a quiet beer together in the Good Nature Saloon when they heard the offer.

"That ain't much of a bet, Stacey," one of the others in the saloon said. "Hell, there ain't nobody ever stayed on him for more'n ten seconds. Can't nobody stay on him for a full minute."

"I'll try it, if you give odds," another cowboy said.

"What kind of odds?" Stacey asked.

"Two to one," the cowboy answered. "I'll put up twenty. If I can stay on for a whole minute, you'll pay me forty."

"You got twenty dollars, cowboy?" Stacey asked.

"I got twenty," the cowboy answered.

"Take 'im up on it, Stacey. I'd like to see if anyone really could ride Cannonball."

"Yeah, give us a show," another shouted.

Stacey stroked his mustache for a second; then he nodded.

"All right," he said. "Put up the twenty dollars. Let's see what you can do."

"Yahoo!" one of the others shouted, and everyone poured out of the saloon to see the ride.

"Come on, Cal, let's go see this," Pearlie said, standing and tugging on Cal's arm.

There had been no more than twenty men in the saloon when the challenge was issued, but as they started down the street toward the corral, word spread through the rest of the town so that many more joined. By the time they reached the corral, which was at the far end of the street from the Good Nature Saloon, there were nearly one hundred spectators.

Pearlie and Cal found a seat on the top rail of the corral fence and watched as they saddled Cannonball.

Cannonball was a big horse with a well-defined musculature. He was also a very aggressive horse, fighting even against being saddled.

"Hey, Stacey, if Pete can't do it, can I give it a try?" one of the cowboys shouted.

"Have you got 'ny money?" Stacey replied.

"I've got money."

"All right, you're next."

When, at last, they got the saddle on Cannonball, Pete climbed up on the top rung of the fence and crouched there, ready. Pete nodded toward the two men who were handling Cannonball, and they led the horse over.

Pete pounced onto the horse's back, and the two

handlers let go, then jumped out of the way. Cannonball exploded away from the fence, then went through a series of gyrations, bucking, twisting, coming down stiff-legged, and ducking his head. Pete was thrown in less than ten seconds.

"Whooowee, that's some horse!" someone shouted.

"My turn," the one who had put in the bid to be second said. But like Pete, he was thrown in a matter of seconds.

"I'll try it for twenty dollars," another said, and Pearlie and Cal watched as the third rider was thrown even faster than the first two.

"Look," Cal said to Pearlie as still a fourth man tried to ride the horse. "See how he ducks his head to the left there, then sort of leans into it? If a man would sort of jerk his head back to the right, he could stop that."

"You think you could ride him, Cal?" Pearlie asked.

Cal didn't answer right away. Instead, he watched another rider try and get thrown.

"Yeah," Cal said. "I think I could."

"Do you think you could a hundred dollars worth?"

"Ha! Are you kidding? I don't have a hundred dollars."

"*I* do. I'll give it to you to bet, if you think you can ride him."

Cal shook his head. "No, Pearlie, that's your money. That's money you said you were going to give to Smoke and Miss Sally."

"Yes, it is," Pearlie said. "But if you could win two hundred dollars more, don't you think that would be even better?"

"Well, yeah, sure, but . . ."

"Do you think you can ride him, or don't you?"

Cal looked at the horse just as it threw another rider.

"Yeah," Cal said. "I think I can ride him."

The two wranglers grabbed Cannonball and brought him back to the end of the corral.

"Anybody else?" Stacey called, holding up a fistful of money, all of it won from would-be riders within the last few minutes.

Nobody responded.

"This is your last chance, boys. Anybody else want to try before we put Cannonball back in his stall?"

There was still no answer.

"All right, men, get the saddle off him," Stacey said to his wrangler.

"Here, Cal, here's the money," Pearlie said.

Cal hesitated but for one second; then he called out loudly.

"I'll have a go at it for one hundred dollars," he said.

Several had started to leave the corral, but when they heard Cal call out, they stopped and came back.

"What did you say?" Stacey asked.

Call held up the one hundred dollars that Pearlie had given him.

"I said I would ride him," Cal said. "And I'm betting one hundred dollars that I can stay on him for an entire minute."

"Who is that fella?" one of the men in the crowd asked.

"I don't know," another answered. "I think he must've just come into town. I ain't never seen him afore now."

"Where did you get a hundred dollars?" Stacey asked.

"What difference does it make where I got it?" Cal

answered. "You didn't ask anybody else where they got the money."

"And you want to wager that one hundred dollars that you can stay on Cannonball for a minute?"

"Yes, sir."

"That's one whole minute, mind you," Stacey said. "Not fifty-nine seconds."

"An entire minute," Cal agreed.

"All right, I'll bet you a hundred," Stacey said.

"Huh-uh," Cal replied, shaking his head.

"What do you mean, huh-uh? That's what you're wantin', ain't it? To bet a hundred dollars?"

"I am betting one hundred dollars," Cal said. "You are betting two hundred dollars."

"Two hundred dollars is a lot of money," Stacey said.

"The boy's right, though, Stacey," Pete said. Pete was the cowboy who was the first to try to ride Cannonball. "That's what you said. You said you was givin' two to one. If the boy bets a hunnert and he stays on the horse for a whole minute, you give him two hunnert."

"Pete's right," one of the others called out.

"All right," Stacey said. "All right, it don't matter none. There ain't no way this boy, or anyone, can stay on Cannonball for a whole minute."

"Ride 'im, boy!" someone shouted.

"Yeah! Let's see you take Stacey's money!" another called.

"Who is this fella Stacey anyway?" Pearlie asked as several men gathered around Cal to offer him their best wishes.

"He owns the mercantile here in town," someone

said. "He got rich during the winter by sellin' his goods at about three or four times what they was worth."

"They ain't nobody here but what wants to see him ride that horse and take some of his money away from him," Pete said to Pearlie.

"Well, come on, boy!" Stacey called. "Are you goin' to ride or not?"

"I'll ride," Cal said. He gave the one hundred dollars back to Pearlie. "Hold onto it."

"Well, get over here and do it," Stacey said.

"Ride 'im, cowboy," the others said by way of encouragement.

Cal walked down to the other end of the corral, climbed up on the fence, then dropped down onto Cannonball's back.

Cannonball leaped away from the fence, throwing Cal into the air as he did so. The others groaned as they saw the saddle slipping to one side. Then Cal did an amazing thing. Instead of coming back down on the saddle, he came back on the horse's hindquarters, just behind the saddle. He held on as the saddle slipped off; then he moved forward and riding bareback, stayed with the animal.

The horse tried every maneuver to throw Cal off. He porpoised and sunfished; he twisted and turned; he reared on his hind legs, then jumped up on his forelegs; he dipped his head and leaned, a maneuver that had been successful with all previous riders. Cal countered that move just as he told Pearlie he would, by jerking the horse's head back and kneeing him in the neck on the opposite side.

Unable to lose his rider any other way, Cannonball began galloping around the corral, running close to the fence trying to rake him off. Those who were on the fence had to jump back to get out of the way.

When the horse reached the end of the corral, he leaped over the fence, and continued his bucking out in the street. The spectators hurried out into the street to watch.

Cannonball leaped up onto the front porch of Stacey's Mercantile Store.

"No!" Stacey shouted, running out into the street in front of his store. "Get him down from there!"

Cannonball twisted and kicked, and when he did, he kicked out one of the front windows of the store. A second kick took out the door and a third kick took out the other window. Then, coming down off the porch, Cannonball hit the pillars, causing the porch roof to collapse.

Cannonball came out into the street and, seeing Stacey, started galloping toward him.

"No!" Stacey shouted again. He leaped to the left just in time to keep from being run down, and he landed face-first in a pile of horse apples. He screamed in anger and frustration as he stood up with gobs of manure sticking to him.

Cannonball ran at full speed to the far end of the street, then came to a sliding stop. Cal stayed on his back.

Everyone watched as horse and rider remained motionless at the far end of the street. Then Cal turned Cannonball around, and they walked back up to the corral at a leisurely pace. When they got back, Cal was sitting sideways on the horse's back.

"How long has it been?" Cal asked.

"One minute and thirty-seven seconds," the timer said.

"You owe me two hundred dollars," Cal said as he slid down. He reached up and patted the horse, which stood calmly beside him.

"I never thought you would be able to stay on," Stacey said.

"Yeah," Pete said. "Especially after you loosened the saddle.

"I did not loosen the saddle."

"Then I guess you did it on your own, huh, Jerry?" Pete asked one of the two wranglers.

"I . . . I . . ." Jerry began nervously. Then he looked over at Stacey and pointed. "I didn't do it on my own," he said. "Mr. Stacey, he told me to do it."

"You're fired, Jerry," Stacey said with an angry growl.

"No need for you to be firin' me," Jerry replied. "I quit." Jerry looked at Cal. "Sorry, fella, I ought'n to have done that. I reckon I was just tryin' to hang onto my job."

"No need to apologize," Cal said. "I won't be holdin' onto any hard feelings. I just want my money, that's all."

Stacey stared at Cal for a long moment; then, with a loud, audible sigh, he pulled a roll of money from his pocket and counted off two hundred dollars. "Here!" he said angrily. "Here's your damn money!"

"Hey, Mr. Stacey," one of the cowboys called out. "Does that bet still hold? I think I could ride ole Cannonball now."

"You go to hell!" Stacey said gruffly as all the cowboys laughed.

* * *

"Four hundred twenty-six dollars," Pearlie said as he and Cal counted their money that night.

"That ain't the two thousand Smoke needs to save the ranch," Cal said.

"Maybe it ain't," Pearlie agreed. "But it ain't no small potatoes either. And it might help him. If nothin' else, it'll give 'em a little money to start with, if they have to start all over again."

"Yeah," Cal said.

"You're all right with this, ain't you, Cal?" Pearlie asked. "I mean, givin' our money to 'em and all. When you think about it, this is a lot of money to be givin' away like this. In fact, I don't know as I've ever had that much money on my own before."

"I know I ain't," Cal said.

"Are you goin' to be able to give it up? 'Cause if you don't, I don't think anyone would fault you."

"I'm goin' to give it up," Cal said.

Pearlie smiled, then reached out his hand and took Cal's hand in his.

"Good man," he said. "Good man."

Chapter Thirteen

Smoke was lying on the bunk in the small, hot, and airless cell, listening to the sound of the carpenters at work as they were busily constructing a gallows.

The hammers banged and the saws ripped through the lumber.

"Joe? Hey, Joe, hand me up that two-by-four, will you?"

"You are going to need more than one two-by-four there. Jensen is a big man. Hell, he could fall through the floor and break his neck," Joe called back.

Smoke heard the exchange, as well as the laughter that followed it.

Turnball stepped up to the cell.

"Sorry 'bout all the noise out there," Turnball said.

"Yeah, well, it's not like it's keeping me awake," Smoke replied.

Turnball chuckled. "I'll say this for you. For a man who's about to be hung, you've got a sense of humor. Anyway, your lunch will be here in a few minutes. The jail has a deal with Emma's Café to furnish meals for the prisoners."

"Thanks," Smoke said.

"Oh, and I also have some paper and a pencil here," Turnball said. "If there's anyone you'd like to write a letter to, I'll see to it that it gets mailed."

"Any chance of sending a telegram?" Smoke asked.

Turnball shook his head. "The line is still down. If you want to send word out to anyone, a letter is the only way you can do it."

"All right, let me have the paper and pencil," Smoke said.

Turnball nodded, walked over to his desk and got the paper and pencil, then brought them back and passed them between the bars. Smoke took them, then returned to his bunk and sat down. He lifted the pencil to write, but didn't begin right away.

He didn't want to hurry into the letter. He realized that by the time Sally got this letter, he would be dead. Because of that, he needed to think, very carefully, about what he would say.

His lunch came before he started writing, so Smoke ate the ham, fried potatoes, and biscuits while he contemplated what he would say to Sally. Then, with his lunch eaten and the sound of construction still ringing in his ears, he began to write.

My Dearest Sally,

If you are reading this letter, it means I am dead.

That's a very harsh thing to be telling you, so maybe you should pause for a minute so you can catch your breath.

I know this isn't the kind of opening sentence

*you would expect to read in a letter from me, and
believe me, it's not one I wanted to write. But
there is no other way to say it, other than to come
right out and say it.*

*I also realize that some explanation is in order
so, as well as I can, I will bring you up on just what
has happened to me since I left home a week ago.*

*The trip up from Sugarloaf was a lot more diffi-
cult than I expected, as there is still a lot of snow
in some of the higher elevations. Coming through
Veta Pass, which normally should take only a
matter of hours, took two days. Stormy had to
break through snow that was up to his chest, and
by the time we did get through, I had to give both
him and me a pretty long breather.*

*We did not see another living soul for those two
days. And that is bad, because if we had seen
anyone else, anyone at all, I probably wouldn't be
in this fix.*

*It's time now for me to explain just what kind of
fix I am in. I am, as of this writing, sitting in a jail
in Etna, Colorado. It seems that the Bank of Etna
was robbed on the morning of the sixth of this
month. As it happens, on the sixth I did see someone else. But by pure coincidence, and the worst
luck, the people I encountered were the very men
who had robbed the Bank of Etna.*

*Stormy had picked a stone, and I was in the
process of taking it out of his shoe when the six men
rode up. I was not expecting anything out of the
ordinary from my encounter with them, so I was not*

nearly as vigilant as I should have been. As a result, I was caught off guard and knocked out.

Sally, I know this was a dumb, you might even say a tenderfoot, thing for me to do. And you know me better than that. You know that, normally, I am much more alert.

I suppose my only excuse is that I was tired from the travel. And to be honest, I wasn't in the best of spirits, due to the fact that I was on my way to Denver to lease our ranch. That is something I know we needed to do, but it wasn't something I was looking forward to.

Anyway, thanks to my own dumb poor judgment, I was knocked out. But the story gets even stranger, Sally, because when I came to, I realized that I was wearing the shirt of one of the men who had waylaid me. I didn't have time to wonder about it, though, because almost from the moment I came to, I was face-to-face with a posse from Etna.

It was then that I found out what the shirt was all about, because the posse, seeing me in that very shirt, assumed that I was one of the ones they were looking for. I was arrested, and taken into town.

I was certain that I would be able to prove my innocence, but because I had not encountered anyone during my time on the trail, I was unable to establish an alibi. The posse had not believed me when they picked me up, and neither did the jury. I was found guilty, not only of the robbery, but of the murder of the banker, a man named Rob Clark.

*That brings us back to the opening line of this
letter. As a result of the verdict, I was sentenced to
death by hanging. And now, as I write this letter, I
can hear them building the gallows out in the
street.*

Putting down the tablet and pencil, Smoke climbed up
onto the bunk so he could look out through the high
window. He couldn't actually see the gallows, though as
it was now late afternoon, he could see its shadow against
the side wall of the apothecary. The men had quit work
for the day, but Smoke could tell from the projected
shadow that they had completed the base of the gallows.

When Pearlie and Cal rode into Big Rock, Pearlie
pointed to a buckboard and team that was parked in
front of the telegraph office.

"Isn't that rig from Sugarloaf?"

"Yes," Cal said. "Smoke must be sending a telegram."

"Let's go surprise him," Pearlie suggested.

Dismounting alongside the buckboard, Pearlie and
Cal stepped into the telegraph office. Rather than sur-
prising Smoke, they were themselves surprised to see
Sally there.

"Hello, Miss Sally," Cal said.

There was a look of concern on Sally's face when she
turned, but that was replaced by a big smile the moment
she saw Pearlie and Cal.

"Pearlie! Cal!" she said happily. Opening her arms, she

embraced each of them in turn. "Oh, I'm so happy to see you. I am so glad you are back!"

"Where's Smoke?" Cal said. "We've got something for him."

The smile left Sally's face to be replaced, once more, by a look of concern.

"I don't know where he is," she said. "He is supposed to be in Denver, meeting with a land broker. He was going to send me a telegram to tell me that he had arrived safely, but I haven't heard anything."

"Well, maybe the telegraph lines are down," Pearlie suggested. "You know, this was an awful bad winter."

"The direct lines are down," Sally said. "But Cody was able to get a message through by relaying it through Wichita. And If I can get through to Denver that way, you know he can get through to me."

Pearlie was quiet for a moment, then he nodded. "Yes, ma'am, I reckon if there was a way to send you a telegram, Smoke would figure it out," he said. "I was just tryin' to keep you from worryin' too much, that's all."

"You say you got through to Denver?" Cal asked.

"Yes. I sent a telegram to the broker, asking if Smoke had arrived. I'm waiting now for the reply."

Behind them, they heard the telegraph begin clacking. The telegrapher hurried over to the instrument, sat down in front of it, grabbed the key, then sent something back.

"Cody, is that my telegram?" Sally asked.

"Yes, ma'am, I believe it is," Cody replied.

The machine began clacking again, and Cody picked up a pencil and started recording the message on a little yellow tablet. The instrument continued for several seconds while Cody wrote; then the machine grew silent.

Once again, Cody put his hand on the key to send a message back. Then, clearing his throat, he tore the page from the tablet, stood up, and brought it over to Sally.

"I wish I had somethin' better to report, Miss Sally," Cody said as he handed the message to her.

HAVE NOT SEEN SMOKE JENSEN STOP EXPECTED HIM
TWO DAYS AGO STOP WILL HAVE HIM SEND MESSAGE
IF HE ARRIVES STOP

"Now I am beginning to get worried," Sally said.

"You want us to go look for him?" Pearlie asked.

"I don't want you to go without me," Sally said. "But I want to give it a couple more days. I would hate to be out looking for him, and not be here to get his telegram when it comes."

"All right," Pearlie said.

"Thank you, Cody," Sally called back to the telegrapher.

"Miss Sally, if anything comes for you in the next day or so, I promise I'll get it out to your ranch," Cody said.

"I appreciate that," Sally said. Then to Pearlie and Cal: "Well, I take it you two are back. Shall we go home?"

"We're back," Cal said. "And guess what we brung you."

"What you *brung* me?" Sally scolded.

"Uh, what we brought you?"

"That's better. And it doesn't matter what you brought

me. I'm just happy to see the two of you back where you belong."

"Four hunnert dollars," Cal said.

"What?" Sally responded with a gasp, surprised by the comment.

"We brung . . . uh, that is, we brought you four hunnert dollars," Cal said. "To help save the ranch."

"Where on earth did you get . . . no, never mind, it doesn't matter where you got it. However you got it, it's your money. Please don't feel any obligation toward Sugarloaf."

"Miss Sally, you don't want to hurt our feelings, do you?" Pearlie asked.

"What? No, of course not."

"Well, then, you must know that we consider Sugarloaf our home too. I know we don't own any of it, or nothin' like that. But it is our home nonetheless. And like you said, this here money is our money, which means we can pretty much do with it as we please. Ain't that right?"

Sally sighed. She wasn't even going to consider the poor grammar.

"Yes," she said. "It's your money to do with as you like. And yes, Sugarloaf certainly is your home."

"Then, we want to give you this money to help save it."

"Thank you," Sally said. "I couldn't be more touched."

Smoke did not finish writing the letter the first day. For a while, he considered scrapping the entire letter, but realized that, while he was actually writing, it almost seemed as if he were with Sally. So, late in the afternoon of the second day, he picked up the tablet and continued the letter.

As I am sure you have learned by now, I did not get to Denver to see the broker, so I have not been able to rent out Sugarloaf. Maybe you can make all the arrangements by telegraph. Or maybe it would even be better for you to sell Sugarloaf. You should be able to get a lot more money than we owe on the ranch. Then you could move into town somewhere and live comfortably on the money you would get from the sale.

I know that right now, as you read this letter, money is probably the furthest thing from your mind. But it is one of the foremost things on my mind. If something like this had to happen, I wish it could have happened last year, or even the year before. The ranch was solvent then, and you would not have been as foolish as I was to risk so much on the greedy ambition of growing even larger. My only comfort now is in knowing that you are smart enough to be able to salvage what value there remains of the ranch.

I hope Pearlie and Cal return sometime soon. I think having them around will help you deal with this. Or maybe you will help them deal with it. For some reason, women seem to be stronger than men about such things.

I have been writing this letter for two days now, not because I am having a hard time in writing it, but because while I am writing it, I feel myself closer to you.

When Smoke heard the sound of construction halt for the day, he put the letter aside and, once more, climbed up onto his bunk to see what he could see. The sun was low in the west, and as it had done the day before, it projected the shadow of the gallows-in-progress onto the wall across the alley from the jail. Today he could see the base and the steps, and just the beginning of the gibbet.

On the third day, Smoke finished his letter.

Sally, I have faced death many times before, and just as I was not afraid then, I am not afraid now. You cannot spend your life in this magnificent country and not be aware that death is a part of life, or that there is something higher than we are. And because I believe in that higher power, I do not think this is the end. It is only a door from this life into whatever God has in store for me. If there is a balance sheet of my life, I am comfortable with the idea that I will be received into His Glory.

My only regret is that I did not have more time to spend with you. You, Sally, have been the purpose and the love of my life. Know that, even though you may not see me, I will find a way to be with you from now on.

Your loving husband,
Smoke

At about the same time Smoke finished his letter, the hammering and sawing stopped, and when he climbed up on his bunk to look at the shadow against the wall, he could see the entire gallows. The instrument of execution was complete, to include the gibbet and dangling rope. The hangman's noose was already tied.

Having faced death many times before, Smoke was convinced that he had come to an accommodation with it. But he was about to be hanged for something he did not do, and there was something about that prospect that bothered him even more than the actual dying. It wasn't just that he was going to be executed, though that was bad enough. It was that those who actually were guilty were getting away with it.

Smoke folded his letter and put it in the envelope Turnball had given him. He had just finished addressing it when Deputy Pike stepped up to the cell and looked in.

"Who'd you write that letter to?" Pike asked.

"I wrote it to my wife."

"Your wife, huh?" Pike said. He giggled. "Is your wife a good-lookin' woman? I mean, bein' as she's goin' to be a widder-woman, why, just maybe I'll go meet her."

"Why don't you do that?" Smoke said.

"Hah! You want me to go meet your widder?"

"Yes," Smoke said. "Tell her how much you enjoyed watching me die." Smoke smiled, a cold, hard smile. "Then I suggest you duck."

"Why? Is she goin' to hit me with a fryin' pan?"

"No. She is more likely to shoot you with a forty-four," Smoke said.

"Really?"

"Really."

"Well, we'll just see about that." Pike stuck his hand

in through the bars of the cell. "If you'll give me your letter, I'll see to it that it gets mailed."

"No, thanks."

"What do you mean no, thanks? Don't you want it mailed?"

"Not unless I'm dead."

"Well, don't you be worryin' none about that. You're goin' to be dead by a little after ten o'clock tomorrow mornin'."

"You can mail it then," Smoke said.

"Pike, get away from that cell and quit bothering the prisoner," Turnball called from his own desk.

"I was just . . ." Pike started.

"I don't care what you was just," Turnball said. "Just get away from the cell like I told you to."

"All right, Marshal, whatever you say," Pike replied.

That night, Deputy Pike was on duty. As it grew dark, he lit a kerosene lantern, but the little bubble of golden light that the lantern emitted barely managed to light the office. Although the cell was contiguous to the office, very little of the light from the lantern reached it. The cell, while not totally dark, was in deep shadows.

Just as the clock struck ten, Pike came over to the cell. Smoke was lying on the bunk with his hands laced beside his head. Because Pike was backlit by the lantern, Smoke could see him quite clearly. However, the dark shadows inside the cell made it more difficult for Pike to see Smoke.

"Hey, Jensen," Pike called. "Jensen, you awake in there?"

"I'm awake," Smoke replied, his low, rumbling voice floating back from the shadows.

"It's ten o'clock," Pike said. He giggled. "You know what that means, don't you? That means you only got twelve hours left to live."

Pike put his fist alongside his neck, representing a hangman's noose. Then he jerked his fist, tipped his head over to one side, and made a gagging sound in his throat.

"Shhhiiick!"

Laughing, Pike walked back into the office.

He came back at eleven. "Eleven hours," he said.

"Thanks so much for reminding me," Smoke said sarcastically.

"Oh, don't you worry none about that," Pike said. "I plan to come here ever' hour on the hour all night long. What's the good of hangin' somebody if you can't have a little fun with it?"

True to his word, Pike came back at midnight, and again at one. And each time, he told Smoke the time left with particular glee.

As it so happened, Smoke had a good view of the clock from his cell, so, just before two o'clock in the morning, he climbed up to the very top of the cell and hung on with feet and hands. As he expected, Deputy Pike came to the cell just as the clock was striking two. But because Smoke was in the shadows at the top of the cell, Pike didn't see him.

"Jensen?" Pike called. "Jensen, where are you?"

Smoke was in an awkward and uncomfortable position, and he didn't know how much longer he would be able to hold on. He watched Pike's face as the deputy studied the inside of the cell, and he could tell that Pike was both worried and confused.

"Where are you?" Pike asked again. "Where the hell did you go?"

Pike hurried back to get the key; then he returned and opened the door to step inside.

Smoke wasn't sure if he could have held on for another moment, but he managed to hold on until Pike was well inside the cell and clear of the door.

Then Smoke dropped down behind him.

"What the hell?" Pike shouted, turning around quickly to face Smoke. That was as far as he got. Before his brain had time to register what was going on, Smoke took him down with a powerful blow to the chin.

Working quickly, Smoke dragged the deputy over to the bunk. Then he pulled off the deputy's socks and stuffed them in his mouth to keep him from shouting the alarm after he left.

"Whew," Smoke said as he pulled the socks off Pike's smelly feet. "Those socks are pretty strong. Sorry about stuffing these in your mouth like this, Pike, but maybe you should think about washing your feet a little more often."

Smoke handcuffed the deputy to the bunk so he couldn't get rid of the socks. Then he closed and locked the door.

By then, Pike was conscious, and he lay on the bunk, glaring at Smoke with hate-filled eyes. He tried to talk, but could barely manage a squeak.

"Deputy Pike, it has been fun," Smoke said. "We'll have to do this again sometime."

Chapter Fourteen

Smoke retrieved his guns and saddlebags from the office. Then, almost as an afterthought, he took the red and black plaid shirt that had played such a role in his trial. After that, he let himself outside. The cool night breeze felt exceptionally refreshing to him, especially after several days of being cooped up in a cell.

As he stepped out into the street, he saw in actuality what he had only seen in shadow before now. The gallows was rather substantial, consisting of thirteen steps leading up to a platform that was about ten by ten. He didn't go up the steps for a closer examination, but he knew there would be a trapdoor at the center of the platform. Gabled over the top of the platform was the gibbet, and hanging from the gibbet was the rope and noose.

There was a sign in front of the gallows:

TO BE HUNG
AT TEN O'CLOCK OF THE MORNING
ON THE 15TH INSTANT

FOR THE MURDER OF ROBERT CLARK
KIRBY JENSEN

PUBLIC INVITED.

Taking out the pencil he had used to write his unsent letter to Sally, Smoke drew a large X across the sign. Then at the bottom he added:

HANGING CANCELLED

Chuckling to himself, Smoke hurried down to the livery stable. Although the night was moon-bright, it was very dark inside the stable where his horse was being kept.

He knew that Stormy was in here because he overheard Turnball telling someone that the town of Etna was going to sell Smoke's horse in order to pay for the expense of his trial and hanging.

As he moved down through the center corridor of the stable, he could smell straw and oats, as well as the manure, urine, and flesh of a dozen or more horses. The animals were being kept in stalls on either side of the center passage, but in the darkness of the building they were little more than large, looming, indecipherable shadows and shapes to him. He would have to depend upon Stormy to help him.

"Stormy?" Smoke called quietly. "Stormy, are you in here?"

Smoke heard a horse whicker in response, and going toward the sound, he found his horse with his head sticking out over the door of the stall.

"Good boy," Smoke said, rubbing his horse behind its ears. "Did you miss me?"

In response, Stormy nudged his nose against Smoke.

Smoke saw that his saddle was draped over the side of the stall. With a silent prayer of thanks for it being so convenient to him, he picked up the saddle and put it on his horse. Then, very quietly, he opened all the other stall doors in the stable and, clucking at the horses, called them out. Mounting Stormy, he then rode around to the corral and opened the gate. Within moments he had gathered a small herd of some thirty horses, and he started moving them out of town. He kept the herd going until he was at least two miles away. Then he pulled his pistol and fired into the air, causing the horses to break into a gallop.

The lead stallion started running in a direction that would take the herd farther away from Etna, and the others followed instinctively. Smoke was certain that after they tired of running, the herd would dissipate and the horses would probably return, one at a time, to the corral.

But for now they were in a panic, following the leader, and he knew it would be at least one day, maybe more, before the horses got back. He was certain that this wasn't every horse in town, but it represented a sizable number of them, enough to make the immediate raising of a posse difficult.

Once Smoke escaped from jail, he knew better than to go back home to Sugarloaf, or to even try to get in touch with Sally. There was no doubt in his mind but that Turnball would have notified Sheriff Carson back in Big Rock. And while Smoke and Carson were close friends, Carson was a man of great integrity, and Smoke's presence there under these circumstances would be very difficult for him.

The only way Smoke could avoid going back to jail, and keeping a date with the hangman, would be to find the real bank robbers and murderers. And it was that, his determination to find the real outlaws and clear his own name, that drove him now.

Tracking six riders on a trail that was a week old would be a task so daunting for most men that they would never even think to try. But Smoke wasn't most men, and he never gave the task before him a second thought. He had learned his tracking skills from a master tutor. The classes began during his days of living in the mountains with the man called Preacher,

"He's a good one to learn from," another mountain man once said to Smoke, speaking of Preacher. "Most anyone can track a fresh trail, but Preacher can follow a trail that is a month old. In fact, I've heard some folks say that he can track a fish through water, or a bird through the sky. And I ain't one to dispute 'em."

Now, as Smoke started on the trail of the bank robbers, the words of his tutor came back to him.

"Half of tracking is in knowin' where to look," Preacher told the young Smoke. *"The other half is looking.*

"Reading prints on a dirt road is easy. But if you know what you are doing, you can follow the trail no matter where it leads. Use every sense God gave you," Preacher explained. *"Listen, look, touch, smell. Taste if you have to."*

* * *

Smoke never was as good as Preacher, but if truth be told, he was second only to Preacher, and he could follow a cold trail better than just about anyone. Returning to the place where he had encountered the bank robbers, he managed to pick up their trail.

It was difficult, the trail being as old as it was, but he was helped by the fact that the robbers were trying to stay out of sight. Because of that, they avoided the main roads, and that made their trail stand out. The funny thing is, if they had stayed on the main roads, Smoke might not have been able to find them because their tracks would have been covered over, or so mixed in with the other travelers that he wouldn't be able to tell which was which.

But cutting a trail across fresh country the way they did led Smoke just as straight as if they had left him a map. Also, since they were isolated from the other traffic, Smoke was able to study each individual set of hoofprints. To the casual observer, all the prints would look alike, just the U shape of the horseshoes. But a closer examination showed that each set had its own peculiar identifying traits. That would be very helpful to him once they got back onto a major trail, for then he would be able to pick out the individual prints from among many others.

Tracking became even easier once he reached high country because there was still snow on the ground, and it was almost as if they were leaving him road signs.

Then, just on the other side of a large patch of snow,

the riders went their separate ways. When that happened, Smoke had to choose which trail he was going to follow.

"What the hell?" Marshal Turnball said when he came into his office the next morning and found Deputy Pike gagged and handcuffed to the bunk and locked in the cell.

"Uhhnnn, uhhhnn," Pike grunted. He was unable to speak because of the socks that were stuffed in his mouth.

"Oh, shut up your moaning," Turnball said, his irritation showing in his voice. "Where are the damn keys?"

"Uhnnn, uhnnn," Pike grunted again.

"Oh, shut up," Turnball repeated.

Finding the keys lying on his desk, Turnball unlocked the cell door, then pulled the socks from Pike's mouth.

"Now, Deputy Pike, would you please tell me just what the hell happened?" Turnball asked as he started looking through the key ring for the one that would unlock the handcuffs.

Pike coughed and gagged for a moment after the socks were removed. "The son of a bitch got away!" he finally blurted out.

"I can see that, Pike," Turnball said. "The question is, how did he get away? When I left last night, he was locked in this cell. Now I come in here this morning and what do I find? Jensen? No! I find you all trussed up like a calf to be branded. Now I want to know how that happened."

"He jumped me," Pike said.

"He jumped you?"

"Yes, sir."

"You were outside, he was locked in the cell, and he jumped you?"

"I, uh, wasn't exactly outside the cell when he jumped me."

"Go on."

"Well, you see, I come into the cell," Pike said. He went on to explain how he had looked in the cell and, not seeing the prisoner, went in to investigate. He left out the fact that he had been harassing the prisoner every hour on the hour.

The front door to the jail opened then, and Syl Jones came in. Jones was the owner of the corral.

"Marshal, the horses is gone," Jones said.

"The horses? What horses?"

"Your horse, my horse, just about ever' horse in town. They're all gone."

"What the hell are you talking about? Gone? Gone where?"

"I don't know gone where. All I know is, when I come to work this mornin' the stable door was open, all the stalls was open, and the corral gate was open. They ain't one horse left."

"Jensen," Turnball said angrily.

"Jensen? Are you talkin' about Smoke Jensen? The fella we're goin' to hang this mornin'?" Jones had been a member of the jury that had convicted Smoke.

"Yes, that's exactly who I mean. The fella we *was* goin' to hang this morning," Turnball said. He looked at Pike, the expression on his face showing his anger.

"That is, we was goin' to hang him before Pike, here, just opened the door and let 'im go."

"You let 'im go? What the hell did you do that for?" Jones asked.

"Shut up, Jones," Pike growled. "You think I done it of a purpose?"

"Well, even if he did escape, why would he steal ever' horse in town?" Jones asked.

"He didn't steal them, he just ran them off," Turnball said. "He figured it would keep us from comin' after 'im."

"Oh, yeah, I guess that's right," Jones said. "Well, if he just run 'em off, like as not they'll all be back before the day's out."

"In the meantime, that gives him a full day's head start." Sighing audibly, Turnball ran his hand through his hair. "Damn you, Pike," he said.

Turnball started for the front door.

"Where you goin'?" Pike asked.

"To the telegraph office. There has to be some way to get a message out."

"Yes, we've got a line through to Omaha," James Cornett said. "Just got put back up yesterday."

"Could you send a message to the sheriff of Hinsdale County through Omaha?"

"Well, if they are connected to anyone, I suppose we can. We could go through Omaha to Wichita to Denver to . . ."

Turnball waved his hand. "I don't need you to build the telegraph line for me, Cornett. Just send the message."

"All right," Cornett replied. "What's the message?"

"I'll write it out for you," Turnball said as he began writing. "Actually, two messages, one to the sheriff of Hinsdale County and one to Big Rock, down in Rio Grande County."

Half an hour later, just after Turnball got through explaining to a disappointed crowd that there would be no hanging today, Cornett came into his office with a message.

"We heard back from the sheriff of Hinsdale County," Cornett said, handing the message to Turnball.

Turnball read it, then shook his head. "What have we gotten ourselves into?" he asked.

"What is it?" Pike asked.

Without a word, Turnball handed Pike the telegram.

ANY SUCH REWARD POSTER ON KIRBY JENSEN AS MAY EXIST HAS LONG BEEN RESCINDED STOP KIRBY JENSEN IS ONE OF THE LEADING CITIZENS OF THE STATE STOP IT IS HIGHLY UNLIKELY THAT JENSEN WOULD PARTICIPATE IN A BANK ROBBERY STOP EXPECT INVESTIGATION FROM STATE ATTY GENERAL OFFICE STOP GOVERNOR PITKIN PERSONALLY INTERESTED IN CASE STOP

Cody Mitchell, the Western Union operator in Big Rock, Colorado, was sweeping the floor of his office when the instrument began clacking to get his attention.

Putting the broom aside, he moved over to the table, sat down, and responded that he was ready to receive.

Cal was filling a bucket at the water pump when he saw a boy of about fifteen riding toward the house.

"Can I help you with somethin'?" Cal called out to him.

"This here's the Jensen spread, ain't it?" the boy replied.

"It is."

"I got a message for Mrs. Jensen from Mr. Mitchell."

"Mitchell?" Cal asked.

"Mr. Cody Mitchell, the telegrapher."

"Oh!" Cal said. He smiled broadly. "It must be from Smoke. Give the telegram to me, I'll take it to her."

The boy shook his head. "I ain't got no telegram. All I got is a message, and Mr. Mitchell says I'm to tell it to her personal."

"All right," Cal said, picking up the bucket. "Come on, I'll take you to her."

An hour after the message was delivered, Sally, Pearlie, and Cal were in Sheriff Carson's office.

"You didn't have to come into town, Miss Sally," Carson said. "I was goin' to come out there to see you."

"What's this all about, Sheriff?" Sally asked.

Sheriff Carson stroked his chin. "All I can tell you is what I heard from the marshal up in Etna. He said that they arrested Smoke for murder and bank robbery, and they tried him and found him guilty. He was supposed to hang this mornin', but he got away."

"Thank God," Sally said, breathing a sigh of relief.

"Yes," Carson said. "Well, he did get away, but it's my understanding that Marshal Turnball has sent word out all over the West sayin' Smoke is a wanted man."

"Sheriff, you know there is no way Smoke would hold up a bank, or murder someone," Sally said. "How could a fair jury find him guilty of such a thing?"

"I reckon they don't know him like we do," Carson said. "Sally, uh, they want me to arrest him if he comes back. I'm legally and morally bound to do it, so if he comes to the ranch first, you tell him to just keep on going and not to come into town."

"Don't worry, Sheriff," Sally said. "I don't think Smoke will come back until he has this mess all cleared up."

That night in the bunkhouse, Pearlie woke up in the middle of the night. When he awoke, he saw Cal sitting at the window, just staring outside.

"Damn, Cal, what time is it?" Pearlie asked from his bed.

"I don't know," Cal answered. "It's some after midnight, I reckon."

"What are you doin' up?"

"Can't sleep."

"You're thinking about Smoke, ain't you?"

"Yeah."

"Smoke will be all right. He can take care of himself, you know that."

"Yeah, I know it."

"And he'll find out who done this and get that set right too."

"Unless . . ." Cal answered, allowing the word to hang, pregnant with uncertainty.

"Unless what?"

Cal turned to look at Pearlie for the first time. "Pearlie, have you stopped to think that maybe Smoke, that is, maybe he . . ."

"Did it?" Pearlie responded.

Cal nodded his head, but said nothing. His eyes were wide, worried, and shining in the moonlight.

"Cal, believe me, I've known Smoke longer than you have. He didn't rob that bank and he didn't kill that banker."

"I mean, if he did, why, I wouldn't think no less of him," Cal said. "What with the winter we just come through, and the danger of him maybe losin' Sugarloaf an' all."

"He didn't do it," Pearlie said again.

"How can you be so sure?"

"I told you how I can be so sure. It's because I know him."

"Pearlie, you know how I come to be here, don't you? I mean, how I tried to rob Miss Sally that time? If it had been anyone else but her, I would of probably got away with it. Then, there's no tellin' where I would be now. I might even be a bank robber. But I ain't, 'cause she took me in."

"Yes, I know that."

"The point is, I ain't a thief. I mean, I ain't no normal

thief, but I was pretty desperate then, so I done somethin' I never thought I would do. I could see how Smoke
might do the same thing if he thought he had to."

"All right, Cal, do you want me to tell you how I
know he didn't do this?"

"Yes."

"It's easy," Pearlie said. "The sheriff said there were
six of 'em robbed the bank, right?"

"Right."

"If Smoke was going to rob a bank, he wouldn't need
no five other men to help him get the job done. He
would'a done it alone."

Cal paused for a minute; then he broke into a big smile.

"That's right!" he said. "He would'a done it alone,
wouldn't he? I mean, Smoke, there ain't no way he
would need someone else to help him do a little thing
like rob a bank."

"Are you satisfied now?"

"Yeah," Cal said. "Yeah, you're right. Smoke didn't
rob that bank."

"So, you'll go to bed now and let me get some sleep?"

"Yeah," Cal said. "Good night, Pearlie."

"Good night, Cal."

Chapter Fifteen

It was just growing dark when Smoke rode into the little town of Dorena. He passed by a little cluster of houses that sat just on the edge of town and as he came alongside them, he could smell the aroma of someone frying chicken. That reminded him that he was hungry, not having eaten anything for the entire day.

Smoke had never been in Dorena before, but he had been in dozens of towns just like it, so there was a familiarity as he rode down the street, checking out the false-fronted buildings: the leather goods store, the mercantile, a gun shop, a feed store, an apothecary, and the saloon.

The saloon was called Big Kate's, and when Smoke stopped in front of it, he reached down into the bottom of his saddlebag, moved a leather flap to one side, and found what he was looking for. He had put one hundred dollars in the saddlebag before he left Sugarloaf, keeping it in a way that a casual examination of the pouch wouldn't find it. Fortunately, it had escaped detection when he was arrested and his horse and saddle were taken.

The smell of bacon told him that Big Kate's offered an opportunity for supper, so he went inside.

One of the amenities the customers could enjoy at Big Kate's was a friendly game of cards. On the wall there was a sign that read: THIS IS AN HONEST GAMBLING ESTABLISHMENT——PLEASE REPORT ANY CHEATING TO THE MANAGEMENT.

In addition to the self-righteous claim of gambling integrity, the walls were also decorated with animal heads and pictures, including one of a reclining nude woman. There was no gilt-edged mirror, but there was an ample supply of decent whiskey, and several large jars of pickled eggs and sausages placed in convenient locations.

From a preliminary observation, Big Kate's appeared to be more than just a saloon. It was filled with working girls who all seemed to be attending to business. Smoke saw one of the girls taking a cowboy up the stairs with her.

The upstairs area didn't extend all the way to the front of the building. The main room, or saloon, was big, with exposed rafters below the high, peaked ceiling. There were a score or more customers present, standing at the bar talking with the girls and drinking, or sitting at the tables, playing cards.

A large, and very bosomy, woman came over to greet Smoke.

"Welcome to Big Kate's, cowboy," she said. "I don't believe I've seen you before. Are you new in town?"

"I am," Smoke answered. "I take it that you are . . ." He hesitated, then left out the descriptive word. "Kate?"

Big Kate laughed, a loud, guffawing laugh. "It's okay,

honey, you can call me big. Hell, I've got mirrors and I ain't blind. Now, could I get you something to drink?"

"Yes," Smoke answered.

"Wine, beer, or whiskey?"

"Beer," Smoke said. "And something to eat, if you've got it."

"Beans and bacon is about it," Big Kate replied. "And cornbread."

"That'll be fine," Smoke said

"Kim, do keep the cowboy company while I get him something to drink," Big Kate said, adroitly putting Smoke with one of her girls.

Kim was heavily painted and showed the dissipation of her profession. There was no humor or life left to her eyes.

"You were in here last week, weren't you?" Kim asked. "Or was it last month?"

Smoke shook his head. "You've never seen me before," he said.

"Sure I have, honey," Kim answered in a bored, flat voice. "I've seen hundreds of you. You're all alike."

"I guess it might seem like that to you."

"Would you like to come upstairs with me?"

"I don't think so," Smoke said. He smiled. "I'm just going to have my dinner and play some cards. But I appreciate the invitation."

"Enjoy your dinner, cowboy," Kim said in a flat, expressionless voice that showed no disappointment in being turned down. Turning, she walked over to sit by the piano player.

The piano player wore a small, round derby hat and

kept his sleeves up with garter belts. He was pounding out a rendition of "Little Joe the Wrangler," though the music was practically lost amidst the noise of a dozen or more conversations.

"What's the matter? you didn't like Kim?" Big Kate asked, returning with Smoke's beer.

"Kim was fine," Smoke said. "I've just got other things on my mind, that's all."

"It must be somethin' serious to turn down a chance to be with Kim. She's one of our most popular girls," Big Kate said, laughing. "If you'll excuse me now, I see some more customers just came in and I'd better go greet them. Oh, there's a table over there. Your food will be right out."

"Thanks," Smoke said.

Ebenezer Dooley had stepped out through the back door to the outhouse to relieve himself. He was just coming back in when he saw Smoke Jensen talking with Big Kate.

What the hell? he thought. How the hell did he get out of jail?

Dooley backed out of the saloon before he was seen.

Kim brought Smoke another beer and supper, then left to ply her trade among some of the other customers. Smoke ate his supper, then, seeing a seat open up in a card game that was in progress, took the rest of his beer over to the table.

"You gents mind if I sit in?" he asked.

"We don't mind at all. Please, be our guest," one of the men said effusively, making a sweeping gesture. "The more money there is in a game, the better it is, I say."

"Thanks," Smoke said, taking the proffered chair.

Some might have thought it strange for Smoke to play a game of cards under the circumstances, the circumstances being that he was a man on the run. But he was also a man on the hunt, and he had learned, long ago, that the best way to get information was in casual conversation, rather than by the direct questioning of people. He knew that when someone started questioning people, seriously questioning them, the natural thing for them to do was to either be very evasive with their responses, or not say anything at all.

Smoke had already drawn his first hand before he saw the badge on the shirt of one of the other men who was playing.

"You the sheriff?" Smoke asked.

"Deputy," the young man answered with a broad smile. "The name is Clayton. Gideon Clayton. And you?"

"Kirby," Smoke replied, using his first name that no one ever used. Then, in a moment of inspiration, he decided to make that his last name. "Bill Kirby," he added.

For a moment, Smoke felt a sense of apprehension, and part of him wanted to just get up and leave. But he knew that doing something like that would create quite a bit of suspicion.

On the other hand, with Deputy Clayton being here, he might learn right away if any telegraph message of his escape had reached the sheriff's office. But when

Deputy Clayton made no move toward him, nor gave any indication of being suspicious of him, Smoke knew that, for now, he was safe to continue his search.

To the casual observer it might appear that Smoke was so relaxed as to be off guard. But that wasn't the case, as his eyes were constantly flicking about, monitoring the room for any danger. And though he was engaged in convivial conversation with the others at the table, he was listening in on snatches of dozens of other conversations.

"I believe it is your bet," Deputy Clayton said to Smoke. Smoke missed the challenge when it was first issued because he was looking around the room to see if he could spot any familiar faces. "Kirby?" the deputy said again.

"I beg your pardon?"

"I said, I believe it is your bet," Clayton said.

"Oh, thank you," Smoke said. He looked at the pot, then down at his hand. He was showing one jack and two sixes. His down card was another jack. He had hoped to fill a full house with his last card, but pulled a three instead.

"Well?" Clayton asked.

Smoke could see why Clayton was anxious. The deputy had three queens showing.

"I fold," Smoke said, closing his cards.

Two of the other players folded as well, and two stayed, but the three queens won the pot.

"Thank you, gentlemen, thank you," Clayton said, chuckling as he raked in his winnings.

"Deputy Clayton, you have been uncommonly lucky tonight," one of the other men said good-naturedly. Smoke had gathered from the conversation around the table that the one speaking was Doc McGuire.

"I'll say I have," Clayton agreed. "I've won near a month's pay just sittin' right here at this table."

"What do you think, Beasley?" Doc asked one of the other players. "Will our boy Clayton here give up the deputy sheriffin' business and go into gambling full-time?"

"Ho, wouldn't I do that in a minute if I wasn't married?" Clayton replied.

"Where's Sheriff Fawcett tonight?" Beasley asked.

"The sheriff's taking the night off," Clayton said. "I'm in charge, so don't any of you give me any trouble or I'll throw you in jail," he teased. The others laughed.

"Where you from, Mr. Kirby?" Doc McGuire asked as he shuffled the cards.

"Down in Laplata County," Smoke lied.

"Did you folks have a hard winter down there?"

"Yes, very hard."

"I was reading an article in the Denver paper a few weeks ago," Clayton said. "According to the article this was the worst winter ever, and it was all over the West. Hundreds of thousands of cows were lost."

"It was a bad one all right," Beasley said as he dealt the cards. "Some folks think that bad weather only hurts the farmers and ranchers, but I can tell you as a merchant that it hurts us too. If the farmers and ranchers don't have any money to spend, we can't sell any of our goods."

"I reckon it was the winter that made those folks hold up the bank over in Etna," Smoke said, taking a chance in bringing up the subject.

"There was a bank robbery in Etna?" Beasley asked. "I hadn't heard that."

"Yes," Deputy Clayton said. "We didn't get word on it until yesterday. Six of 'em held up the bank and killed the banker."

"They killed the banker?" Beasley asked. "Wait, I know that banker. His name is Clark, I think."

"Yes, Rob Clark," Clayton said. "But I understand they caught one of the ones who did it."

"Good. I hope they hang the bastard," Beasley said. "From what I knew of him, Clark was a good man."

"Oh, I expect the fella that killed him is already hung by now," Clayton said.

"You haven't heard anything on any of the others, have you?" Smoke asked.

"No, as far as I know they're still on the run," Clayton said as he pulled in another winning hand.

Smoke won the next hand, which brought him back to even, and the way the cards were falling, he decided he had better stop now. When Clayton started to deal, Smoke waved him away.

"Are you out?"

"Yeah, I'd better quit while I have enough money left to pay for my hotel room," Smoke said, pushing away from the table and standing up. "I appreciate the game, gentlemen, but the cards haven't been that kind to me tonight. I think I'll just have a couple of drinks, then turn in."

* * *

Ebenezer Dooley was standing just across the street from the saloon, tucked into the shadows of the space between Lair's Furniture and Lathum's Feed and Seed stores. He had been there for just over an hour when he saw Smoke step outside.

"Well now, Mr. Jensen," Dooley said quietly. "It's time I settled a score with you, once and for all."

Dooley pulled his pistol and pointed it, but just as he did so, a wagon passed between him and Smoke. By the time the wagon had cleared, he saw Smoke going into the hotel.

"Damn!" he said, lowering his pistol.

Chapter Sixteen

The hotel clerk was reading a book when Smoke stepped up to the desk. He looked up.

"Yes, sir, can I help you?"

"I'd like a room."

"Would you prefer to be downstairs or upstairs?"

"Upstairs, overlooking the street if possible."

"Oh, I think I can do that for you," the clerk said. He turned the book around. "The room will be fifty cents."

Smoke gave him the half-dollar, then signed the book, registering as Bill Kirby.

The clerk turned the book back around, checked the name, then wrote the room number beside it. He took a key down from the board and handed it to Smoke.

"Go up the stairs, then back to your left. The room number is five; you'll see it right in front of you."

"Thanks," Smoke said, draping his saddlebags over his shoulder.

The stairs were bare wood, but the upstairs hallway was covered with a rose-colored carpet. The hallway was illuminated by wall-sconce lanterns that glowed dimly with low-burning flames, putting out just enough light to allow him to see where he was going.

The number 5 was tilted to one side, but Smoke didn't have any difficulty making it out. He unlocked the door, then went inside. The room was dark, illuminated only by the fact that he had left the door open and some light spilled in from the hall. He saw a kerosene lamp on the bedside table, as well as several matches.

Dooley was frustrated that Smoke had managed to go into the hotel before he was able to take a shot at him. He put his pistol back in his holster while he contemplated what to do next.

Dooley had a room in the hotel himself. Maybe the best thing to do would be to wait until much later, then sneak down the hall into Smoke's room and kill him in the middle of the night.

Dooley had just about decided to go back to the saloon and have a few drinks while he was waiting, when he saw a lantern light up in one of the windows facing the street on the second floor of the hotel. That had to be Smoke Jensen.

As it happened, the stable was just across the street from the hotel, so Dooley ran back to the alley, then down to the stable, coming in through the back door. Going to the stall where his horse was boarded and his saddle waited, he snaked his rifle from the saddle holster. Then, with rifle in hand, he climbed into the hayloft and hurried to the front to look across the street into the hotel. He smiled broadly when he saw that the shade was up and the lantern was lit. Just as he had thought it would be, the occupant of the room was Smoke Jensen.

He had an excellent view from the hayloft.

It was a little stuffy in the room, so Smoke walked over to the window, then raised it to catch the night breeze. That was when he saw a sudden flash of light in the hayloft over the livery across the street.

Instinctively, Smoke knew that he was seeing a muzzle flash even before he heard the gun report. Because of that, he was already pulling away from the window, even as the bullet was crashing through the glass and slamming into the wall on the opposite side of the room.

Smoke cursed himself for the foolish way he had exposed himself at the window. He knew better; he had just let his guard down. He reached up to extinguish the lantern, and as he did so, a second shot came crashing through the window.

He extinguished the lamp, and the room grew dark.

"Damn!" Dooley said aloud. He jacked another round into the chamber of his rifle and stared across the street into the open, but now dark, window of Smoke Jensen's room.

Dooley was very quiet, very still, and very observant for a long time, and it paid off. He saw the top of Jensen's head appear just above the windowsill. He fired a third time.

* * *

This bullet was closer than either one of the other two, so close that he could feel the concussion of the bullet. But this time he had seen the muzzle flash from across the way, so he had a very good idea of where the shooter was, and he fired back.

Dooley hadn't expected Jensen to return fire. For one thing, Dooley was well back into the loft, so he was convinced that he couldn't be seen at all. He hadn't counted on Jensen being able to use the muzzle flash of his rifle to locate his position.

The bullet from Jensen's pistol clipped just a little piece of his ear, and he cried out and slapped his hand to the shredded earlobe.

"You son of a bitch," he muttered under his breath.

"What was that?" Smoke heard someone shout.

"Gunshots. Sounded like they came from down by the . . ."

That was as far as the disembodied voice got before another shot crashed through the window.

"Get off the street!" another voice called. "Everyone, get off the street!"

Smoke heard the command, loud and authoritative, floating up from below. "Everyone, get inside!"

Smoke recognized the voice. It belonged to Deputy Clayton, the man he had been playing cards with but a few minutes earlier. On his hands and knees so as not to present a target, Smoke crept up to the open window and looked out again. He saw the deputy running up the street.

"Clayton, stay away!" he shouted down to him. Clayton headed for the livery stable with his pistol in his hand. "Clayton, no! Get back!"

Smoke's warning was not heeded. A third volley was fired from the livery hayloft, and Clayton fell facedown in the street.

With his pistol in his hand, Smoke climbed out of the window, scrambled to the edge of the porch, then dropped down onto the street. Running to Clayton's still form, he bent down to check on him. Clayton had been hit hard, and through the open wound in his chest, Smoke could hear the gurgling sound of his lungs sucking air and filling with blood.

"Damnit, Clayton, I told you to get down," Smoke scolded softly.

"It was my job," Clayton replied in a pained voice.

At that moment, another rifle shot was fired from the livery. The bullet hit the ground close by, then ricocheted away with a loud whine.

"He's still up there," Clayton said.

"Yeah, I know," Smoke said.

"What's going on?" someone shouted.

"What's all the shootin' about?" another asked.

"Get back!" Smoke yelled. "Do what the deputy told you! Get back!"

"Is the deputy dead?"

Another shot from the loft of the stable did what Clayton and Smoke had been unable to do. It forced all the curious onlookers away from the street and out of the line of fire.

Smoke fired back, shooting once into the dark maw of the hayloft. Then, taking Clayton's pistol and sticking it down in his belt, he ran to the water trough nearest the livery, diving behind it just as the man in the livery fired again. He heard the bullet hit the trough with a loud popping sound. He could hear the water bubbling through the bullet hole in the water trough, even as he got up and ran toward the door of the livery.

Smoke shot two more times to keep the shooter back. Then, when he reached the big, open double doors of the livery, he ran on through them so that he was inside.

Once inside, he moved quietly through the barn itself, looking up at the hayloft just overhead. Suddenly he felt little pieces of straw falling on him and he stopped, because he realized that someone had to be right over him. That's when he heard it, a quiet shuffling of feet. He fired twice, straight up, but was rewarded only with a shower of more bits and pieces of straw.

"That's six shots. You're out of bullets, you son of a bitch," a calm voice said.

Smoke looked over to his left to see a man standing in the open on the edge of the loft. It was one of the bank robbers.

"Well," Smoke said. "If it isn't the pockmarked droopy-eyed son of a bitch who set me up."

"How the hell did you get out of jail, Jensen?" he asked. "I figured they'd have you hung by now. I must confess that I was some surprised when I seen you come in the saloon tonight."

"You're going to shoot me, are you?" Smoke asked.

"Seems like the logical thing to do, don't you think?"

"What's your name?"

Dooley laughed. "What do you need to know my name for?"

"I don't know. Maybe because I'd like to know the name of the man that wants to kill me."

"It ain't just wantin' to, Jensen. I'm goin' to kill you. And to satisfy your curiosity, my name is Dooley. Ebenezer Dooley."

"Since you are in a sharing mood, Mr. Dooley, where are the others?" Smoke asked.

Dooly laughed. "You got some sand, Jensen," he said. "Worryin' about where the others are when I'm fixin' to shoot you dead."

"Where are they?"

"I don't know where they all went, but the Logan brothers was goin' to Bertrand. Not that it'll matter to you. You got 'ny prayers, now's the time to say them."

Slowly, and deliberately, the outlaw raised his rifle to his shoulder to take aim.

Smoke raised his pistol and fired.

Dooley got a surprised look on his face as he reached down and clasped his hands over the wound in his chest. He fell forward, tumbling over once in the air, then landing on his back in a pile of straw in the stall right under him. The horse whinnied and moved to one side of the stall, barely avoiding the falling body.

Smoke stepped into the stall and looked down at Dooley. The outlaw was gasping for breath, and bubbles of blood came from his mouth.

"How did you do that?" Dooley asked. "I counted six shots."

Smoke held out the pistol. "This is the deputy's gun," he said. "I borrowed it before I ran in here."

"I'll be go to hell," Dooley said, his voice strained with pain.

"I expect you will," Smoke said as Dooley drew his last breath.

Smoke saw that the horse was still pretty agitated, and he petted it on the neck to try and calm it down.

"I'll be damned," he said. "No wonder you are upset. You're his horse, aren't you?"

The horse continued to show its agitation.

"Don't worry, I'm not going to shoot you. You can't help it because your owner was such a bastard."

As Smoke continued to try and calm the horse, he saw a twenty-dollar bill lying in the straw over by the edge of the stall, just under the saddle.

"Hello, what's this?" he said, leaving the horse and going over to retrieve the bill. That's when he saw another bill sticking out of the rifle sheath.

Smoke stuck his hand down into the rifle holster and felt a cloth bag. Pulling the bag out, he saw that it was marked BANK OF ETNA. There were five packets of bills in the bag, each packet wrapped by a band that said $1000. Four of the packets were full, and one was partially full.

Smoke looked back toward the door of the stable to make certain that he wasn't being watched; then he took the money bundles from the bag and stuck them inside his shirt. After that, he stuffed the empty bag back down into the rifle boot, then walked out into the street.

The street was still empty.

"It's all right, the shooter's dead!" Smoke called. "Someone get Doc McGuire to come have a look at the deputy!"

At his call, several people began appearing from inside the various buildings and houses that fronted the street. One of the first to show up was Doc McGuire, who, carrying his bag, hurried to the side of the fallen deputy. Kneeling beside the deputy, Doc McGuire put his stethoscope to the young man's chest. He listened for a moment, then, with his face glum, shook his head.

"He's dead," he said.

One of the others to hurry to the scene was the sheriff. The sheriff, who had gotten out of bed, was still tucking his shirt into his trousers as he came up. His badge gleamed in the moonlight.

"Damn," he said as he saw his deputy lying on the ground. "Anybody know who did this?"

"His name was Dooley. Ebenezer Dooley, and you'll find him in the barn," Smoke said.

"In the barn?" the sheriff said, pulling his pistol.

"It's all right. He's dead."

The sheriff looked at Smoke. "Did you kill him?"

"Yes."

"And who might you be?"

"The name's Kirby. Bill Kirby," Smoke said, continuing to use his alias.

"Tell me, Kirby, did you have a personal grudge with this fella?" Sheriff Fawcett asked.

"No."

"Then how come it was that you and him got into a shootin' war?"

"You'd have to ask Dooley that, Sheriff," Smoke said. "He's the one that started the shooting."

"What are you pickin' on him for, Sheriff?" one of the townspeople asked. "He's right, the man in the barn started the shootin' and Deputy Clayton come after him, only he got hisself kilt. Then this fella"—he pointed at Smoke—"went in after him. "I seen it. I seen it all."

"Did you know this man?" Sheriff Fawcett asked Smoke.

"No."

"Then, how'd you know his name was Dooley?"

"He told me his name before he died."

Sheriff Fawcett had a handlebar mustache, and he curled the end of it for a moment. "Seems to me like I've heard that name before. There may be a wanted poster on him. Are you a bounty hunter?"

"I'm not a bounty hunter. I just happened to be here when this all started happening."

"Mr. Kirby would you be willing to stop by my office tomorrow and answer a few questions for me?"

"I don't mind," Smoke said.

"In the meantime, if some of you fellas would get these bodies over to the undertaker, I'll go see Mrs. Clayton and tell her about her husband." Sheriff Fawcett sighed. "I'd rather take a beating than do that."

Smoke hung around until the two bodies were moved; then he walked back across the street and into the hotel.

The hotel clerk was standing at the front door when Smoke went inside.

"Mister, that's about the bravest thing I ever seen, the way you run into that barn like that. It was the dumbest too, but it sure was brave."

"You're half right," Smoke said with a little chuckle. "It was dumb."

When Smoke went up to his room, he took the money out of his shirt, counted it, then put it in his saddle bags. He'd counted 4,910 dollars, which was nearly half of what had been stolen. He wasn't exactly sure how he was going to handle it, but he had it in mind that, somehow, returning the money might help him prove his innocence.

But this was only half the money. For his plan to work, he would have to track down every remaining bank robber and retrieve whatever money was left.

Chapter Seventeen

The next morning Dooley's corpse was put on display in the front window of Laney's Hardware Store. He was propped up in a plain pine box, and was still wearing the same denim trousers and white shirt he had been wearing at the time of his death.

Dooley's eyes were open and opaque, and his mouth was drawn to one side as if in a sneer. When the viewers looked closely enough, they could see that, although the undertaker had made a notable effort, he had not been able to get rid of all the blood from the repaired bullet hole in the shirt.

A sign was hanging around the corpse's neck.

EBENEZER DOOLEY
THE MURDERER OF
DEPUTY GIDEON CLAYTON
SHOT AND KILLED BY BILL KIRBY
ON THE SAME NIGHT

After the money was divided, the five remaining bank robbers went their separate ways. Dooley went off by himself, but the Logan brothers left together, and so did Fargo Masters and Ford DeLorian, who were first cousins.

Ford was relieving himself while Fargo remained mounted, his leg hooked around the saddle horn.

"Hey, Fargo," Ford called up from his squatting position. "You know what I been thinkin'?"

"Ha," Fargo teased. "I didn't even know you could think, let alone what you were thinkin'."

"I'm thinkin' it don't do no good to have this here money if we ain't got no place to spend it."

"Yeah, I've give that a little thought myself," Fargo replied.

Ford grabbed a handful of leaves and made use of them. "So, how about we go into the next town and spend a little of this money?" he said as he pulled his trousers back up.

"Sounds fine by me," Fargo replied. "Where is the closest town?"

"Closest town is Dorena," Ford said, "But we can't go there."

"Why not?" Fargo asked.

"'Cause that's where Dooley was goin'."

"So?"

"I thought he said it wouldn't be good for us to all go to the same place."

"We won't all be in the same place," Fargo said. "Just you'n me and Dooley."

"Yeah, you're right," Ford said as he remounted. "Ain't no reason he gets to go to the closest town and we got to ride over hell's half acre, just to find us a place to spend some money."

"That's what I was thinkin'. You been to Dorena before?" Fargo asked.

"Yeah, once, a long time ago."

"I've never been there. What's the best way to get there from here?" Fargo asked.

"It's just on the other side of that range of hills there," Ford said, pointing. "We should be there by noon."

"First thing I'm goin' to do when we get there is get me a big piece of apple pie," Ford said. "With cheese on top."

Fargo laughed. "You just give me an idea about what I aim to get me."

"What is that?" Ford asked.

"A cold piece of pie and a hot piece of ass," Fargo called back over his shoulder as he slapped his legs against the side of his horse, causing it to break into a trot.

Ford laughed, then urged his horse into a trot as well.

The sun was high in the sky as Fargo and Ford reached Dorena. A small, hand-painted sign on the outer edge of the town read:

Dorena
Population 515
Come Grow With Us

No railroad served the town, and its single street was dotted liberally with horse apples. At either end of the street, as well as in the middle, planks were laid from one side to the other to allow people to cross over when the street was filled with mud.

The buildings of the little town were as washed out and flyblown up close as they had seemed from some distance. The first structure they rode by was a blacksmith's shop.

TOOMEY'S BLACKSMITH SHOP

Ironwork Done.

Tree Stumps Blasted.

That was at the east end of town on the north side of the street. There, Ford and Fargo saw a tall and muscular man bent over the anvil, the ringing of his hammer audible above all else. Across the street from the blacksmith shop, on the south side of the street, was a butcher shop, then a general store and a bakery. Next were a couple of small houses, then a leather shop next door to an apothecary. A set of outside stairs climbed the left side of the drugstore to a small stoop that stuck out from the second floor. A sign, with a painted hand that had a finger pointing up, read:

Roy McGuire, M.D.

Next to the apothecary was the sheriff's office and jail, then the bank, a barbershop and bathhouse, then a hotel.

On the north side of the street, next to the blacksmith shop, was a gunsmith shop, then a newspaper office, then a café, then several houses, followed by a seamstress shop, then a stage depot, the Brown Dirt Saloon, several more houses, then the stable, which was directly across from the hotel.

Fargo pointed to the café. "There!" he said. "Let's go in there 'n get us somethin' good to eat."

"All right," Ford agreed. The two men cut their horses to the side of the street toward the café, then dismounted and tied them off at the hitching rail. When they stepped inside the building, some of the patrons reacted visibly to the filth and stench of the two visitors.

They found a table and sat down. A man and woman who were sitting at a table next to them got up and moved to another table.

"What you reckon got into them folks?" Ford asked.

"I guess they don't like our company," Ford answered.

A man wearing an apron came up to them. "You gentlemen just coming into town, are you?" he asked.

"Yeah, and we're hungry as bears," Fargo said. "What you got to eat?"

"Oh, we have a lot of good things," the man replied. "But, uh, being as you just came in off the trail, perhaps you would enjoy your meal better if you cleaned up first? There is a bathhouse just across the street."

"Yeah, we seen it," Ford said. "But we're hungry. We'll eat first, then we'll go take us a bath."

"Go take a bath first," the waiter said. "Trust me, you will enjoy your meal much more."

"How do you know?" Ford asked.

"Because in your present condition, you are offensive to my other customers, and I don't intend to serve you until you have cleaned up."

"The hell you say," Ford replied angrily.

The waiter turned away from the table and started back toward the kitchen.

"Look here, mister, don't you walk away while I'm a'talkin' to you!" Ford called after him, reaching for his gun.

Fargo reached across and grabbed Ford's hand, preventing him from drawing.

"You don't want to do that, Ford," he said sternly, shaking his head.

"I ain't goin' to let no son of a bitch talk to me like that," Ford said angrily.

"Come on, let's go take a bath," Fargo said. "Our money ain't goin' to do us no good if we're in jail."

"You heard what . . ."

"Come on," Fargo said again, interrupting Ford's grumbling. "We'll board our horses, then take a bath."

As the two left the livery, they saw a crowd of people gathered in front of the hardware store, about halfway down the street.

"What do you reckon that's all about?" Fargo asked, pointing toward the crowd.

"I don't know," Ford said. "What do you say we go down there an' take a look?"

"All right," Fargo agreed.

The two men started down the street toward the hardware store, but stopped when they got close enough to see what everyone was looking at.

"I'll be damned," Ford said as he spit a stream of tobacco, then wiped the dribble from his chin. "That's ole Dooley up there in that pine box."

"It sure as hell is," Fargo replied.

"How'd he wind up there?" Ford asked.

"It tells you right there on the sign they got hangin' around his neck," Fargo said.

"Hell, Fargo, you know I can't read," Ford said. "What does the sign say?"

"It says he was kilt by a fella named Bill Kirby."

"Bill Kirby? I ain't never heard of no Bill Kirby, have you?"

Fargo shook his head. "Can't say as I have," he said.

"What for do you think this fella Kirby kilt 'im?"

"I don't know. Says on the sign that Dooley kilt a deputy sheriff, then this Kirby fella kilt him."

Ford studied the corpse for a long moment.

"What you lookin' at?" Fargo asked.

Ford chuckled. "Hell, the son of a bitch is even uglier dead than he was while he was alive."

Fargo laughed as well. "He is at that, ain't he?" He paused for a moment before he spoke again. "Wonder where at is his share of the money," Fargo said.

"He prob'ly spent it all already," Ford said.

"He couldn't of spent it this fast," Fargo insisted.

"Then he must'a hid it," Ford said.

"What do you say we hang around town long enough to find out just what happened?" Fargo suggested. He smiled. "Ha, the son of a bitch got most of the money; now he ain't even around to spend it. What do you say we find it and spend it for 'im?"

"Yeah," Ford agreed. "I would like that."

When Sally, Pearlie, and Cal rode into Etna, they saw a gallows in the middle of the street, just in front of the marshal's office. A rope was dangling from the gibbet, the noose at the end ominous-looking.

"That kind of gives you chills lookin' at it, don't it?" Cal said. "I mean, knowin' it was for Smoke."

"It wasn't used," Sally said, "so it doesn't bother me."

"Where do we start?" Pearlie asked.

"Why don't you two go on down to the saloon and see what you can find out?" Sally asked. "I'll check in the marshal's office."

"Uh, you want me'n Cal to go on down to the saloon?" Pearlie asked.

"Yes. Smoke always says you can find out more about what's going on in a saloon than you can from the local newspaper."

Pearlie smiled broadly. "Yes, ma'am, I've heard 'im say that lots of times. All right, me'n Cal will go on down there and see what we can find out. We'll all get together later," Pearlie added.

Pearlie and Cal continued to ride on down to the saloon, while Sally reined up in front of the office, dismounted, then went inside. A man with a badge was sitting at the desk, dealing poker hands to himself. He looked up as she entered.

"Somethin' I can do for you, little lady?" he asked with a leering grin.

"Are you Marshal Turnball?"

"No, I'm his deputy. The name is Pike."

"Where can I find Marshal Turnball?" Sally asked.

"What for do you need him?" Pike asked. "I told you, I'm his deputy." Pike moved around to the front of the desk, to stand uncomfortably close to Sally. "You want anything done . . . why, all you got to do is just ask."

"All right," Sally said. "I want you to tell me where I can find Marshal Turnball."

"I tell you what," Pike said, putting his hand on Sally's shoulder. "Maybe if you'd be nice to me, I'll be nice to you."

Pike moved his hand down to her breast.

Pearlie and Cal stepped up to the bar and ordered a beer apiece. When they were delivered, Pearlie blew some of the foam away, then took a long, Adam's apple-bobbing drink.

"You're pretty thirsty, cowboy," the bartender said.

"We rode a long way today," Pearlie answered.

"That'll make you thirsty all right," the bartender agreed.

"Say, we noticed the gallows out in the street as we came into town," Pearlie said. "You folks about to have a hangin'?"

"Well, we thought we was," the bartender said. "But the fella we was goin' to hang, a man by the name of Kirby Jensen, got away."

"How did he do that?"

The bartender laughed. "Hey, Marshal Turnball," the bartender called across the room. "Here's two fellas wantin' to know how Jensen got away."

"Ain't nobody's business how he got away," Turnball replied gruffly.

Pearlie and Cal turned toward the man who had

answered the bartender. They saw a big man filling a chair that was tipped back against the wall. He was wearing a tan buckskin vest over a red shirt. The star of his office was nearly covered by the vest, though it could be seen.

Pearlie took his beer and started back to talk to the marshal. Cal followed him.

"Mind if we join you?" Pearlie asked when he reached the table.

"It's a free country," the marshal replied, taking in the empty chairs with a wave of his arm. "What can I do for you?"

"We're looking for Smoke Jensen," Pearlie said.

"Who?"

"Kirby Jensen," Pearlie clarified.

"Ha," Turnball said. "Ain't we all? What do you want him for?"

"We don't want him for nothin'," Cal said. "He's our friend."

"Your friend, huh? Well, mister, your friend robbed a bank and killed our banker."

"Was he caught in the act of robbin' the bank?" Pearlie asked.

"Near'bout," Turnball said.

Turnball explained how he and the posse found Smoke out on the prairie. "There was some of them empty wrappers, like's used to bind up money, on the ground around him, and they was marked 'Bank of Etna.' Besides which, he was still wearin' the same plaid shirt he was wearin' when he robbed the bank."

"Plaid shirt?" Cal said. He chuckled. "Smoke ain't got no plaid shirts. He don't even like plaid."

"Yeah? Well, he was wearin' one when he robbed the bank, and he was wearin' that same shirt when we caught him."

"Did he confess to robbin' the bank?" Pearlie asked.

"No." Turnball laughed, a scoffing kind of laugh. "He said he was set upon out on the prairie by the ones who actual done it, and one of 'em changed shirts with him."

"But you didn't believe him," Pearlie said. It was a statement, not a question.

"It wasn't just me that didn't believe him," Turnball said. "Your friend was tried legal, before a judge and jury, and found guilty."

"Did you think to send a telegram back to Rio Grande County to check with Sheriff Carson?" Pearlie asked.

"We couldn't. The telegraph line was down."

"If the line was down, how is it that you was able to send a telegram a few days ago sayin' that Smoke had escaped?"

Turnball squinted. "Are you fellas deputies to Sheriff Carson?"

"We ain't regular deputies, but we've been deputies from time to time," Pearlie said. "So I'll repeat my question. How is it that you could send a telegram after he escaped, but you didn't think to send one to check on him?"

"They got a line put up that we was able to use," Turnball explained.

"If you had just waited, I think the sheriff would have told you that Smoke couldn't have done what you said he done."

"Let me ask you this," Turnball said. "Is it true that Jensen is bad in debt? That he's about to lose his ranch?"

"He owes some money, yes," Pearlie said. "But he wasn't about to lose the ranch. He was goin' to Denver to make arrangements to lease Sugarloaf out for the money that he needed."

"That's what you say. But sometimes folks change. Especially if they get desperate."

"How did Smoke escape?"

"What do you mean, how did he escape? He escaped, that's all. I had him in jail; then when I come back to the jail the next mornin', he was gone."

"Was there anyone guardin' him while he was in jail?" Pearlie asked.

"Yeah, my deputy was. Why?"

"A few minutes ago you said that Smoke robbed your bank and killed a banker. But you didn't say anything about him killin' your deputy."

"I didn't say that 'cause he didn't kill 'im," Turnball said.

"If Smoke is the killer you think he is, don't you think he would have killed the deputy when he was getting away?"

"What? I don't know," Turnball said. He was silent for a moment. "Maybe he would have."

"Marshal, we brung Mrs. Jensen with us," Cal said. "Would you like to meet her?"

"What do I want to meet her for?"

"She rode a long way to get here, Marshal," Pearlie said. "It wouldn't hurt you to meet her."

Turnball sighed and stroked his chin; then he nodded and reached for his hat.

"All right," he said. "I'll meet her. Where is she? At the hotel?"

"We left her down at your office," Cal said. "She might still be there."

"Oh, damn," Turnball said. "I hope she didn't tell Pike who she is."

"Pike?"

"Pike is my deputy," Turnball said. "He is as dumb as dirt, and he was . . . well, he was . . ."

"He was what?"

"He was ridin' Jensen pretty hard while he was in jail, carryin' on about how he was goin' to go back to Jensen's ranch and tell his widow first-hand what happened to him."

"That would be all the more reason for Smoke to kill your deputy, wouldn't it?" Pearlie said. "But he didn't do it, did he?"

"No, he didn't," Turnball said. "But now I'm worried about the woman bein' down there with Pike. There's no tellin' what that dumb son of a bitch might do if he knows who she is."

"Might do?" Pearlie asked.

"To Mrs. Jensen."

Pearlie and Cal looked at each other; then both laughed.

"What is it?" Turnball asked. "What's so funny?"

"What's funny is you worryin' about Miss Sally," Cal said.

* * *

When Pearlie, Cal, and Turnball stepped into Turnball's office a few minutes later, they saw Sally sitting at the desk, calmly dealing out hands of cards. She looked up and smiled.

"Hello, Pearlie, Cal," she said. She turned her smile toward Turnball. "And you must be Marshal Turnball," she said.

"Yes, ma'am, I am," Turnball said. "I'm sorry you had to wait here all alone. My deputy was supposed to be here."

"Oh, he is here," Sally said.

"He is? Where?"

"I'm afraid Mr. Pike was a bad boy," Sally said. "So I had to put him in jail."

Looking toward the jail cell for the first time, Turnball saw Pike, handcuffed to the bed. His socks had been stuffed into his mouth.

"I'm sorry about sticking his socks in his mouth like that," Sally said. "But his language was atrocious. I just didn't care to listen to it anymore."

Chapter Eighteen

Fargo and Ford were in adjacent bathtubs. They had agreed to spend some of their money on new duds, so a representative of the mercantile store came to the bathhouse to show some of the clothes the store carried. He was standing alongside the two tubs, displaying his shirts.

"Them's just ordinary work shirts," Ford said. "Ain't you got nothin' fancier than that?"

Like Fargo, Ford was wearing his hat, even though he was in the tub. And like Fargo, he was smoking a cigar.

"These are very good shirts, sir," the store clerk said defensively.

"I was just lookin' for somethin' a little fancier is all."

"We only had one dress shirt in stock," the clerk said. "And the merchants all went together to buy it and a suit of clothes for Deputy Clayton to wear for his funeral."

"Oh, yes, that's the man Bill Kirby shot, ain't it?" Fargo asked.

The clerk shook his head. "No, Mr. Kirby shot the man who shot the deputy. Dooley, his name was. Ebenezer Dooley."

"Do you know this here fella Bill Kirby?" Fargo asked. "Does he live here in town?"

"I don't know him. I believe he is just passing through," the clerk said. "He has a room down at the hotel."

"Hand me that bottle of whiskey," Ford said, pointing, and the clerk complied.

"Will you gentlemen be making a purchase then?" the clerk asked.

"Yeah," Fargo said. He pointed to the pile of dirty clothes they had been wearing. "I tell you what, you take them old ones, and leave us the new ones, and we'll call it an even trade."

The store clerk looked shocked. "I beg your pardon, sir?"

Fargo laughed out loud at his joke. "I was just funnin' you," he said. He reached down on the floor beside the tub and picked up a billfold, then took out some money and handed it to the clerk. "This here ought to do it."

"Yes, thank you," the clerk said.

"And you can also have the old clothes," Fargo said.

The clerk looked at the old clothes with an expression of distaste on his face. "You, uh, want me to take the old clothes?" he asked. "And do what with them, sir?"

"Do anything you want to with them," Fargo said. "Clean them up and wear them if you want to. Or burn them."

"Burn them, yes. Thank you, I'll do that," the clerk said. Looking around, he saw a stick and he used the stick to pick the clothes up, one item at a time. Then he dropped them into the paper in which the new clothes had been wrapped. "I'll take care of them for you," he said.

After the clerk very carefully and hygienically collected the old clothes, he wrapped them in the packing material, then left the bathhouse. Ford took a big drink of the whiskey, then tossed the bottle into an empty tub.

"Did you see the way he got into a piss soup when you told him you wanted to trade even for them duds?" Ford asked, laughing out loud.

"Yeah," Fargo said, laughing with him. "He was so old-maidish the way he was handlin' them clothes, I should'a made him put them on and wear them out of here."

Ford lifted his arm and began rubbing the bar of soap against his armpit. "Hey, Fargo, how do you figure we ought to go about lookin' for Dooley's money?" he asked.

"We could start by goin' over to the hotel where he was stayin' at and lookin' through his room," Fargo suggested.

"Ha! Like they're goin' to let some strangers look through his room."

"We ain't strangers," Fargo said. "We're Dooley's brothers."

"What? No, we ain't," Ford said.

"We are if we say we are," Fargo said. "And who's going to know the difference?"

"Oh," Ford said. Then, as he understood what Fargo was saying, he smiled and nodded. "Oh!" he said again.

"Five hundred dollars?" Smoke said.

"Yes, sir," Sheriff Fawcett said. "Turns out I was right. I had heard Dooley's name before. There's a reward poster on my wall right now offerin' five hundred dollars for anyone who kills or captures him. By rights, that money should go to you. Unless you have something against taking bounty money."

"No, believe me, I don't have anything against it," Smoke said.

"Well, then, if you hang around town for another twenty-four hours, I'll have authorization from the governor's office to pay you the reward," the sheriff said.

"Thanks," Smoke smiled. "You've got a nice, friendly town here. I don't mind staying another twenty-four hours."

Ford belched loudly as he finished eating. A plate filled with denuded chicken bones told the story of the meal he had just consumed. In addition to fried chicken, mashed potatoes, biscuits, and gravy, he had also eaten two large pieces of apple pie, each piece topped by melted cheese.

"Let's go get drunk," he suggested.

"Not yet," Fargo said. "First things first."

"Yeah? What could possibly come before getting drunk?"

"Finding the money," Fargo said.

"Oh, yeah. So, where do we start?"

"We start at the hotel."

"Will that be all, gentlemen?" the waiter asked, approaching their table then.

"Yeah."

"And don't you both look so nice now that you are all

cleaned up?" the waiter said obsequiously. Using a towel, he bent over Ford and began to brush at his shirt.

"Here? What are you doing?" Ford said in an irritable tone of voice.

"I'm just brushing away a few of the crumbs," the waiter said. "It is part of the service one performs when one is in a position to receive gratuities."

"Receive what?" Ford asked.

"Gratuities."

"What is that?"

"Tips?" the waiter tried.

Ford shook his head. "I don't know what you are talking about."

"Oh, well, then, let me explain, sir," the waiter said. "It is customary in a place like this that when one provides a service that is satisfactory, the customer will leave a gratuity, that is, leave some money as a"—the waiter struggled for the word—"gift, as a token of his appreciation for that service."

"What you are sayin' is, you expect us to give you some money above the cost of the meal," Fargo said. "Is that it?"

The waiter broke into a wide smile. "Yes, sir. I'm glad you understand, sir. Ten percent is customary."

"A gratuity?"

"Yes, sir."

"But that's not part of the bill, is it? I mean, if we don't leave you anything, that's not against the law?" Fargo asked.

"Oh, no, sir, not at all. That's why it is called a gratuity."

"Well, if the law don't say I've got to, I ain't goin' to,"

Fargo said. "Come on, Ford, we've got work to do," he added.

"Good-bye, gentlemen," the waiter said with a forced smile. He watched them until they stepped out into the street; then the smile left his face. "You cheap bastards," he added under his breath.

Fargo and Ford were standing in front of the registration desk at the hotel.

"Would you tell me what room Mr. Ebenezer Dooley is a'stayin' in?" Fargo asked. "He's our brother."

The clerk blinked a few times in surprise.

"I beg your pardon," he said. "Who are you asking for?"

"Mr. Ebenezer Dooley," Fargo said. "We was all supposed to meet up here in this hotel today, and we figured he'd be down here in the lobby waitin' for us by now, but he ain't here." Fargo chuckled. "Course, as lazy as ole Eb is, like as not he's lyin' up there sleepin' like a log."

"Oh," the clerk said. "Oh, dear, this is very awkward."

"Ain't nothin' awkward about it," Fargo said. "He's our brother, and he's expectin' us. Tell you what, just give me the key and we'll go wake him up our ownselves."

"You haven't heard, have you?"

"We ain't heard what?" Fargo replied, playing out his role. "What are you talkin' about? Look, just give us the key so we can go wake up our brother and then we can get on our way."

The hotel clerk shook his head. "I'm talking about

your br . . . uh, about Mr. Dooley. I can't believe you haven't heard yet."

"What's there to hear?"

"I'm sorry to have to tell you gentlemen this, but Mr. Dooley was killed last night."

"Kilt? Did you hear that, Ford? Our brother was kilt," Fargo said, feigning shock and concern.

"That's real bad," Ford said, though neither the expression in his voice nor his face reflected his words.

"How was he kilt? What happened?" Fargo asked the hotel clerk.

"He was involved in a shoot-out," the clerk answered. "It seems that your brother killed our deputy sheriff; then he was killed himself."

Fargo pinched the bridge of his nose and shook his head. "Oh," he said. "Mama ain't going to like this, is she, Ford."

"No," Ford said, his voice still flat and expressionless. "She ain't goin' to like it."

"You can, uh, view your brother down the street if you'd like," the hotel clerk said. "His remains are on display in the window of the hardware store."

"What? What kind of town is this that they would put our brother in the window for ever'one to gape at?" Fargo asked.

"Believe me, sir, it wasn't my doing," the clerk said, frightened. He held up his hands and backed away, as if distancing himself from the issue.

"Where at's our brother's things?" Fargo asked. "We'll just get them and be on our way."

"Your brother's things?"

"His saddlebags, or suitcase, or anything he might have had with him. I want to take 'em back to Mama. You got 'em down here?"

"No, they are still in the room. I'm waiting for the sheriff to tell me it is all right to take them out."

"What's the sheriff got to do with it? I told you, we're his brothers. If Brother Eb's still got some things in his room, then we're the ones should get them, not the sheriff."

"Well, I don't know," the clerk said. "I'm not sure about this."

"Just give me the key to his room," Fargo said, more forcefully this time. "We'll go up there and have a look around our ownselves."

"Sir, how do I know you are his brother?"

"How do you know? 'Cause I told you I am his brother."

"Just the fact that you tell me that doesn't validate it."

"Doesn't what?"

"Doesn't prove it."

"Well, hell, why didn't you say you needed proof? Ford, tell him I'm Dooley's brother."

"Yes, sir, he's Dooley's brother all right," Ford said.

"And Ford is his brother too," Fargo said. "So there, you've got all the proof you need."

"That's not really proof, that's just the two of you vouching for each other," the clerk said. "Maybe we should wait for the sheriff. I could send for him if you like."

"Tell you what," Fargo said. "My brother had a drooping

eye right here." Fargo put his hand over his right eye. "Now, how would I know that if I wasn't actual his brother?"

The clerk sighed. The two men were getting a little belligerent with him and they were frightening-looking to begin with. What was he protecting anyway? As far as he knew, there was nothing up there but a set of saddle-bags anyway.

The clerk took a key from the board and handed it to Fargo. "Very well, Mr. Dooley. This goes against my better judgment, but go on up there and look around if you must."

"Thanks," Fargo said.

Fargo took the key; then he and Ford went up to the room. Dooley's saddlebags were hanging over a hook that stuck out from the wall.

Fargo grabbed the bags and dumped the contents onto the bed. One shirt, one pair of denim trousers, a pair of socks, and a pair of long underwear tumbled out.

"You pull out all them drawers and have a look," Fargo ordered, and Ford started pulling out the drawers from the single chest.

Finding nothing, Fargo stripped the bed, then turned the straw-stuffed mattress upside down.

"Nothin' here," Fargo said angrily. "Not a damn thing!"

Ford started to put the drawers back in the chest.

"What are you doin'?"

"Puttin' these back."

"To hell with 'em, just leave 'em," Fargo said. "We can't be wastin' no more time here."

When the two men came back downstairs, the clerk

looked up. He was surprised to see that they weren't carrying anything with them.

"You didn't find his saddlebags?" he asked.

"We found 'em, but there weren't nothin' there that Mama would want," Fargo said as they left.

"What'll we do now?" Ford asked when the two men went out into the street.

"I don't know," Fargo said, taking his hat off and running his hand through his hair. "I figured for sure he would have had the money hid out in his room somewhere," Fargo said.

"Maybe he had it with him, and the undertaker took it," Ford suggested.

"Good idea. Let's go down there and talk to him," Fargo said.

"You think the undertaker would keep the money if he found it?" Ford asked.

"We'll soon find out."

Chapter Nineteen

Gene Prufrock, the undertaker, had done nothing to prepare the outlaw's body but wash the shirt, then put him in a pine box. He didn't like the idea of making a public show of the dead, no matter how despicable a person he might have been. So when the sheriff asked him to stand Dooley's body up in the hardware store window, Prufrock tried to talk him out of it. But the sheriff prevailed, and Dooley's body was now on display.

It was a different story with Gideon Clayton, though. The young deputy had been very popular among the citizens of the town, and Prufrock was taking his time to do as good a job as he possibly could. Several of the merchants had gotten together to buy a special coffin for Clayton. It was finished with a highly polished black lacquer and fitted with silver adornments. Those same merchants had also bought him a suit, so that Gideon Clayton's body lay on Prufrock's preparation table, dressed in a suit and tie that he had never worn in life. The undertaker made the final touches, combing Clayton's hair and powdering and rouging his cheeks.

Prufrock had just stepped back to admire his work when he was suddenly surprised by the entry of two men.

"Is there something I can do for you gentlemen?" Prufrock asked.

"Yeah, we want to ask you some questions," Fargo said.

"Could the questions wait? As you can see, I'm working on a subject."

"Is that what you call them? Subjects? Why don't you just call them what they are? Dead meat?" Ford asked with a laugh.

"I'm sorry, sir, but I do not find your joke at all funny. I believe, very strongly, in maintaining the dignity of the departed," Prufrock said.

"I hear that when somebody dies, you take all the blood out of them," Ford said. "Is that true."

"Yes."

"What do you do that for?"

"So we can replace the blood with embalming flood. It preserves the body."

"What do you do with the blood?"

"We dispose of it," Prufrock said impatiently. "Gentlemen, please, I don't like people back here. Is there something I can do for you?"

"Who is this fella you're workin' on here?" Fargo asked, pointing to the body on the table. "Was he rich or somethin'?"

"No. Why would you think he is rich?"

"Well, look at him. He's all decked out in a new suit. And I'm lookin' at that real pretty coffin over there and figurin' you're about to put him in it. Is that right?"

"That's right."

"Then he must'a been rich."

"He wasn't rich, he was just well respected. He was our deputy sheriff."

"Your deputy sheriff, huh? So what you are saying is that this is the man our brother killed."

Prufrock gasped. "Good heavens! Mr. Dooley is your brother?"

"Yeah," Fargo said.

The mortuary was in the same building as the hardware store, but behind it. Fargo pointed toward the front. "The man you have standin' up in that window out there, showin' him off like a trussed-up hog, is our brother. Is that what you mean when you say you like to maintain the dignity of the departed? Our brother is a departed, ain't he? Where at's his dignity?"

"I . . . I'm sorry. I don't think anyone knew that he had kin in town."

"We just come into town this mornin'," Fargo said, indicating himself and Ford. "Didn't find out about our brother until we saw him standin' there in that store window for all the world to see."

"I'm sorry about your brother," Prufrock said.

"Yes, well, like I say, he was our brother. So that means that anything you found on him is rightly our'n."

"I beg your pardon?" Prufrock said, surprised by the sudden change in the direction of the conversation.

"His belongin's," Fargo said. "Ever'thin' he had on him is rightly our'n now. Well, 'cept he can keep them clothes on he's a'wearin'. Wouldn't want him to have to show up in hell butt naked."

Both Fargo and Ford laughed.

"That'd be funny all right," Ford said. "Ole Dooley walkin' around in hell naked as a jaybird."

"Dooley?" Prufrock said.

"What?"

"You called him Dooley."

"Well, hell, that's his name," Ford said. "What else am I supposed to call him?"

"It's just that, within the family, people normally use first names."

"Yeah, well, Eb, bein' the oldest, was just always called Dooley," Fargo said, trying to smooth over Ford's mistake. "Now what about his belongings? Do you have any of 'em here?"

"Well, of course there's his gun and his boots," Prufrock said. "Only other thing he had was the clothes he is wearing. But of course, you have already indicated that you don't want those."

"What about the money?"

"Yes, I'm glad you brought that up," Prufrock said. "That will be five dollars."

"Five dollars? That's all he had on 'im, was five dollars?" Fargo asked.

"Oh, no, you misunderstand. He had less than one dollar on him. The five dollars is what you owe me."

Fargo looked confused. "Why the hell should I owe you anything?"

"You did say that he was your brother, did you not? That means that someone owes me for the preparation of his body. As you two gentlemen are his next of kin, you are responsible for his funeral."

"Far as I'm concerned, he ain't goin' to have no funeral,"

Fargo said. "We may be his next of kin, but you ain't goin' to get no money from us."

"Then, what do you propose that I do about burying your brother?"

"What would you do about buryin' him if I hadn't'a come along today?"

"He would be declared an indigent, and I would collect the fee from the town council. Of course, that would also mean that he will be buried in a pauper's grave."

"That's fine with me. Go ahead and get your money from the town," Fargo said. "Come on, Ford, let's go."

"Aren't you even interested in when and where he is to be buried?" Prufrock called out as Fargo and Ford left the mortuary.

"No," Fargo yelled back over his shoulder.

"My word," Prufrock said quietly as the men left.

"The only place we ain't looked yet is the stable," Ford said. "Are we goin' to tell the fella watchin' the stable that Dooley was our brother?"

"No," Fargo said. "If Dooley owes any money for boardin' his horse, the son of a bitch might try to make us pay."

"Then how are we goin' to look?"

"We'll just have to find another way," Fargo replied.

Fargo and Ford hung around the stable until they saw the stable attendant go into the corral to start putting out feed for the outside horses. Then the men slipped into the barn.

"How will we find what stall he was in?" Ford asked.

"You know his horse, don't you?"

"Yeah, sure I know his horse."

"We'll just look around until we see whichever horse is his."

The two men started looking into the stalls. Then, at the fifth stall they examined, Ford said, "There he is. I'd recognize that horse just about anywhere."

Opening the door, they stepped inside; then Fargo picked up a pitchfork and handed it Ford. "Get to work," he said.

"Get to work doin' what? What's this here pitchfork for?"

"Start muckin' around in the straw, make sure he don't have it hid there."

"Yeah, well, while I'm shovelin' straw and shit, what are you going to do?"

"I'm going to look at his saddle and blanket roll."

"How come you get to look in his saddle, while I have to muck around in the straw and horseshit?"

"That's just the way it is," Fargo said.

Grumbling, Ford began tossing the straw aside while Fargo examined the saddle. Finding nothing there, he unrolled the blanket. When his search of the blanket turned up nothing, he stuck his hand down into the empty rifle sheath.

"Ha!" he said happily. "I feel somethin' here! I think this is it!"

Ford tossed the pitchfork aside and hurried over to watch Fargo as he retrieved a bag. But as soon as he brought the bag out for a closer examination, his smile changed to a frown.

"What the hell?" he said. "The bag is empty. There ain't no money here!"

"Well, where is it?" Ford asked. "Somebody's got it. He wouldn't of just kept an empty bag."

"Bill Kirby," Fargo said.

"Who?"

"The man they say shot Dooley. His name is Bill Kirby. And I'd bet you a hunnert dollars to a horseshoe that he's the one that got the money."

"So what do we do now?"

"We find the son of a bitch," he said.

Chapter Twenty

When Fargo woke up the next morning, he saw that he was in one of the rooms upstairs over Big Kate's saloon. There was a whore sleeping beside him and as he looked at her in the harsh light of day, he marveled at how different she looked now from the way he'd thought she looked last night. There was a large and disfiguring scar on one cheek. She was missing three teeth, and her breasts were misshapen and laced with blue veins.

"Damn," he said to himself. "How'd you get so ugly so fast? I must'a been pretty damn drunk last night."

Turning the covers back, he stepped out on the floor, put on his hat, and then, totally naked except for the hat, walked over to the window and looked at the back of the building behind the saloon. Feeling the need to urinate, he lifted the window and let go, watching as a golden arc curved down. A cat, picking through the garbage below, was caught in the stream and, letting out a screech, started running down the alley.

"Ha!" Fargo laughed out loud.

At that moment the door to the room opened and Ford came in.

"Son of a bitch!" Ford DeLorian said. "I seen 'im! I seen 'im when he come out of the sheriff's office."

"You seen who?" Fargo asked.

"I seen the fella that kilt ole Dooley."

"You seen Kirby?"

Ford smiled broadly. "Yeah, I seen 'im," he said. "Only his name ain't Kirby."

"What do you mean, his name ain't Kirby?"

"I mean his name ain't Kirby 'cause it's Jensen. He's the same fella that we put Logan's shirt on," Ford said. "Smoke Jensen, Dooley said his name was then. You recollect him, don't you, Fargo? He's a big man."

"Yes, I recollect him all right," Fargo said. "But how do you know he's the one that kilt Dooley?"

"Well, he's the one they give the reward for doin' it," Ford said. "They was talkin' about it downstairs, how Kirby was goin' to get a reward from the sheriff this mornin'. That's why I went down there so I could see what he looked like."

"You went down to the sheriff's office?"

"Yeah. I was out workin' this mornin', while you was in here layin' up with the whore."

"Well, you had her first. If you hadn't been so tight about it, we could'a each had our own whore 'stead of sharin' one."

"Is she still asleep?" Ford asked, looking toward the bed.

"Yeah, she's either asleep or passed out," Fargo replied.

"She did drink a lot last night," Ford said.

"She couldn't of drunk as much as we did. Otherwise, we wouldn't of brought her up here. Did you get a good look at her? She is one ugly woman."

"Yeah, well, me'n you ain't exactly what you would call good-lookin'," Ford replied. "Damn, Fargo, you just goin' to stand there naked all day?"

"Oh, yeah," Fargo said. "I guess I'd better get dressed."

"You know what I don't understand?" Ford asked as Fargo began pulling on his long underwear. "I don't understand what Jensen's doin' here. How come he ain't in jail?"

"He must'a broke out."

"Yeah, well, that's the trouble with jails these days," Ford said. "Hell, a citizen can't even count on 'em to keep the outlaws locked up."

"Are you sure it was Jensen you saw?"

"Yeah, I'm sure. And if you don't believe me, you can see for yourself. He's downstairs right now. But you better hurry, 'cause he ain't goin' to be there long."

"How do you know?"

"'Cause I heard him askin' someone how to get to Bertrand."

Fargo look up sharply. "Bertrand, you say?"

"Yeah."

"That's where the Logans was goin'."

"Yeah, that's what I was thinkin' too," Ford said. "You reckon Jensen is goin' after them?"

"Of course he is. Damn, you know what I think the son of a bitch is doin'?"

"No, what?"

"Well, what he is plannin' on doin' is runnin' us down and killin' us one at a time," Fargo said.

"For revenge?"

"Probably some revenge," Fargo agreed. "But more'n likely, it's to get his hands on the money that we stole."

"Damn! That mean he plans to kill *us,* don't it?"

"Yeah," Fargo replied. "Unless we kill him first."

"How we goin' to do that? We can't just walk downstairs and shoot him where he's sittin'."

"No, but if he's goin' to Bertrand, we can set up an ambush along the way."

As Smoke rode out of Dorena, he thought about the reward money he had received from killing Ebenezer Dooley. Five hundred dollars was still quite a way from having enough money to pay off the note on his ranch, but it was a start. If there had been a reward for Dooley, maybe there was a reward on the others. If each of them was worth five hundred dollars, finding them all would be worth three thousand dollars. Three thousand dollars would not only pay off the note on his ranch, it would give him a little operating capital to start the next year with.

Smoke had never been a bounty hunter, had never even considered it. But this was a different situation from hunting men just for the bounty. He needed to find each of these men in order to prove that he was innocent of the bank robbery in Etna.

On the first night on their way back to Sugarloaf Ranch, Sally, Pearlie, and Cal made camp on the trail. They found a place next to a fast-flowing spring of clear water where there was abundant wood for their fire and grass for the horses. Cal had gathered the wood, Pearlie had made the fire, and now Sally was cooking their supper.

Pearlie started laughing.

"What ever are you laughing about?" Sally asked.

"I was thinkin' of the way you had the deputy all trussed up and gagged like that."

"Yeah," Cal said. "And what was real funny was the way the marshal was laughin' at it. He said Smoke done the same thing to him."

"*Did* the same thing," Sally corrected.

"Yeah," Cal said. "But you have to admit, whether he done it or did it, it was funny, especially you doin' it too."

"He had such a dejected look about him that I almost felt sorry for him," Sally said.

The others laughed again, then Cal inhaled deeply. The aroma of Sally's cooking permeated the camp.

"They ain't nothin' no better'n bacon and beans when you're on the trail," Cal said as he walked over to examine the contents of the skillet that was sitting on a base of rocks over the open fire. A Dutch oven of biscuits was cooking nearby. "It sure makes a body hungry."

"Cal, you are incorrigible," Sally said, shaking her head. "What you mean is, there isn't *anything* better than bacon and beans," she said, correcting him.

"Yes, ma'am, I reckon that is what I meant," Cal said contritely.

"And when have you not been hungry?" she added with a chuckle.

"Well, you're right about that, Miss Sally," Cal said. "But there ain't . . . isn't," he corrected, "anything any better than bacon and beans cooked out on the trail."

"'Ceptin' maybe bear claws," Pearlie said. "Too bad you can't make us a batch of them out on the trail."

Sally smiled. "Well, maybe I will make some tomorrow night," she suggested.

Pearlie smiled broadly. "That would be . . ."

"Help me, somebody," a voice called, interrupting Pearlie in mid-sentence.

"What was that?" Sally asked.

"Help me," the voice called again.

"Can anyone see him?" Cal asked, looking all around them.

"Who is it? Who's out there?" Pearlie called. He pulled his pistol and cocked it. "Answer up. Who's out there?"

"Don't shoot," the voice called. "I ain't got no gun."

"Come toward the camp," Pearlie said. "Come slow, and with your hands up in the air, so we can see you as you come in."

"I'm comin'," the man's voice answered.

The three campers looked toward the sound of the voice until a man materialized in the darkness. As he came toward them, he kept his hands raised over his head, just as Pearlie had ordered.

"That food sure smells awful good," he said. "It's been near a week since I've et 'nything other'n some roots and bugs."

"Who are you?" Sally asked.

"The name is Yancey, ma'am," the man said. "Buford Yancey." His hands were still raised.

"You can put your hands down, Mr. Yancey," Sally said. "And you are welcome to some of our beans."

"Thank you, ma'am, that's mighty decent of you," Yancey said.

"What happened to your horse?" Cal asked.

"He stumbled and broke his leg," Yancey said. "I had to put him down."

"How'd you do that? You don't have a gun," Pearlie said.

"Oh," Yancey replied. "Well, I, uh, lost my gun. It must'a fell out of my holster. Uh, if you don't mind, I'm goin' to go over there an' get me a drink of water."

Yancey went over to the side of the stream, lay on his stomach, stuck his mouth down into the water, and drank deeply.

A few minutes later Sally took the food off the fire, then distributed it to the others. Pearlie noticed that she took less for herself than she gave anyone else.

After they had eaten, Pearlie found a moment to talk to Sally without being overheard.

"Miss Sally, what do you aim to do about this man?" he asked.

"Do? What do you mean what do I aim to do about him?"

"What I mean is, he's eaten. Don't you think it's time to send him on his way?"

"Look at the man," Sally said. "He's half dead. We can't just send him away."

"Well, what do you plan to do with him?"

Sally sighed. "I don't know exactly," she said. "As far as I know, the closest town is still Etna. I guess we should take him back there."

"That'll make it two extra days before we get back to the ranch," Pearlie said.

"I realize that, but it can't be helped."

"So that means you're going to let him spend the night here with us?"

"Pearlie, I told you, we can't just run him off," Sally insisted.

"I don't like it. There's somethin' about him that I don't trust."

"I'll tell you what," Sally suggested. "We can take turns staying awake all night. That way, someone will always be watching him. Do you think that would make you feel better?"

"Yes, ma'am," Pearlie said. "I think that would be a good idea."

"All right, I'll take the first watch. I'll stay awake until midnight. You take the second watch, from midnight to four, and we'll get Cal to take the watch from four until dawn."

"You know your problem, Miss Sally? Your problem is you are too decent to people," Pearlie said. "Your first notion is to just take ever'one at their word. But that hasn't been my experience."

"Pearlie?" Sally said. She put her hand on his shoulder and gently shook him. "Pearlie?"

"What?" Pearlie asked groggily.

"It's your time on watch," Sally said.

"Oh," Pearlie groaned.

Sally chuckled. "Don't blame me. You said we shouldn't trust our visitor, remember?"

"Yes, ma'am, I remember," Pearlie said. He sat up

and stretched, then reached for his boots. He nodded toward Yancey, who was wrapped up in a spare blanket. "Has he been quiet?"

"Sleeping like a log," Sally replied.

"It don't seem—"

"It doesn't seem," Sally corrected.

"Yes, ma'am. It doesn't seem fair that he gets to sleep all night, while we have to take turns lookin' out for him."

"Don't forget to wake Cal at four," Sally said.

During Pearlie's watch he sat very still, just listening to the snap and pop of the burning wood. For the first hour he stared into the fire. He looked at the little line of blue flame that started right at the base of the wood, watching as the blue turned to orange, then yellow, and finally into twisting ropes of white smoke as it streamed up from the fire. Orange sparks from the fire rode the heat column high into the night sky, where they added their tiny, red glow to the blue pinpoints of the stars.

Pearlie didn't know when he fell asleep, but he did know when he woke up. He woke up when he heard the metallic click of a pistol being cocked. Opening his eyes, he saw Buford Yancey standing in front of him, holding a pistol that was pointed directly at him.

"I figured if I stayed awake long enough, I'd catch one of you asleep," Yancey said.

"Where did you get the pistol?" Pearlie asked.

Yancey pointed to one of the two bedrolls.

"The boy over there had it lying on the ground

alongside him. It wasn't hard to get. No harder than it's goin' to be for me to take one of them horses."

"You don't need to do that," Pearlie said. "Miss Sally was plannin' on us takin' you into Etna tomorrow. She figured you could get back on your feet there."

"Ha!" Yancey said, laughing out loud. "Now that would be a fine thing, wouldn't it? For you to take me back into Etna, after I just robbed the bank there little more'n a week ago."

"You?" Pearlie said. "You are the one who robbed the bank?"

"Yeah, me'n some pards," Yancey said. "Only they ain't much my pards now. The stole my share of the money from me."

"Was one of your pards Smoke Jensen?" Pearlie asked.

"Who? No, he ain't . . . wait a minute," Yancey said. "I think Jensen was the name of the fella we put Curt's plaid shirt on. Leastwise, that's what Dooley said his name was."

"So you admit you framed him?"

"Slick as a whistle," Yancey said with a laugh.

"Thank you, Mr. Yancey," Sally's voice said. "I will expect you to tell Marshal Turnbull that."

"What the hell?" Yancey said, spinning around quickly, only to see Sally holding her pistol on him.

"Drop your gun," Sally ordered.

Yancey smiled. "You think I'm going quake in my boots and drop my gun just because some woman's holding a pistol on me? Why, you'd probably pee in your pants if you even shot that thing." Yancey reached for her gun. "Why don't you just hand that over to me before you hurt yourself?"

Sally fired, and the tip of Yancey's little finger turned to blood and shredded flesh.

"Oww!" Yancey shouted, dropping his gun and grabbing his hand. "What the hell? You shot my finger off."

"Just the tip of it," Sally replied. "And I chose your little finger because I figure you use it less. It could be worse."

"Are you trying to tell me that you aimed at my little finger? That it wasn't no accident that you hit it?"

"Miss Sally always hits what she aims at," Pearlie said, picking up the pistol Yancey dropped.

"Get over there and sit down," Sally ordered.

"Miss Sally, I'm sorry about this," Pearlie apologized. "I must've fallen asleep. The next thing I knew, he was holding a gun on me."

"That's all right," Sally answered. "I'm sorry I didn't pay more attention to you. You said there was something about him you didn't trust. It turns out that you were right."

Chapter Twenty-one

Ford lay on top of a flat rock, looking back along the trail over which he and Fargo had just come.

"Do you see him?" Fargo asked.

"Yeah, he's back there, comin' along big as you please. He's trailin' us, Fargo. I mean he's stickin' to us like stink on shit. We can't get rid of him."

"I don't want to get rid of him," Fargo said.

"What do you mean you don't want to get rid of him? You said yourself that you thought he was trackin' down ever'one of us to kill us."

"Why did I suggest that we come through Diablo Pass? It's twenty miles farther to Bertrand this way than it would have been by going through McKenzie Pass."

"I thought it was to throw him off our trail," Ford said.

"No. It was to get him to come through here. I can't believe the son of a bitch was dumb enough to take the bait. We're playin' him like you'd play a fish."

"If you say so," Ford said, though it was clear that he still didn't understand what Fargo had in mind.

"Think about it, Ford," Fargo said. "This is the perfect

place to set up an ambush. I'll stay on this side of the pass, you go on the other side. When he gets between us, we'll open up on him. We'll have him in a cross fire."

"Why do I have to go over the other side?" Ford asked. "That means I've got to climb down, go over, then climb back up."

"Want the money he took from Dooley, don't you?"

"Yeah."

"Then just do what I tell you without all the belly-aching."

"All right," Ford answered. "But after all this trouble, he better be carryin' that money with him, is all I can say."

"He's got the money," Fargo said. "It couldn't be any-where else. But even if he didn't have it, we'd have to kill the son of a bitch before he killed us. Remember?"

"Yeah," Ford said. "I remember. All right, I'll go over to the other side."

"Get a move on it. Looks like he's comin' along pretty steady," Fargo ordered.

Smoke had noticed the hoofprints shortly after he left Dorena. Because he had identified each set of prints from his original tracking, he recognized these prints as belonging to two of the bank robbers.

Smoke was actually going to Bertrand to follow up on Dooley's declaration that two of the robbers had gone there. He had not expected to cut the trail of two of the very people he had been tracking.

Could these tracks belong to the Logan brothers? At first he thought they might. Dooley had told him they were in

Bertrand, but clearly, these tracks were fresh. In fact, they were made within the last hour. If they belonged to the Logan brothers, what were they doing out here? Especially if they were holed up in Bertrand? These tracks didn't seem to be going to Bertrand, or at least, if they were going there, they weren't going by the most direct route.

As a result of having come across the fresh hoof-prints, Smoke's journey to Bertrand changed from a normal ride to one of intense tracking. But within an hour after he first came across the trail, he realized, with some surprise, that they weren't trying to cover their tracks. On the contrary, it was almost as if they were going out of their way to invite him to come after them.

Why would they do that? he wondered.

Then, as he contemplated the question, the answer came to him.

They wanted him to find them, and they wanted him to find them so they could kill him. They must have been in Dorena while he was there. That meant that they probably knew that he killed Dooley. They probably also knew that he took Dooley's share of the loot.

Smoke saw that the trail was leading to a narrow draw just ahead of him. He had never been in this exact spot before, but he had been in dozens of places just like this, and he knew what to expect.

He stopped at the mouth of the draw and took a drink from his canteen while he studied the twists and turns of the constricted canyon. If the two men he was following were going to set up an ambush, this would be the place for them to do it.

Smoke pulled his long gun out of the saddle holster;

then he started walking into the draw, leading his horse.
Stormy's hooves fell sharply on the stone floor and echoed
loudly back from both sides of the narrow pass. The draw
made a forty-five-degree turn to the left just in front of
him, so he stopped. Right before he got to the turn, he
slapped Stormy on the rump and sent him on through.

Stormy galloped ahead, his hooves clattering loudly
on the rocky floor of the canyon.

"Ford, get ready!" Fargo shouted. "I can hear him a
'comin'!"

"I see 'im!" Ford shouted back.

The canyon exploded with the sound of gunfire as
Ford and Fargo began shooting from opposite sides.
Their bullets whizzed harmlessly over the empty saddle
of the horse, raising sparks as they hit the rocky ground,
then ricocheted off the opposite wall, echoing and re-
echoing in a cacophony of whines and shrieks.

"Son of a bitch!" Ford shouted. "Did we get him? We
must've got him! I don't think I saw nobody on the horse!"

"I don't know," Fargo replied. "I didn't see him go
down. Look on the ground. Do you see him anywhere?"

"No," Ford replied. "I don't see him. Where is the son
of a bitch?"

From his position just around the corner from the
turn, Smoke looked toward the sound of the voices,
locating one of the two ambushers about a third of the
way up the north wall of the canyon. The man was
squeezed in between the wall itself and a rock out-
cropping that provided him with a natural cover.

"Fargo, where is he?"

The one who called out this time was not the one he had located, so looking on the opposite side of the draw, toward the sound of this voice, Smoke saw a shadow move.

Smoke smiled. Now he had both of them located, and he not only knew where they were, he knew who they were. At least, he knew their first names.

"Fargo? Ford?" he called. "I'm right here. If you're looking for me, why don't you two come on down?"

"You know our names?" Ford called down to him. "Hey, Fargo, the son of a bitch knows our names! How does he know our names?"

"Oh, I know all about you two boys," Smoke called back. "I know that you robbed the bank back in Etna. I know that you killed the banker."

"Weren't us that killed the banker," Ford called back. "It was Ebenezer Dooley and Curt and Trace Logan that done that. We was across the street from the bank."

"Ford, will you shut the hell up?" Fargo called across the canyon.

"Dooley cheated the rest of you, didn't he?" Smoke called. "There was ten thousand dollars taken from the bank, but he kept half of it."

"How do you know he kept half the money?" Fargo called down to him.

"Well, now, how do you think I know, Fargo?"

"You took it, didn't you? You've got the money with you right now."

"That's right," Smoke said.

"You son of a bitch!" Fargo said. "By rights, that's our money."

Smoke laughed. "It's not your money. It belongs to anyone who can hold onto it. And right now I'm holding onto it. You know what I'm going to do now?"

"What's that?"

"I'm going to take *your* money," Smoke said.

"The hell you are," Fargo replied. "You might'a noticed, mister, they's two of us and they's only one of you."

All the while Smoke was keeping Fargo engaged in conversation, he was studying the rock face of the wall just behind the outlaw. Then he began firing. His rifle boomed loudly, the thunder of the detonating cartridges picking up resonance through the canyon and doubling and redoubling in intensity. Smoke wasn't even trying to aim at Fargo, but was, instead, taking advantage of the position in which his would-be assailant had placed himself.

Smoke fired several rounds, knowing that the bullets were splattering against the rock wall behind his target, fragmenting into deadly missiles.

"Ouch! You son of a bitch, quit it! Quit your shootin' like that!" Fargo shouted.

As Smoke figured it would, the ricocheting bullets made Fargo's position untenable and Fargo, screaming in anger, stepped from behind the rock. He raised his rifle to shoot at Smoke, but Smoke fired first.

Fargo dropped his rifle and grabbed his chest. He stood there for a moment, then pitched forward, falling at least fifty feet to the rocky bottom of the canyon.

"Fargo?" Ford shouted. "Fargo?"

"He's dead, Ford," Smoke shouted. "It's just you and me now."

Smoke watched the spot where he knew Ford was hiding, hoping to see him, but Ford didn't show himself. Smoke took a couple of shots, thinking it might force him out as it did Fargo, but he neither saw nor heard anything except the dying echoes of his own gunshots.

"Ford? Ford, are you up there?"

Then, unexpectedly, Smoke heard the sound of hoofbeats.

Damn! he thought. He should have realized that they would have their horses on the other side. Ford had slipped away.

Smoke started to step around the turn, then halted. Ford could have sent his empty horse galloping up the trail, just to fool him.

He looked cautiously around the corner, then saw that his caution, though prudent, was not necessary. Ford was galloping away.

Smoke also saw Stormy standing quietly at the far end of the draw. He whistled and Stormy ducked his head, then came trotting back up the draw toward him.

A second horse joined Stormy, and Smoke realized that it must be Fargo's horse.

In a saddlebag on Fargo's horse, Smoke found a packet of bills bundled up in a paper wrapper. The name of the bank was printed on the wrapper, along with the notation that the wrapper held one thousand dollars.

The bills were so loosely packed within the wrapper that Smoke knew there was considerably less than one thousand dollars, which, he knew, had been Fargo's share of the take.

Smoke put the roll in his saddlebag where he was keeping the money he had taken from Dooley. After that, he led the horse over to Fargo's body.

"Sorry to have to do this to you, horse," Smoke said as he lifted Fargo up and draped him over the saddle. "I know this is none of your doing, but we can't just leave him out here."

Marshal Turnball, with his chair tipped back and his feet propped up on the railing, was ensconced in his usual place in front of Dunnigan's Store. He was rolling a cigarette and paying particular attention to the task at hand when he felt Billy Frakes's hand on his shoulder.

"That's one of 'em," Billy said.

"What?"

"That's one of the bank robbers," Billy said excitedly. "He was one of the fellers that was in front of Sikes Leather Goods lookin' at the boots when the bank was robbed."

When Turnball looked in the direction Billy Frakes had pointed, he saw four people coming toward him. There were four people, but only three horses. The woman, whom he recognized as Sally Jensen, was riding double with Cal, the younger and smaller of the two men who had come to Etna to see about her husband.

The fourth person, the one Frakes had pointed out, was riding alone. He also had a rope looped around his neck, and riding next to him, holding onto the other end of the rope, was Pearlie.

"Damn," Turnball said with a long-suffering sigh. "I thought they had left town."

Turnball tipped his chair forward and stood up.

"Maybe they come back to bring the bank robber," Frakes said.

"You're sure that fella with them is one of the bank robbers?"

"I was standin' not more'n twenty feet from him when it all happened," Frakes said. "And I got a good look at him 'cause he wasn't wearin' no mask like the ones that went into the bank. But he was waitin' outside and, when the robbers rode out of town, all of 'em shootin' and such, he was ridin' along with 'em, shootin' his gun and screamin' like a wild Indian."

The riders, seeing Turnball standing on the porch in front of Dunnigan's Store, headed his way.

"Mrs. Jensen," Turnball said politely, touching the brim of his hat. "Gents," he said to the others.

"Marshal," Sally replied.

"Who have you got here?" Turnball asked.

"This man's name is Buford Yancey," Sally said.

"Yancey has something to tell you," Sally said.

"Arrest this woman, Marshal," Yancey said. He held up his little finger, which was covered by a bandage. The bandage was reddish brown with dried blood. "She shot my finger off."

"You're lucky she didn't shoot something else off," Pearlie said. "Now tell the marshal what you told us."

"I don't know what you're talkin' about," Yancey said. "I ain't got nothin' to say."

"Are you sure about that?" Pearlie asked as he gave a hard jerk on the rope.

"Easy there," Yancey said fearfully. "You could break my neck, messin' around like that."

"Get down off my horse, Yancey," Cal said.

Scowling, Yancey got down.

"You're goin' to tell the marshal what you told us, or I aim to drag you from one end of this street to the other," Pearlie said, backing his horse up and putting some pressure on Yancey's neck.

"All right, all right," Yancey said. "I'll talk to him."

"You was one of them, wasn't you?" Frakes said. "You was one of the bank robbers. I seen you."

Yancey looked over at Sally. "I don't reckon I need to say much," he said. "The boy here's done said it for me."

"He hasn't said it all," Sally said.

"You got more to say, Yancey?" Turnball asked.

"I wasn't one of 'em what went inside," Yancey said. "Like the boy here said, he seen me standin' in front of the store across the street from the bank. I didn't go inside."

"What about the others? The ones who did stay inside? Who was they?" Turnball asked.

Yancey thought for a moment, then he nodded. "Yeah," he said. "Hell, yeah, you want to know who they was, I'll tell you. Ain't no need in coverin' up for them. Them sons of bitches stole my share of the money, and you better believe I don't intend to go to jail while they're wanderin' around free."

"First, Mr. Yancey, tell them who was not with you," Sally demanded.

"Who was not with me?" Yancey replied, a little confused by Sally's remark. Then, realizing what she was saying, he nodded. "Oh, yeah, I know what you mean. You're talkin' about Jensen," Yancey said. Yancey looked back at the marshal. "Jensen wasn't with us. He wasn't no part of the robbin' of the bank."

"What do you mean he wasn't with you? I saw him," Turnball said. "We all saw him. Nobody is likely to miss that shirt he was wearing."

"Yeah, that was Dooley's idea," Yancey said. "We put Curt Logan's shirt on him. Then we dropped a couple of them paper things that was wrapped around the money by him. We seen you and the posse when you found him. You took the bait like a rat takin' cheese." Yancey laughed. "Dooley's an evil son of a bitch, but he sure is smart."

"Dooley," Turnball said. "Would that be Ebenezer Dooley?"

The smile left Yancey's face. "Yeah, Ebenezer Dooley. He was the one behind it all, and he's the one that stole from me. I tell you true, I hope you catch him."

"We don't have to catch him," Turnball said. "He's dead."

"He's dead? The hell you say," Yancey said.

"It came in by telegram," Turnball said. "He was shot by a man named Kirby."

"Kirby?" Sally said.

"That's the name that was on the telegram," Turnball said. "Seems that Dooley shot the deputy sheriff over in Dorena, and this fella Kirby shot Dooley."

"This man Kirby," Sally said. "Is he another deputy, or something?"

"Not unless it's someone they've put on recently," Turnball said. "I've never heard of him."

"I see."

"Come on, Yancey," Turnball said. "Oh, and Mrs. Jensen, you might want to come down to the jail with me."

"Why?" Sally asked.

Turnball chuckled. "Don't worry, I ain't arrestin' you or nothin'. But I've got a feelin' that there's a reward out on Yancey. I thought you might be interested in it if there was."

"You thought right, Marshal. I would be very interested in it," Sally said.

Deputy Pike was standing by the stove, pouring himself a cup of coffee, when he heard the door open.

"You want some coff . . . ," Pike began, speaking before he turned around. He stopped in mid-sentence when saw that Turnball had a prisoner. "Who is this?" he asked.

"This is one of the bank robbers," Turnball said. "Put him in jail."

"Yes, sir!" Pike said. "Come on, you, we've got just the place for you." Grabbing the key from a wall hook, Pike took the prisoner back to the cell, opened the door, and pushed him in. "Where'd you catch 'im?" Pike asked as he closed the door.

"I didn't catch him," Turnball answered. "She did."

"What?" Pike asked. Turning back again, he saw

Jensen's wife and the two men who were traveling with her. "You!" he said. "What are you doing here?"

"Why, Mr. Pike," Sally said. "Aren't you happy to see me?"

"I'd be happy if I never saw you again," Pike said.

Turnball chuckled. "Don't worry. I won't let her throw you in jail again."

"She tricked me," Pike said.

"Yeah, I'm sure," Turnball said. He began going through several circulars. Then finding what he was looking for, he held it up for Sally. "I was right. Mr. Yancey is worth five hundred dollars."

"You said somethin' about the town offerin' two hundred and fifty dollars as well?" Pearlie said.

"I did say that, didn't I? Mrs. Jensen, it looks like you'll be getting out of here with seven hundred and fifty dollars. That ought to make you feel a little better about us."

"I'll feel much better when you send out telegrams informing everyone that my husband is no longer wanted for bank robbery and murder."

"Yes, ma'am, all the lines are open now, so I'll do that right away," he said.

"Do you think there was a reward for Ebenezer Dooley?"

"I'm sure there was."

"Good."

"Why do you say good? He's already been killed."

"I said good because I'm sure Smoke is the one who killed him."

Turnball shook his head. "No, ma'am. I told you, it

was somebody named Kirby." Then he stopped. "Wait a minute. Your husband's name is Kirby, isn't it? Kirby Jensen."

"Yes."

"Do you really think it was him?"

"If Smoke was found guilty for something he didn't do, I've no doubt but that he is hunting down the bank robbers right now in order to clear his name."

"Well, I tell you what, Mrs. Jensen. If your husband is the one who took care of Dooley, and he can have the sheriff of Dorena vouch for him, we'll be sending on another two hundred fifty dollars reward on him as well."

"Thank you," Sally said. "When will I get the reward due me?"

"I'll get a telegram off to Denver today. I figure by tomorrow we'll have authorization back. You should get all your money then."

"Hey, Marshal, if you're through talkin' about how much money you're goin' to give this woman for shootin' my little finger off, maybe you'll get the doctor to come take a look at it," Yancey called from his cell.

"Looks to me like Mrs. Jensen did a pretty good job of doctorin'," Turnball said.

"I know my rights," Yancey insisted. "I'm your prisoner. That means I got a right to have a doctor treat me."

"All right, I'll get the doc down here for you," Turnball said. "I ought to tell you, though, he likes to amputate. More'n likely he'll chop that finger clean off. Maybe even your hand."

"What?" Yancey gasped. He stepped back away from

the bars. "Uh, no, never mind. She done a good enough job on me. I won't be needin' no doctor."

"I didn't think you would," Turnball said.

Pearlie and Cal were laughing at Yancey as they left the marshal's office.

"You know what, Miss Sally? With your reward money and what we have, there's almost enough money to save Sugarloaf right there," Pearlie said.

"Yes, there is."

"I tell you this. The trip back home tomorrow is going to be a lot more joyful than it was when we started out yesterday," Cal said.

"It would be if we were going back home. But we aren't going to Sugarloaf yet," Sally said.

"Where are going?"

"We're going to find Smoke."

"How are we going to find him? I mean, where will we start?" Cal asked.

"We'll start in Dorena," Sally said. "First thing tomorrow, after we collect the reward money."

"Do you think Smoke is the one who killed Dooley?" Cal asked.

"I'd bet a thousand dollars he was," Sally said.

Chapter Twenty-two

Smoke looked back over his shoulder as he led the horse across the swiftly running stream. The horse was carrying Fargo's body, belly down, across his back. The horse smelled death and he didn't like it one little bit.

Stormy and Fargo's horse kicked up sheets of silver spray as they trotted through the stream. Smoke paused to give them an opportunity to drink. Smoke's horse, Stormy, was a smart horse and knew from experience that he should take every opportunity to drink when he could. He put his lips to the water and drank deeply, but Fargo's horse just tossed its head nervously. The horse was obviously anxious to get to where it was going so it could rid itself of its gruesome cargo.

Smoke reached over and patted Fargo's horse on the neck a few times.

"Hang on just a little longer, horse," Smoke said gently. "If what they told me back in Dorena is right, it won't be much longer, then you'll be rid of your burden."

The horse whickered, as if indicating that it understood.

"Come on," Smoke said when Stormy had drunk his fill. "Let's be on our way."

Sheriff Fawcett was sitting at his desk with a kerosene lantern spread out before him. He was cleaning the mantle when Sally, Pearlie, and Cal stepped through the door. Seeing a beautiful woman coming into his office, the sheriff smiled and stood.

"Yes, ma'am," he said. "Is there something I can do for you?"

"I hope you can help me find my husband," Sally said.

The smile left, to be replaced by a troubled frown. "Is he missing?"

"Well, not missing in that he is lost," Sally said. She smiled to ease his concern. "He is missing in that I don't know where he is."

"You think he is here in Dorena?"

"I think he has been here," Sally said. "His name is Kirby Jensen, though most people call him Smoke."

"Jensen?" Sheriff Fawcett said. "Jensen? Wait a minute. I just heard something about someone with that name." He walked over to a table that was up against the wall and started shuffling papers around. He picked up a yellow sheet of the kind that was used for telegrams. "Here it is," he said. He read the message; then his face grew very concerned and he looked up at Sally.

"Did you say Jensen was your husband?"

"Yes. My name is Sally Jensen."

"And you are looking for him?"

"I am."

Sheriff Fawcett shook his head and sighed. "Well, evidently, so is every lawman in Colorado," he said. He held up the paper. "According to this, he is an escaped prisoner, convicted of murder and robbery."

"No, he ain't!" Cal shouted in a bellicose voice.

"Cal," Sally said, holding up her hand as if to calm him down, "it's all right." She maintained her composure as she smiled at the sheriff. "What my young friend is trying to say is that the wanted notice has been rescinded."

"It's been what?"

"It has been canceled," Sally explained. "Marshal Turnball, back in Etna, sent out telegrams rescinding the notification that my husband was a wanted man."

"Why would he do that?"

"'Cause Smoke wasn't guilty, that's why," Cal said, his voice holding as much challenge as it had earlier.

"It seems that one of the bank robbers was caught," Sally said.

"Ha! It wasn't the law that caught him. Tell the sheriff who it was that caught 'im, Miss Sally," Pearlie said.

"*She* caught him," Cal answered, pointing proudly to Sally. "She caught 'im, and we took him in and got a reward for him."

"His name was Buford Yancey," Sally said.

Sheriff Fawcett nodded. "Yancey," he said. "Buford Yancey. Yes, I've heard that name. He's a pretty rough customer, all right."

"He ain't so rough now," Cal said. "He's over in Etna behind bars."

"And he has not only confessed to the robbery," Sally

said, "he has also confessed that my husband was not involved. The actual bank robbers framed him so people would think he was guilty."

"And you say that word has been sent out to all the law agencies around the state calling back the wanted notice?" Sheriff Fawcett asked.

"He was supposed to have sent word out by telegraph," Sally said.

Again, Fawcett began looking through all the papers on his desk. After a moment or two of fruitless search, he shook his head.

"I'm sorry. There's nothing here."

"What about your telegraph service? Is your line still up?"

"As far as I know it is," Fawcett answered. "If you'd like, Mrs. Jensen, we could walk down to the telegraph and check this out."

Sally nodded. "Yes, thank you, I would like that," she said.

The four walked from the sheriff's office down to the Western Union office. The group was unremarkable enough that no one paid them any particular attention as they passed by, other than to take a second glance at the very pretty woman who was obviously a stranger in town.

The little bell on the door of the Western Union office caused the telegrapher to look up. He stood when he saw the sheriff, and smiled when he saw the pretty woman with him.

"Can I help you, Sheriff?"

"Danny, have you got any telegrams you haven't brought down to my office yet?" Sheriff Fawcett asked.

"As a matter of fact, I have," the telegrapher said. "I didn't think there was any rush to it, so I hadn't gotten around to it yet."

The telegrapher picked up a message from his desk, then handed it to Sheriff Fawcett. Fawcett read it, then nodded.

"You're right, Mrs. Jensen," he said. "Your husband is no longer wanted."

"Except by me," Sally said. "I have to find him. You see, he doesn't know that he is no longer a wanted man."

"I see. And you are afraid of what he might do while he thinks he is wanted?"

"I'm sure that whatever he does will be justified by the law," Sally said. "For example, I am sure that he killed a man called Ebenezer Dooley right here in your town."

Sheriff Fawcett shook his head. "No, that was a man named Kirby. We have eyewitnesses who say they saw Bill Kirby engage Ebenezer Dooley . . . in self-defense, I hasten to add . . . and shoot him down."

"Was he a big man with broad shoulders, a narrow waist, blue eyes?"

"Well, yes, that sounds like him, all right," Sheriff Fawcett said.

"That's him."

"So his name isn't Kirby?" Sheriff Fawcett asked. Then he stopped in mid-sentence and chuckled. "Wait a minute, I get it now. He's calling himself Kirby from Kirby Jensen, right?"

"That's right," Sally said. "Did you say you paid him a reward?"

"Yes. Dooley had a five-hundred-dollar reward on him."

"Seven hundred fifty," Sally corrected.

"No ma'am, it was only five hundred," Sheriff Fawcett said.

"Dooley was one of the bank robbers," Sally explained. "The town of Etna added two hundred fifty dollars to the reward."

"Uh, Mrs. Jensen, if you are asking me to pay the additional two hundred fifty dollars, I got no authority to do that," the sheriff said.

"I don't need the money from you, just your verification that my husband is the one who killed Dooley."

"Well, uh, I don't know as I could actually . . ." Fawcett began, but Sally interrupted him.

"Is this the man?" she asked. She was holding an open locket in her hand, and Fawcett leaned down to look at the picture. He studied it for a moment, then nodded.

"Yes, ma'am, that's him all right," he said.

"You'll write the letter validating that he is the one who killed Dooley?"

"Yes, ma'am, I'll be glad to do that," the sheriff said. He smiled. "I'll do better than that. Danny," he called to the telegrapher.

"Yes, Sheriff?"

"Send a telegram to the city marshal in Etna, Colorado," he said. "In the message, say that Kirby Jensen is the man who killed Ebenezer Dooley. As this was a justifiable killing, there are no charges against Jensen, and he was paid a reward for bringing Dooley to justice. Then put my name to it."

"Yes, sir," the telegrapher said as he sat down to his instrument.

"You know," the sheriff said with a smile. "Now that I know who you are talking about, I think I might even be able to help you find him. At least, I can tell you where he went from here."

"Where?"

"Bertrand," the sheriff answered.

"How far is it to Bertrand?"

"Well, there are two ways to go. Some folks go through Diablo Pass because the pass isn't quite as high. But most folks go through McKenzie Pass, which is about ten miles closer."

"Thanks," Sally said.

Chapter Twenty-three

After several hours of riding on a bumping, rattling, jerking, and dusty stagecoach, the first view of Bertrand could be quite disconcerting to its passengers. Especially to someone who had never seen the town before. Experienced passengers were often called upon to point out the town, for from the top of the pass it looked like nothing more than a small cluster of the brown hummocks and hills common to this country.

Five years after founding the town, a saloon keeper named John Bertrand was shot down in the street of his own town. The drunken drifter who killed him was lynched within an hour of his foul deed. Now, without the entrepreneurial spirit of its founder, the little town was dying, bypassed by the railroad and visited by the stagecoach but two times per week. Its only connection to the outside world was a telegraph wire, and though it was recently restrung, even it had been down for most of the winter.

Smoke stopped on a ridge just above the road leading into Bertrand. He took a swallow from his canteen and watched the stage as it started down from the pass into the town. Then, corking the canteen, he slapped his legs against the side of his horse and sloped down the long ridge, leading the horse over which Fargo's body had been thrown.

Smoke was somewhat farther away from town than the coach, but he knew he would beat it there because he was riding down the side of the ridge, whereas the coach had to stay on the road, which had many cutbacks as it came down from the top of the pass.

Smoke passed by a sign that read: WELCOME TO BERTRAND. Behind it, another sign said: THE JEWEL OF COLORADO.

Smoke wasn't at all sure that the person who wrote that sign was talking about the same town he was riding into about then. He didn't see much about the little town that would classify it as the "Jewel of Colorado."

Two dirt roads formed a cross in the middle of the high desert country. The town consisted of a handful of small shotgun houses, and a line of business buildings, all false-fronted, none painted. The saloon was partially painted, though, with LUCKY NUGGET painted in red high on its own false front.

As he rode into town, the fact that he was bringing in a corpse caused him to be the center of attention. Several people, seeing him, began to drift down the street with him to see where he was going.

Smoke was heading for one particular building, identified by a black letters on a white board sign that said:

TATUM OWENS, *Sheriff.*

Bertrand, Colorado.

By the time he reached the front of the sheriff's office, more than twenty people had gathered around. Even the sheriff had come out of his office, summoned by someone who had run ahead to tell him about the strange sight of someone riding into town bringing with him a dead body.

As Smoke dismounted and tied Fargo's horse to the hitching rail, Sheriff Owens lit his pipe.

"Did you kill 'im?" the sheriff asked around the puffs that were necessary to get his pipe started.

"I did."

"I figure you must think you had a good reason to kill 'im," the sheriff said. "Otherwise, you would have left him."

"He was trying to kill me," Smoke said.

"Sounds like reason enough," Sheriff Owens said. "And if there ain't nobody to back you up, there ain't nobody here to say any different. What you plannin' on doin' with him?"

"I figured the sheriff's office was as good a place as any to leave him," Smoke replied.

"Would you happen to know his name?"

"I don't know his last name. But I heard him called Fargo," Smoke said. "He robbed a bank in Etna," Smoke added.

The sheriff nodded. "Ah, then that would be Fargo Masters."

Smoke looked up in surprise.

"How do you know that?" he asked.

The sheriff nodded. "The telegraph is up again, and word come through this mornin' tellin' about the robbery. It also named all the robbers, and put out a reward of two hundred fifty dollars for each one of them. That means you've got money comin', if we can prove this is who you say he is."

"What if I show you the money he had on him?" Smoke asked.

"You got the money from him?"

Smoke nodded. "From him, and from Ebenezer Dooley."

"If you've got the money, I'd say that's pretty good proof."

"Sheriff, what do you want me to do with the body?" a tall, skinny man asked. His long black coat and high-topped hat identified him as an undertaker.

"Find a pine box for him," the sheriff said. "If nobody claims him within a few days, you can bury him."

"Is the town going to pay?"

"Five dollars, Posey," the sheriff said. "Same as with any indigent."

"Sometimes the town don't pay," Posey complained as he took the horse by the reins and started leading it down the street to the mortuary.

"I admit we're late sometimes," Owens called after Posey. "But when you get down to it, we've always paid."

Having satisfied their curiosity as to who the corpse was, most of the gathered townspeople began moving away. The coach that Smoke had seen several minutes earlier was just arriving in town now, and it pulled to a stop at the stage depot, which was next to the sheriff's office.

"Hey, Walt, how was your trip?" the sheriff called up to the driver.

"The trip was fine, no problems," Walt replied as he set the brake and tied off the reins of his six-horse team. "Folks, this is Bertrand!" he called down.

The door to the coach opened and the passengers stepped outside. One of them glanced over toward the sheriff, then seeing Smoke, smiled broadly.

"Why, Smoke Jensen!" the passenger called over to him. "What are you doin' here? You're a long way from home, aren't you?"

Smoke knew the passenger only as Charley. Charley was a salesman who from time to time had come into Longmont's Saloon when he was in Big Rock.

Smoke considered pretending that he didn't know what the passenger was talking about, but decided it would be less noticeable to just respond and get it over with.

"Hello, Charley," Smoke said. "I haven't seen you in a while."

"No, Big Rock isn't my territory anymore," Charley replied. "But I sure had me some friends over there. Listen, when you get back over there, you tell Louie Longmont and Sheriff Carson that ole Charley Dunn said hi, will you?"

"Sure, Charley, I'll do that," Smoke replied. He was aware that Sheriff Owens was staring hard at him.

"You're Smoke Jensen?" the sheriff asked. "Is your real name Kirby Jensen?"

"Yes," Smoke said. He poised for action. He didn't

want to kill the sheriff, but he wasn't going to go back to jail either. Especially for a crime he didn't commit.

"Oh, then you must've already got the word. Otherwise, you'd still be running."

"I've already got the word?" Smoke asked. "Got what word?"

"Why, that you've been cleared," the sheriff said. "That message that come in this morning also canceled the wanted notice that went out on you." Owens laughed. "But, since we didn't have a telegraph line through to anyplace else until just the other day, we wasn't gettin' much news anyway. I found out that you was wanted and not wanted on the same day."

Smoke smiled broadly. "Well, that's good to know, Sheriff," he said.

"So, what are you going to do now? Go back home?" Sheriff Owens asked.

Smoke shook his head. "You say there is a two-hundred-fifty-dollar reward for every one who took part in the bank robbery?"

"That's right."

"That's good to know," Smoke said. He smiled. "It's also good to know that I don't have to worry about you wanting to lock me up while I go about my business."

"What business?"

"Finding the other bank robbers."

Bidding the sheriff good-bye, Smoke started toward the saloon, as much to slake his thirst as to find out more information. He tied his horse off in front, then on a whim, took the plaid shirt out of his saddlebag and put it on.

Pulling his pistol from its holster, Smoke spun the cylinder to check the loads, then replaced the pistol loosely and went inside. He had long had a way of entering a saloon, stepping in through the door, then moving quickly to one side to put his back against the wall as he studied all the patrons. Over the years he had made a number of friends, but it seemed that for every friend he made, he had made an enemy as well. And a lot of those enemies would like nothing better than to kill him, if they could. He didn't figure on making it easy for them.

As Smoke stood there in the saloon with his eyes adjusting to the shadows, he saw one of the men he was looking for. He might not have even noticed him had the man not been wearing the shirt Smoke was wearing when the men jumped him. It was a shirt that Sally had mended when Smoke tore it on a nail in the barn.

As Smoke thought about it, he began to get angrier and angrier. He was not only angry with the man for being one of those who framed him, he was angry because the man was wearing a shirt that Sally's own hands had mended and washed.

What right did that son of a bitch have to be wearing, next to his foul body, something that Sally had touched?

The man was talking to a bar girl, and so engaged was he that he noticed neither Smoke's entrance, nor his crossing the open floor to step up next to him.

"Would you be Curt or Trace Logan?" Smoke asked.

"I'm Curt. Do I know you?"

"Let's just say that's my shirt you are wearing," Smoke said.

"What?" the man replied. For a moment he was confused; then, perhaps because Smoke was wearing the very shirt *he* had been wearing, he realized who Smoke was. Smoke saw the realization in the man's eyes, though he continued to protest.

"What do you mean I'm wearing your shirt? I don't know what are you talking about."

"You know what I'm talking about," Smoke said. "You, your brother, and four others set me up to take the blame for a bank you robbed in Etna. I've already taken care of two of your friends. You and Trace are next. Where is Trace, by the way?"

Curt's eyes widened, then he turned toward the bartender. "Bartender, send somebody for the sheriff," he said. "This man is an escaped convict."

"Go ahead, send somebody for the sheriff," Smoke said. "I just left his office." Smoke gave a cold, calculating smile. "I'd like him to come down here and take charge. According to the sheriff, Curt Logan is worth two hundred fifty dollars to me."

The bartender looked back and forth between the two men, not knowing who to believe.

"Dan, this man is Smoke Jensen," someone called out from the door. Although Smoke didn't realize it, Charley, the salesman, had followed him to the saloon from the sheriff's office, and was now standing just a few feet away. "I've known Mr. Jensen for years, and I'll vouch for him. And I was just down at the sheriff's office while Jensen and the sheriff were talking.

Jensen's telling the truth. This man," he said, pointing toward Curt, "is lying."

"You're crazy," Logan said.

"I don't know that he is so crazy," the bartender said to Logan. "I've been wonderin' where you and your brother got all the money you two been throwing around ever since you come to town. Besides which, Jensen is wearing a shirt just like the shirt your brother is wearing. To me, that means that the story he's tellin' makes sense."

"We . . . we sold some cows, that's where we got the money. And the shirt's just a coincidence."

"Where is your brother?" Smoke asked.

Suddenly Curt went for his pistol. Smoke drew his as well, but rather than shooting him, he brought it down hard on the top of his head.

Logan went down like a sack of feed.

Smoke stared at the man on the floor. "Do you have any idea where his brother is?"

"Yeah, I know. He's upstairs," the bartender said. "Like I told you, they been spendin' money like it was water. He and this one have been keepin' the girls plumb wore out ever since they got here."

"Which room is he in?"

"Well, he's with Becky, so that'd be the second room on your left when you reach the head of the stairs. And you better watch out for Becky too. She's some taken with him now, I think. Though to be truthful, I think it's more his money than it is him."

"Thanks."

The altercation at the bar had caught the attention of all the others in the saloon, and now all conversation stopped as they watched Smoke walk up the stairs to the second floor.

When Smoke reached the room at the top of the stairs, he stopped in front of the door, then raised his foot and kicked it open.

Becky screamed, and Trace called out in anger and alarm.

"What the hell do you mean barging in here?" he shouted.

"Get up and get your clothes on," Smoke said. "There's a two-hundred-and-fifty-dollar reward out for you for robbing a bank, and I aim to collect it. I'm taking you down to the sheriff."

"The hell you are."

Smoke should have been more observant. If he had been, he would have noticed that Trace had a gun in the bed with him. From nowhere, it seemed, a pistol appeared in the outlaw's hand.

Trace got off the first shot, and Smoke could almost feel the wind as the bullet buzzed by him and slammed into the door frame.

Smoke returned fire and saw a black hole suddenly appear in Trace's throat, followed by a gushing of blood. The outlaw's eyes went wide, and he dropped the gun and grabbed his throat as if he could stop the bleeding. He fell back against the headboard as his eyes grew dim.

Becky's screaming grew louder and more piercing.

"You killed him! You killed him!" Becky shouted. She picked up the outlaw's gun and, pointing it at Smoke, fired at him.

Becky's action surprised him even more than the fact

that Trace had had the gun in bed with him. Stepping quickly toward her, he stuck his hand down to grab the gun, just as she pulled the trigger again. The hammer snapped painfully against the little web of skin between Smoke's thumb and forefinger. It brought blood, but it didn't hit the firing pin, so the gun didn't go off.

Smoke jerked the pistol away from Becky, then threw it through the window. Then, just to make certain there were no other hidden weapons, he picked up one side of the bed and turned it up on its end, dumping Trace's body and the naked bar girl out on the floor.

Becky curled up into a fetal position and began crying. Smoke looked at her for a moment, then left the room. When Smoke reappeared at the top of the stairs, he saw that everyone in the saloon was looking up to see how the drama had played out. They watched in silence as he descended the stairs; then several rushed toward him to congratulate him.

Smoke smiled back and nodded at them, but he was very subdued about it. He didn't consider killing a man to be anything you should be congratulated for. Looking toward the floor, he saw that that Curt Logan was gone. Silently, he cursed himself for not tying him up before he went upstairs.

"Where did he go?" he asked.

The bartender looked toward the floor where Curt Logan had been lying, and was genuinely surprised to see that he was no longer there.

"I . . . I don't know," the bartender said. "We was all lookin' upstairs to see what was goin' to happen. I reckon he must've left when nobody was payin' attention to him."

"That's real brotherly love for Curt to leave and let Trace face me alone," Smoke said.

He walked over to the bar. "I'll have a beer," he said.

"Yes, sir, and it's on the house," the bartender replied. As the bartender took an empty mug down to the beer barrel to fill it, Smoke happened to glance toward the mirror that was behind the bar. That was when he got a quick glimpse of the reflection of Curt Logan just outside the front window. The outlaw had a gun in his hand, and he appeared to be sneaking up toward the front door.

When Smoke leaned over the bar for a better look, he happened to see the double-barrel, ten-gauge, sawed-off Greener shotgun that the bartender kept handy. Picking it up, Smoke pulled both hammers back, then turned toward the door just as Curt Logan came through the batwings with his pistol in his hand.

"You son of a bitch!" Logan shouted, shooting toward Smoke. His bullet crashed into one of the many bottles that sat in front of the mirror, shattering the bottle and sending up a spray of amber liquid. The other customers at the bar, suddenly finding themselves in the line of fire, dived to the floor and scooted toward the nearest tables.

Smoke pulled both triggers on the shotgun and it boomed loudly, filling the saloon with smoke. Curt Logan was slammed back against the batwing doors with such force as to tear them off the hinges. He landed on his back at the far side of the boardwalk with his head halfway down the steps just as Sheriff Owens, drawn by the sound of the first shots, was arriving.

When Owens came into the saloon, he saw Smoke standing at the bar, still holding the Greener. Twin wisps of smoke curled up from the two barrels.

The sheriff looked back through the broken door at the body lying on the porch; then he stepped up to the bar.

"Give me a beer, Dan," he said.

Dan drew the beer, then with shaking hands, held it toward the sheriff.

"Better let me take that before you spill all of it," the sheriff said, taking the beer. He blew the foam off, and took a drink before he spoke to Smoke, who by now had put the shotgun down and picked up his own beer.

"Let me guess," the sheriff said. "You've just earned yourself another two hundred fifty dollars."

"Five hundred," Smoke replied. "That's Curt Logan. His brother Trace is upstairs."

Suddenly there was a commotion at the door and, as fast as thought, Smoke drew his gun and turned toward the sound.

"Hello, Smoke," Sally said. "How've you been?"

Sally had a gun in her hand, having just used it as a club. Ford DeLorian was lying facedown on the floor, unconscious. His right arm was stretched out before him, his fingers wrapped around a pistol.

Pearlie bent down and took the pistol from Ford's hand.

Cal came in right behind Sally and Pearlie, and Sally came over quickly to embrace Smoke.

"Sheriff Owens, this is my wife, Sally."

"Sheriff," Sally said, smiling sweetly. "I hope your aren't planning on arresting my husband for bank robbery. Because I'm here to tell you that he has been cleared."

"Yes, ma'am, I know that," Sheriff Owens said. "I was just tellin' him that the state owes him seven hundred fifty dollars."

"Make that a thousand dollars," Smoke said, nodding toward the man who was just beginning to regain consciousness. "His name is Ford DeLorian."

"I guess that explains why he was planning to shoot you," Sheriff Owens said. "All right, I stand corrected. The state owes you one thousand dollars."

"No," Sally said. "You were right the first time. It's just seven hundred fifty."

"What are you talking about?" Smoke asked. "He was one of the bank robbers, and there is a two-hundred-fifty-dollar reward for each of them."

"I know," Sally said. She smiled at Smoke. "But this two hundred and fifty dollars is mine."

As Ford came to, he looked around in confusion, wondering what everyone was laughing at.

Turn the page for an exciting preview of

PREACHER'S QUEST
by William W. Johnstone (with J.A. Johnstone),
USA TODAY bestselling author of
BLOOD BOND and THE LAST GUNFIGHTER!

Coming in January 2007
wherever Pinnacle Books are sold.

Preacher's Quest
January 2007
Pinnacle Books
ISBN 0-7860-1739-2

Chapter One

If there was ever any doubt in the mind of the man called Preacher that the frontier was truly where he was meant to be, it was erased as he rode slowly down a wooded hillside toward a long, green valley. He felt a sense of contentment growing within him. He felt as most men do when they return from a long journey to the place where everything dear to them resides.

Preacher felt like he was coming home, and that was the simple, God's honest truth of it.

Rugged, snowcapped mountains loomed all around the valley, starkly beautiful against the deep blue vault of sky. The snow on the peaks was a reminder that although the weather down in the valley was warm and sunny on this late spring day, winter was never very far off in this mountainous region.

Tendrils of gray smoke from dozens of campfires rose into the air above the valley. Tents and tepees dotted the valley floor on both sides of the little stream that meandered through it. A couple of hundred people were crowded into the encampment, mostly bearded, buckskin-clad men, although quite a few Indian women in beaded buckskin dresses were in evidence, too, most of them stirring the contents of iron pots that simmered over the flames of the campfires. The men stood and talked and smoked their pipes or played cards or passed around jugs. They argued with the representatives of the fur-trading companies who had come out here to bargain for their loads of pelts. A few wrestled or competed at throwing knives and tomahawks.

A grin creased Preacher's lean, weathered face as he looked down the hill at all the goings-on. There was only one word to describe these festivities.

Rendezvous!

Twice each year, at the end of the spring trapping season and also at the end of the fall season, the mountain men who had come here to the Rockies to harvest beaver pelts gathered together to sell the results of their labor to the agents of the fur companies. However, Rendezvous was a lot more than just business. It was also the most important social occasion—often the *only* social occasion—each spring and fall. Friends who hadn't seen each other for months slapped each other on the back and called each other obscene names and roared with laughter. Fiddles scraped and mouth harps wailed and the valley fairly shook from the stomping feet of the mountain men as they danced and capered. The party lasted for three days and nights, and when it was over the buckskinners, most of whom led solitary lives the rest of the year, went their separate ways, hungover, sore from laughing and fighting, back to their lonely existence until the time came for them to head once again for the Rendezvous.

Preacher knew that sometimes the men who lived in these mountains went crazy from the solitude. A lot more probably would have lost their minds if it hadn't been for the Rendezvous twice a year.

With the grace of a natural-born horseman, Preacher rode a rangy, ugly mount known as Horse. At his side padded along a big wolflike cur called Dog. Like Preacher, the animals were starting to get some age on them. Not that any of them were actually *old,* far from it. Preacher, who had been born as the eighteenth century slipped into the nineteenth, hadn't seen thirty-five winters yet. But the rugged life he'd led had put a few silver strands in the thick black hair under the floppy-brimmed hat he wore. The mustache that hung over his mouth and the beard stubble on his lean cheeks were dotted with silver as well.

He led a packhorse that carried the pelts he had taken. This time he had fewer than usual because he hadn't been able to spend a full spring season in the mountains. After wintering in Texas, he had been on his way back to the high country when he'd gotten delayed by some trouble in the Sangre de Cristos, down New Mexico way. He wasn't particularly worried, though. A man who could live off the land like Preacher could didn't need a lot of money.

A frown creased Preacher's forehead as he noticed a large, striped tent near the river. Mountain men usually didn't go in for anything that fancy. The tent probably belonged to some of the fur company representatives, Preacher decided.

As he reached the bottom of the slope and started

across the valley floor toward the encampment, several dogs noticed him coming and bounded toward him, barking. The big cur beside him growled low in his throat, and Preacher said, "Behave yourself, Dog. I don't want to have to be pullin' you out of a ruckus ever' time I turn around."

Dog just looked up at him.

"I know, I know," Preacher said tolerantly. "You're bigger and tougher'n those other dogs. But you know that and I know that, and I reckon that's all that matters."

With dignity and only the occasional growl, Dog padded on, ignoring the canine commotion that went on around him.

Some of the men attending the Rendezvous noticed Preacher's impending arrival, too, and they stopped what they were doing to stride out a short distance from the edge of the encampment and wait for him, long-barreled Kentucky rifles cradled in the crooks of their elbows. Preacher lifted a hand in greeting as he approached them.

"As I live and breathe," one of the buckskin-clad men called, "if it ain't Preacher." He nudged the man next to him with an elbow. "See, I told you I smelled somethin'. Smelled like rotted bear grease, so I knew it had to be Preacher."

"Rather smell like rotted bear grease than a three-hole privy like you, Stump," Preacher said.

The grin disappeared from the man's face and was replaced by a scowl. "Damn it, Preacher, you know I don't like bein' called that." The nickname had come about not because the trapper had lost an arm or a leg or because he was short—although he was—but rather because nature had been less than generous to him when it came to his masculine endowment. Quite a bit less than generous, in fact.

"Yeah, you're right," Preacher said as he reined Horse to a halt and the packhorse stopped, too. He held up a hand with the thumb and forefinger only a couple of inches apart and went on, "It ain't really your fault that you only got—"

Another man had walked up behind the ones who had come out to meet Preacher, and now shouldered through their ranks. That wasn't much of a chore because he was taller and heavier and had broader shoulders than any of them except for Preacher himself.

"Preacher!" the newcomer bellowed. "Nobody's killed you yet? I'm plumb amazed!"

Grinning, Preacher swung down from the saddle and stepped forward to shake hands with the man. "Howdy, Rip," he said. "Good to see you again."

"Good to see you, too, you old scalawag." The man pulled Preacher closer and pounded him on the back before retreating a step.

Rip Giddens was a little younger than Preacher, with shaggy blond hair that hung around his shoulders and a beard of the same shade. He and Preacher had been friends for several years, although the only place they ever saw each other was at Rendezvous.

Looking past Preacher at the packhorse, Rip commented, "Doesn't appear that you had a very good spring."

Preacher grimaced. "I only got up here in time to trap

for a few weeks. I spent the winter in Texas, and when I started back I had to stop for a spell in New Mexico."

"What for?" Rip asked bluntly.

Preacher shrugged. "Helped out a few folks, and shot some others."

"Damned if that ain't just like you."

"Hey, I was talkin' to Preacher!" the trapper called Stump interrupted. He crowded forward, his rifle clutched in both hands now.

Rip turned and said, "Sorry, Stump," ignoring the baleful look the smaller man gave him. He waved a hand at Preacher. "You go right ahead."

Stump glared. "Well, I was just sayin' that, uh, you shouldn't make fun of a fella because of his, uh, short-comin's that he don't have no control over—"

He had to stop because all the other trappers were laughing now, not just Preacher and Rip. Looking mad and frustrated, Stump fumed and muttered under his breath as he stomped off.

Rip put a hand on Preacher's shoulder. "Come on," he said. "I want you to meet the folks I'm workin' for."

"Workin' for?" Preacher repeated as he fell in step with Rip and led the two horses across the encampment. "Ain't you trappin' this year?"

"Oh, yeah, sure. Got a good load o' plews durin' the spring, in fact. But I've got another job comin' up for the summer, guidin' some pilgrims—"

Preacher didn't know where Rip intended to guide those mysterious pilgrims, and didn't get a chance to find out right then, because a frightened scream rang out from not too far away.

A *woman's* scream.

"Damn it!" Rip said. "That sounds like Miss Faith!"

He broke into a run, and Preacher saw that Rip was heading for that fancy striped tent he had noticed earlier.

Preacher followed at a more deliberate pace, not running because he was still leading the two horses, but not wasting any time, either. As he approached the tent, he saw a knot of people in front of the canvas flaps that formed its entrance. Two knots of people, rather, with Rip Giddens between them, evidently trying to keep them apart.

One group, the bunch that Rip faced angrily, was made up of men in buckskins and coonskin caps and floppy-brimmed hats. They were trappers, and Preacher recognized most of them. He wasn't particularly fond of them, either, especially the man who appeared to be their leader. His name was Luther Snell, and Preacher had had a few run-ins with him before. Once he had even suspected Snell of raiding his traps, but he'd never been able to catch the man at it.

The half-dozen or so men with Snell were the same sort, no more honest than they had to be and given to brutality.

It was the group of people clustered behind Rip that drew most of Preacher's attention, though. He knew immediately that they must be those pilgrims Rip had mentioned.

There were four of them, and one of them was a woman—a *white* woman, maybe the only one in more than a hundred miles. She was tall and on the slender side, with a thick mass of auburn curls that tumbled around her shoulders. Her eyes were a vivid, almost startling shade of green. Standing next to her with an arm protectively around her was a slight, sandy-haired man who was several inches shorter than her. On the woman's other side stood a handsome, dark-haired man in his thirties, and behind that trio was a taller man with brown hair. He looked to be the most physically fit of the group, but the spectacles that perched on his nose gave him a bookish look, and he seemed to be the one of the four who was the most nervous.

Preacher's keen eyes took in the whole scene and the people involved at a glance. Rip was saying, "Look, Luther, there ain't no call for trouble. I'm sure that Miss Faith didn't mean to offend you—"

"She called me an uncouth lout!" Luther Snell interrupted angrily. "I ain't exactly sure what that is, but it can't be nothin' good!"

"Perhaps I should have added uneducated as well," the woman said with a defiant look on her pretty face, and Preacher winced a little. Clearly, she wasn't going to go out of her way to ease the tension here.

"If you mean I ain't had no schoolin', that ain't true," Snell shot back. "I went to school for a whole year. I can read a little and cipher some."

"Oh, well, then, you're ready to apply for admission to Oxford."

The man with his arm around her said, "Faith, dear, you're not really helping matters—"

"Oh, hush," the woman snapped at him. "If you were any sort of a decent brother, Willard, you would have stood up to this bully when he first accosted me." She glared at the other two men in their party. "And the same is true for the pair of you. My God, you must have *some* backbone, if you're brave enough to come out here to this filthy wilderness in the first place."

"I didn't have that much choice," the smaller dark-haired man said. "The newspaper for which I work insisted that I come along with your brother's expedition, Miss Carling. A journalist goes where he's told to go, you know."

Faith Carling looked at the third man, who refused to meet her accusatory gaze. Despite his muscular build, he was obviously a peace-loving sort.

That wasn't exactly the same thing as being a coward, Preacher thought—but it wasn't far from it, either.

"Look," Snell said, "I didn't do anything to get the gal upset. I just asked her if she'd be willin' to write one of her pomes about me."

"Poems," Faith said distinctly and scornfully. "I write poems, not *pomes*. And as an artist, I can't be commanded what to write. I have to follow the urgings of my muse."

One of the other trappers said, "I thought the little prissy fella was the artist."

"My brother Willard is a painter," Faith replied. "He captures the beauties of nature in oils, while I use words. But both of us are artists." She looked at Luther Snell. "And you, sir, are *not* one of the beauties of nature."

"That does it!" The burly, black-bearded Snell drew back a fist. "Sorry, Giddens. Since I can't wallop no female, looks like I got to beat the hell outta you!"

Chapter Two

"Hold it, Snell." Preacher's deep, powerful voice wasn't loud, but it cut through the atmosphere of impending violence and stopped Snell before the trapper could launch a punch at Rip Giddens.

Snell and his friends hadn't noticed Preacher coming up behind them. At the sound of Preacher's voice, Snell's head snapped around. "Preacher!" he said in surprise. "I didn't know you'd got here to the Rendezvous yet."

"Just rode in a few minutes ago," Preacher said mildly. "And I'd take it kindly if you'd stop threatenin' my friend Rip, Snell."

Reluctantly, the angry trapper lowered his arm, but he didn't unclench his fist. "This ain't any o' your business, Preacher. I know you like to meddle in other folks' affairs, but this is one time when maybe you ought to back up."

"Funny thing about that," Preacher said as he dropped the reins he had been holding. The horses weren't going to wander off. As Preacher stepped forward, he continued. "When the Good Lord made me, He clean forgot to put much back-up in me."

"Now look here," Snell began to bluster.

"No, *you* look," Preacher said, and his tone was cold and angry now. "You and your pards just leave these folks alone and move on. There's been hard feelin's but never any real trouble between us, Snell. Let's keep it that way."

Snell looked like he wanted to continue the argument, but one of his companions said, "Come on, Luther. We never figured on Preacher bein' mixed up in this. You know what a lobo wolf he is."

"Yeah, well, I can be a wolf, too," Snell said obstinately. But the look of wanting to fight had gone out of his small, piggish eyes, and Preacher knew Snell was going to back down. He wouldn't like it, but he'd do it.

Snell couldn't leave without getting in a parting shot, though. He sneered at Rip and said, "If I was you, Giddens, I'd be ashamed about havin' to get Preacher to fight my battles for me."

With that he turned and stalked away, followed by his friends, before Rip could make any sort of reply.

Rip didn't look happy, though, and Preacher wondered suddenly if he should have stayed out of the confrontation. Ignoring trouble wasn't the sort of thing he was good at, though, especially when the fella threatening to raise a ruckus was a no-account bastard like Luther Snell.

"I appreciate the help, Preacher," Rip said tightly, "but you didn't have to do that. I ain't scared of Snell."

"Nobody said you were," Preacher pointed out. "But him and me don't like each other, and it goes back a while. Still, I didn't mean to mix in where I hadn't ought to."

The woman took a step toward him. "On the contrary,

sir, your participation in this contretemps was quite welcome. Men such as that have no concept of fair play. I'd wager that they would have ganged up on poor Mr. Giddens and given him the thrashing of his life had you not intervened."

Preacher saw Rip's bearded jaw tighten even more, and he wanted to echo what Faith Carling's brother had told her a few minutes earlier—that she wasn't helping the situation. But his natural frontiersman's politeness made him just nod and tug at the brim of his hat. The way words spewed out of this redheaded gal's mouth, he doubted if he could ever keep up with her.

"Preacher, this here is Miss Faith Carling," Rip said, evidently deciding it was better to just move ahead rather than dwelling on what had happened.

She stuck out her hand like a man and asked, "Are you a minister, then? A man of God? A purveyor of the Gospel?"

"No, ma'am," he said as he took her hand. It was surprisingly strong, and her grip was firm. "I'm just a fur trapper like all these other fellas at the Rendezvous."

"Then why do they call you Preacher?"

He didn't much want to rehash the details, but the story would be new to her. "Sometime back, a bunch of Blackfoot grabbed me, took me prisoner, and figured on liftin' my hair. Funny thing about Indians, though. They generally won't bother a man if they think he's touched in the head. I'd seen a street preacher one time, back in Saint Looey, so I started doin' like he would've if he'd been there, preachin' at those heathen Blackfeet at the top o' my lungs. Kept it up all night and the next day, too, until they didn't have any choice but to believe that I was pure-dee crazy." He shrugged. "They let me go, and once the story got around, folks started callin' me Preacher. The name's stuck all this time."

"But what's your real name?" Faith persisted.

"After all these years, I sort of disremember."

That wasn't really true—his name was Arthur, and he knew that perfectly well. But he didn't particularly feel like sharing it with this woman, who he had already sized up as being rather obnoxious, despite the fact that she was good-looking.

Beauty and being a decent human being didn't always go hand in hand.

The short, sandy-haired man introduced himself. "I'm Willard Carling, Mr. Preacher. As my sister mentioned, I'm a painter."

"Pleased to meet you, but it's just Preacher. No mister." Preacher paused, then waved a hand at the magnificent scenery surrounding them. "I reckon you came out here to paint all this?"

"Yes, and the savages, too. It's becoming all the rage back East for artists to paint Western landscapes and portraits of the Indians. I like to see my subjects at first hand before I attempt to capture them on the canvas."

That made sense to Preacher. He was no artist, but he figured it would be a lot easier to paint a picture of something if you'd seen it for yourself, with your own eyes.

"And this is Jasper Hodge," Carling went on. "He's a journalist, you know. Plans to write a book about this expedition, as well as the stories for his newspaper."

"That a fact?" said Preacher as he shook hands with Jasper Hodge.

"Yes, indeed," Hodge replied. He smiled jauntily. "If you'd like, I can put you in the book, Preacher. Wouldn't it be something for your friends to read about you in such a volume?"

"It sure would, considerin' that most of 'em can't read a lick," Preacher said dryly.

Hodge's smile went away and was replaced by a frown. Preacher could tell that the Eastern journalist wasn't sure if he was being made fun of or not—but if he was, he didn't like it.

That just left the bigger, bespectacled man, who wasn't quite as well dressed as the others. "Chester Sinclair," he introduced himself as he briefly shook hands with Preacher. "I'm Mr. Carling's assistant."

"I have to have someone lug all my paints and canvases about, you know," Carling said. "And for that I need a big strapping mule like this lad here."

"Chester may be big, but he's obviously not any more courageous than you two," Faith said. "Otherwise, he would have volunteered to help Preacher and Mr. Giddens when they confronted those ruffians."

"Sorry, Miss Faith," Sinclair said with his eyes downcast. "I didn't think it was my place to interfere."

"That's a handy excuse, anyway," Faith said caustically.

Preacher frowned at her. There weren't many things in this world more annoying than a bossy, tart-tongued woman, he thought. But he didn't say anything. These Easterners were Rip's problem, not his.

At least he supposed that was the case. He said, "These are the folks you've hired on with for the summer, Rip?"

"That's right," Rip replied with a nod.

"Yes, Mr. Giddens has agreed to be our chief scout and guide," Willard Carling said. "We're all quite pleased about that."

Faith gave out with a ladylike little snort. From what Preacher could tell, she wasn't very pleased with much of anything about this trip to the Rocky Mountains.

"I've got Sparrow to cook for us," Rip told Preacher. "You remember her?"

Preacher remembered the Indian woman called Sparrow quite well. She must have gotten the name back when she was a youngster, he had reflected more than once, because there was nothing birdlike about her now. She was short and broad, just about as wide as she was tall. But she was a fine cook, he recalled, and he nodded and said, "That's good, Rip. You folks will be well fed." A concern occurred to him. "What about other fellas to go along and help you watch out for trouble?"

"I've got four gents lined up for that. Switchfoot, Hammerhead Jones, and the Ballinger brothers. But if you're offerin', Preacher, I reckon I could talk Mr. Carling into hirin' you on, too." Rip turned to Carling and added, "I don't want to embarrass him, Boss, but when it comes to the frontier, Preacher's worth more'n all them other boys put together."

"Why, that sounds excellent," Carling said. "Join our little expedition, Preacher, do."

Preacher almost wished now that he hadn't asked Rip who else was going along on the journey. He didn't particularly like any of these four pilgrims, and he surely didn't desire to spend a few months around Faith Carling and her shrewish ways.

But it was true that he didn't have nearly as big a load of pelts to sell this time as he usually did. Whatever Willard Carling would pay to hire him, the money would come in handy sooner or later. But would it be worth the aggravation?

Preacher reached a decision and shook his head. "I appreciate the offer," he said, "but I just come here to sell my plews and move on. I ain't lookin' for work."

"Oh, dear." Carling looked disappointed. "Are you sure?"

"Rip and the others you've hired are good men. They can handle just about any problem that comes up."

"Very well. But I wonder . . . would you be interested in posing for a portrait before we part company, Preacher?"

Preacher's eyebrows went up in surprise. "You want to paint a picture of *me*?"

"Yes, indeed. You're the quintessential woodsman, a perfect archetype."

Preacher wasn't sure exactly what Carling was trying to say, but he figured it was better than being called an uncouth lout. He said, "What would I have to do?"

"Simply stand still."

"I reckon I could do that."

"Excellent! We'll get started this afternoon, if that's all right with you."

Preacher nodded. "Fine. That'll give me time to talk

to some of the agents about my furs and get somethin' to eat."

"Come back here whenever you're ready. I'll have Chester set up an easel and a fresh canvas."

Carling went back into the fancy tent, accompanied by Jasper Hodge. Faith and Sinclair remained outside. Faith sat down on a stool at a small folding table that held a pad of paper, a pen, and an inkwell. Now that she wasn't paying any attention to him, Sinclair's eyes followed her with almost doglike devotion, Preacher noted.

He gathered up the reins of his horses and started back across the encampment toward the tents set up by the fur buyers. Rip trailed along with him.

"Sure you won't change your mind about comin' along, Preacher?" Rip asked. He inclined his head toward the fancy tent where the Easterners were. "Havin' you around might make it a heap easier for me to ride herd on that bunch."

Preacher laughed softly. "I'm afraid that's your lookout, Rip. The lady ain't what you'd call shy and retirin', is she?"

Rip sighed and didn't answer the question. "It's a good job. Mr. Carling's payin' me a mighty good wage."

"You tryin' to convince me . . . or you?"

"I said I'd take 'em on into the mountains, and I figure on doin' what I said I'd do." A stubborn edge had come into Rip's voice.

"I wouldn't expect any less of you. Still, if that gal lets out a scream just because Luther Snell comes up and talks to her, I don't know what she'll do if you run into any real trouble."

"He didn't just talk to her," Rip said. "When she told him to go away, he grabbed her arm and wanted to know what made her think she was so much better'n him."

Preacher stopped and looked over at his old friend. His eyes narrowed. "Is that so? I didn't know he'd laid hands on her." He might not like Faith Carling, but he'd been raised to believe that a man didn't lay hands on a woman in anger.

Rip nodded and said, "That's what she told me when I first come runnin' up, and Snell didn't deny it. I was almost hopin' he'd take a swing at me, so's I'd have an excuse to wallop him some." His broad shoulders rose and fell. "But Miss Faith was prob'ly right. Snell's bunch would've jumped me, too."

They might have discussed the matter further, but at that moment several of the fur company agents noticed Preacher and advanced toward him holding out their hands, ready to shake and make offers on the pelts Preacher had on the packhorse. Rip added, "See you later," and moved on.

Preacher spent the next hour negotiating with the various representatives of the fur companies, and finally settled on a price with one of them. He was always glad to get that transaction concluded. He didn't like haggling over money.

The agent counted out the agreed-upon amount in gold coins. Preacher put them away in a small leather pouch that he stowed under his buckskin shirt. Then the fur company man's hired helpers unloaded the pack-horse and carried the pelts into the tent that was serving as a temporary warehouse. Later, when the Rendezvous was over, they and all the other pelts the agent had bought would be loaded on pack animals and started on the long trip back to St. Louis.

Preacher shook hands with the man, who said, "Pleasure doing business with you." As Preacher turned away, he wondered briefly what he was going to do next.

That question was answered unexpectedly as he found his arms suddenly full of woman and a pair of warm, demanding lips pressed themselves eagerly against his mouth.

GREAT BOOKS,
GREAT SAVINGS!

When You Visit Our Website:
www.kensingtonbooks.com
You Can Save Money Off The Retail Price
Of Any Book You Purchase!

- All Your Favorite Kensington Authors
- New Releases & Timeless Classics
- Overnight Shipping Available
- eBooks Available For Many Titles
- All Major Credit Cards Accepted

Visit Us Today To Start Saving!
www.kensingtonbooks.com

All Orders Are Subject To Availability.
Shipping and Handling Charges Apply.
Offers and Prices Subject To Change Without Notice.